# Faceoff

## ST. CLOUD HOCKEY SERIES

# MARI LOYAL

*This one is for the girlies
who were told they couldn't
and so they did,
and made everyone
eat their words.*

# HEAT LEVEL AND CONTENT WARNINGS

Before reading this book, I really encourage you to first read this section to determine whether it's the right fit for your personal circumstances.

This book is closed door, which means there is innuendo, kisses are descriptive, and characters don't shy away from their attraction. However, there are no on-the-page explicit scenes.

There is mild to moderate use of cuss words, particularly in emotional moments. However, there is no use of f-bombs, religious blasphemies, or known ableist terms.

This book depicts difficult family dynamics including an antagonistic relative to the male main character who verbally abuses him and turns violent once, as well as somewhat neglectful parents.

The characters are college freshmen and are depicted drinking alcohol at a private party.

If any of these topics are troublesome for you, please protect yourself and read a book that better suits your situation.

Visit my website mariloyal.com for general content warnings that apply to all my books.

# CHAPTER 1
# MAX

only feel alive when I'm on the ice. Life is a hazy dream, a succession of disconnected scenes I have to go through to get to moments like this.

As I stand before the door to the arena, my heart pounds at a mid-game rhythm. It can't be explained by the minimal effort of suiting up for my first training session. A cocktail of excitement and nerves swirls in my gut, and I try shaking it off by stretching my neck and shoulders. Orientation at St. Cloud University was meh, but this moment—an hour before my first training session as a newly minted St. Cloud Thunder Bolt—feels like a big freaking deal.

"This is it," I say to myself. The start of my whole future. No presh.

I push the door open and take the first steps into the corridor. The cold seeps through the air, and I breathe it in. Smells like home. And there's nothing better than being the first in to the new digs. That's why I'm here an hour before it will be teeming with guys—to get a feel for the space I'll be living in for the next four years.

A sound stops me. Someone's skating already.

Whatever. Let's not attach some bad omen to this. Second on the ice isn't bad. The other guy may value solitude as much as I do and leave me alone for a while. I stomp all the way down the corridor. The glare of the overhead lights makes me squint until I'm all the way out of the shadows.

My plans are derailed once more when the dude turns out to be skating up a storm. He dashes from one goal to the other like an arrow. Slush rains on the boards as he brakes to turn and skate behind the goal, then back out to the other side. He's doing edge work as he goes, shifting backward and forward every time he crosses a line.

Going hard like this, on my own, was precisely what I wanted to do. And I still intend to do it. I push the door open with my knee and step onto the ice anyway. I may be used to being pushed aside in my private life, but not here. On the ice, I am king.

I glide over to center ice to warm up my ankles. The guy does some figure skating move that would get him a ten in the Olympics. If he plans to pull crap like that during a game, he's going to get eaten alive by the opponent. And he'll have it coming.

A cross between a snort and a laugh escapes from my chest. The echo across the quiet arena grinds him to a halt.

The way he squares up his shoulders screams hostility louder than words, but I don't know who he's trying to shake when he's pocket-sized. If I were a D-man, I'd be pissed about having Tinker Bell here on the team. With guys my size and larger, he'll be a liability no matter how fast he can skirt away.

I catch him approaching from the corner of my eye, but I keep stretching in silence. I make a point of whistling as inno-cently as possible.

"Was that a laugh?" Lil dude has a weird voice, too high pitched. Don't tell me he's a child.

Through the helmet's visor, I catch a scowl so deep it

scrunches up his nose and lifts up his lip. Which is surrounded by the smoothest face I've seen since middle school. I do a double take.

Uh, correction. Tinker Bell is a she.

"What the—You're a girl?" The question spews out of my mouth before I can think better of how it sounds.

She tosses her stick and gloves onto the ice in one motion. "Yeah, you got a problem with that, you jerk?"

At most, she's five-six to my six-three. Her fists ball up like an enforcer about to throw down, but they couldn't hurt a fly. I have to bite my lips to keep from laughing again.

"You can't possibly think you'll fight me."

"I don't think—I will. Someone clearly needs to teach your smug face a lesson." She pushes the sleeves of her jersey up. "And no one who makes fun of me lives to tell the tale."

I lean on one foot, using the stick like a cane. This is considerably more amusing than if she'd turned out to be a guy who beat me to the punch.

"Oh yeah? Can you even reach my face?"

To her credit, she makes an attempt to swing at me. It has no chance of landing when she has to stretch far out of her range to even get close. The second fist I catch in my left glove.

"You may want to introduce yourself with your mouth and not your fist, Tinker Bell," I say with a chuckle.

She splutters for a second. "Tinker—*excuse me?*"

At least the shock made her drop the bravado, and with that, her guard goes all the way down. And she's frozen. The ice is finally mine.

I go from zero to a hundred in a second, taking up the whole span of the two hundred feet like she did earlier. Every cell of my body roars to life. This is what I wanted, to breathe in the icy air until it burns my lungs. To push my muscles until I break a sweat. That's how you break the ice, pun intended.

"What did you call me?"

I startle when I catch her beside me, keeping pace. Her breathing is more labored, but not to the point that would make me think she's about to keel over.

Small but mighty, huh?

"Tinker Bell." I slow down and switch backward to my skates' outside edges, sort of like she did earlier. "You know, because you looked like a tiny fairy figure skating out here." To emphasize the point, I make a twirl, hands up like a ballerina.

"I have a name, and it is definitely not Tinker Bell. But surely yours must be Big Turd on a Stick."

I shrug. "At least I'm big."

"Good thing this isn't a game, because I can do this." With that, she raises her stick as if it's a sword.

"Hold up." I raise a gloved hand as a thought suddenly hits me harder than her stick would have. "This can't mean you're on the team, right?"

"Of course I'm on the damn team."

"No, no." I shake my head. "I didn't sign up for some co-ed team that is supposed to be about warm and fuzzies."

"And what makes you think I did?" She snorts, sizing me up from head to toe. "Besides, if we were on a team together, I'd trip you. Breaking all your teeth is a sure way to shut you up."

I hiss and put my hands over my chest. "So much hatred in that small body. That's not healthy, Tinker Bell."

She grinds her teeth, and every word comes out with a period attached to it. "I am *not* Tinker Bell. My name is Luz Rodriguez, and you best remember that."

"Luz means light, right?" I ask, pulling from my high school Spanish class. "And Tinker Bell is all shiny, so if I make that association…" I pause and grin so wide my face hurts. "Don't worry," I continue, wheezing with the effort not to crack up. "I will never forget your name, Tinker Bell."

Her body tenses from the bottom up, as if it were being

filled with lava about to erupt from her mouth. I skate away before the explosion.

A different kind of noise fills the arena up. Voices draw closer and finally spill onto the ice with the bodies they belong to. A bunch of guys and girls wrestle around for space, as though there isn't enough square footage. Someone shoves someone else, who knocks into a third person, who retaliates by pushing back.

"Get out of the way, meathead, before I clean the floor with your face." A different girl is the author of that line of poetry.

"Why don't you go home and play with your Barbie, princess?" some guy responds, adding in baby noises.

More and more people drop onto the ice. Too many to be from the same team. And, according to the giant clock overhead, a good forty minutes too early for practice. Clearly, there are two teams here. I just have to find mine and send Tinker Bell off to her figure skating squad.

My lungs expand to capacity, taking in air I then release slowly. So much for catching a quiet skate, staking ownership of the place, working up a sweat.

Tinker Bell heads over to the fray, and from what little I know of her, I don't think it's to pour water on the fire but to stoke it. I pick up the pace and get there before her. I don't know any of these people, but I grab the first guy I find from the collar of his jersey and drag him back. Before he gets testy, I wedge my stick between him and the girl he's been heckling.

Someone does the same with the girl, holding her back. Instead of exploding like I expected, Tinker Bell helps pluck the girls from among the boys until there's a clear line between.

I count the girls in front of me. Eighteen. Which means there are seventeen dudes behind me if they're all early.

"Guess you were right, Tinker Bell. We're not on the same team."

The glare she tosses my way reminds me that she's still a volcano about to blow up. Her dark eyes promise murder if I breathe another word.

"I see you've all met each other," says a new voice from behind.

I turn, and from among a wall of heads, I catch yet more people stepping on to the ice. At the helm is the guy who scouted me, Glen Green, who is supposed to be the head coach of the St. Cloud Thunder Bolts. There's a cohort of people behind him, men and women, too many to be the staff of one team alone.

"If you'd all followed instructions instead of arriving early, you'd have learned where you were supposed to go," he says while folding his arms. "Strikes, off the ice. Bolts, with me."

And he stays on the ice.

"But—" Tinker Bell complains, confirming she's a Strike or whatever.

"Follow me," a middle-aged woman says to her and the rest.

As she passes by, Tinker Bell stares daggers at me.

I wave a hand. I don't join in the other guys' taunting, but it does feel like I won the faceoff with her.

Or so I think.

# CHAPTER 2
## LUZ

It figures that Max Cassiano is a jerk. Being dubbed the next Sidney Crosby must have gotten to that huge head of his. Or was the next Sidney Crosby supposed to be his cousin?

Whatever.

Just before stepping off the ice, I pause and turn around. Anyone would think he just won a match with that shit-eating grin on his face. I slice the air before my neck with a hand, a clear declaration of war.

I'm the queen of the ice, not this Tinker Bell crap he keeps yapping about.

Somehow, I'll find the way to make him fall to his knees before me. I don't care that he's poised for the world juniors or the draft. Or that he's a massive wall of muscle and wildly talented. Or that his ridiculously good-looking face appears on the local news all the time. He will learn my name forward and backward. It will give him nightmares.

But first I need to understand what this travesty is.

I follow the rest of the team out of the arena and back into the locker room. Grumbles sound all around me, and I glean that we have one collective thought.

What the hell?

The head coach stops in the middle of the locker room. I recognize her because she was in my interview when I applied for the scholarship. She's surrounded by three other women and one guy who must be part of her staff. A pretty big difference to the ten or so dudes who seem to be the men's team staff.

"I'm Head Coach Elaine Young. Call me Coach Young." Her voice is clear and void of any feeling. I can't read her face either. She could be vibrating with excitement on the inside, like I am, or she could be raging, also like I am. "When I speak, you will *yes, ma'am* me."

"Yes, ma'am," we all say at once, loud and clear.

"Good. Now, take off your gear. We're going to start with dryland training."

"Yes, ma'am."

Except me. My big, fat mouth opens instead with "But why?"

Coach Young's eyes zero in on me as if magnetically pulled by my voice. You could hear a pin drop with how quiet the whole room grows.

I know I'm messing up on my first day, but I'm nothing if not honest. So I take a step forward, puff up my chest with a breath, and more eloquently, ask, "Why do we have to get off the ice, and not them?"

Her eyes flash with thunder.

Hey, very apropos to the team name—the St. Cloud Thunder Strikes.

"Because I say so." She sweeps sharp eyes across the roster. "If there are no further complaints, I'll see you at the gym in five minutes."

"Oh, shit," I mutter as I do quick mental math. That's not

enough time to remove all my gear, put it in place, change my socks, and put on my sneakers.

I drop my gloves and stick, and right here, in the middle of the locker room, I start stripping at lightning speed. I'm not the only one with the same idea. Among muffled curses and squeals, my future teammates also scramble to divest themselves of all the layers.

The floor becomes a cemetery for jerseys, pads, and equipment. Who the hell knows which one belongs to whom anymore. All that matters is leaping over it to find my sneakers.

I run out of the locker room wearing the wrong socks, carrying the shoes in my hands, and in my underclothes. Somehow, I manage to be the first one in the gym. It's brand new, and the machines still gleam, but I have no time to admire it. Hopping on one foot, I put on a sneaker and then the next as the rest of the team arrives. One of the other women has been watching the show from the mats.

"I'm Kaylee McDonald, your strength trainer. And for the next two hours, you will *yes, ma'am* me too."

With the way her T-shirt hugs her biceps, I should've guessed. I dream of having definition like hers.

"Yes, ma'am." This time I don't screw up.

She gives us a grim smile. "Great, we'll officially kick off this program with some light training."

I learn very quickly what the definition of *light* is to this woman. No session that starts with burpees right out of the warm-up is going to be light.

Half an hour later, the girl beside me straight-up faints face down on the mat. I freeze until some disjointed voice barks that I should keep going. I continue the push-ups even as my neighbor's drool reaches my hand. Or it could just be my own sweat pooling beneath me.

Coach McDonald leans over the unconscious girl to check her pulse. "She's fine," she tells someone behind her.

"Wake her up." That I recognize as Coach Young's voice above me. "No one said it's time for a break."

*Mierda*, I think to myself. *Are we training for the Marines?*

After Coach McDonald pats her face a few times, the girl comes back to the waking world. Her eyes are hazy as she pulls herself up and wipes the drool off her face.

"Keep going," I manage to say in a wheeze. "C'mon."

Finally, she gets with the program, and I can stop worrying that I just witnessed a murder.

Someone blows a whistle an eternity later, and my limbs give out. Pretty funny how, despite lying prone and still, absolutely every one of my muscles shakes like a leaf. I wish I could faint. The embarrassment of that would be way better than this feeling.

"You. Rodriguez, was it?"

I can't hold back a groan as I shift my head to look up. Coach Young stands before me, seemingly ten feet tall in my feeble state.

"Yes, ma'am." I sound drunk or high. Or both.

She crouches down. "Go get drinks for everyone. That's your punishment for speaking out of turn."

"Yes," I say as I slide my hands back under my chest and push up on my knees. "Ma'am."

It sounds simple enough, but it does feel like a punishment in my current state. I almost land on my chin when one of my hands slips out from under me. A newborn foal probably has more grace than me as I stand slowly. Painfully. I can't feel my legs, and for a moment, I lose my balance. Reflexes catch me before I can land like a domino over the fallen bodies around me. Somehow, my back is numb, and I'm thankful for that miracle.

The two coaches watch my every step like hawks. I, too, would be holding back laughter if I were them.

"Vamos, que sí se puede." I watch my own feet, crammed

into the sneakers with too-thick socks, carefully making their way through the gym. We got this, guys.

There was a table just outside the locker rooms loaded with a mountain of bottles and two massive coolers. That's where I have to go.

I stop halfway to my goal and clap a hand on my mouth before the explosion.

Looks like I'll just die right here.

No, I demand my stomach stop this riot. I am an elite athlete. I've gone through much worse than this. A little strength training won't kill me.

I swallow it all back down and take a few deep breaths. My eyes are set on the table, so close and yet so far. I know that if I take another step, my gut will betray me again, but I'm already on thin ice with the head coach. I can't return empty-handed. Or not return at all.

Steeling myself, I keep walking. The air is much cooler out here, with floor-to-ceiling windows that overlook the campus on one side and the door to the arena up ahead. I pretend it's the third period of the most challenging game of my life. We're down two to one and it's up to me to save the team.

My hands shake as I grab one of the empty bottles. It almost slips while I struggle to uncap it. The struggle is real as I fill it up with some blue sports drink from the first cooler. At last, I take a sip.

The moan that comes out of my throat is almost R-rated.

"Whoa."

Obviously, I choke.

And, even better, blue drink comes out of my nose.

Chuckling is the background music of my humiliation. I cough away the pain and wipe my nose with the back of my sweaty arm. Only then do I turn the full weight of my glare on the culprit.

"Max Cassiano," I say through gritted teeth.

"You know me, Tinker Bell?"

He's not wearing his helmet, and his dark hair sticks to his head, heavy with sweat. A drop falls from his nose, more still from his chin. I'm glad he's being tortured, too, but he doesn't look to be suffering as much as I am. It pisses me off.

"Who doesn't?" I ask, my voice deadpan. "You're like the best hockey player to come out of this town."

I put my bottle on top of the cooler and grab another one, getting to work before one of the coaches comes out demanding speed.

His hands don't shake as he tops up his bottle from the other cooler. "Not really. There are plenty of players better than me."

His words don't carry any of that sugary sweet false modesty I'd have expected. He really believes this.

"Whatever. And stop calling me that silly name."

"But it's cute and adorable, like you."

"Do you want to die?" I squeeze the bottle I'm filling up as if it were his neck.

I hate that his eyes are as true blue as this freaking drink, and that they twinkle when he makes fun of me. Should I squeeze the contents out of the bottle in his face?

No, that's maybe not the best way to start my college hockey life.

"I have a word of advice for you," I say while I gather as many drink bottles as my arms can carry. Then I smile. "Get bent."

"That's two words, though." He gives me a condescending look. He's lucky my hands are too busy to slap it off his face.

With more energy than I thought I had, I turn around, ready to walk away from this sham of a conversation. As I do, there's a small gasp.

I glance at him over my shoulder. His eyes are glued to my back. Not to my bottom, like I'd expect from some guys.

It takes me a second to remember that I'm in my sports bra, which means everyone can see the paraspinal scar that runs all the way down the base of my neck to my coccyx. The shock in his face is usually the reaction it gets. Without knowing the details, people can guess I went through some shit.

I snort. "Not so tiny and delicate now, huh?"

His eyes snap back up to mine. I flip my long braided hair over my shoulder and walk away. And what a luxury it is being able to do so.

# CHAPTER 3
## MAX

While campus is abuzz with parties during the week before the semester starts, the hockey program is subjected to torture.

The first drill every morning consists of jogging for an hour. Usually, the Bolts head one direction and the Strikes the opposite. If the two groups risk crossing paths, the coaches steer us the opposite way. When we're on the ice, they're at the gym and vice versa. If we meet members from the opposite team in the halls, the insults that get traded range from sailor- to trucker- to elementary-schooler levels. And this petty animosity doesn't stay there.

I'm in the gym, squatting with weights on my shoulders that equate to slightly over my own body mass, listening to the guys go on and on about the girls.

"I can't believe they did that," Nate Garcia, a defenseman, says between pull-ups. "Like, if you pay close attention, you can hear my stomach roaring."

It's not just him. All of us are sluggish with hunger thanks to the little prank the Strikes pulled on us. They made it to lunch before us and polished off all the meat.

On cue, my stomach roars like a lion. Six feet, three inches and two hundred ten pounds can't be sustained on bread and vegetables, like I had for lunch today.

"On the plus side," I say while grunting through the last squat of the series. "They gotta be having the meat sweats."

Which also leads to sluggishness. And we all know coaches *love* it when a team has no energy. They're probably getting their own punishment right now.

"Wish *I* had the meat sweats," says Conor Mahoney, one of the forwards. "As it is, I don't even have enough juice in the tank to sweat."

"Oh yeah?" I snort. "Then why does that barbell keep slipping from your hands?"

"Dude, you could've given me the courtesy of pretending I was right."

"Pretending isn't in my user manual. What you see is what you get."

His eyebrows go up just as his eyes squeeze. "One really big jerk?"

I can't help but laugh, because he's not wrong. And if I've learned anything after one week of bootcamp training with these guys, it's that we're all enormous jerks. Aggressive on the ice, competitive over the smallest thing, obsessive about performance… and really, really arrogant. Coach Green picked great players, and if we can all have the camaraderie Nate, Conor and I have formed, we may just be lucky enough to assemble a kick-ass team.

Or the big personalities of all these characters will shit on the whole enterprise. Either or.

"Or JLo," Nate adds with a laugh.

Conor shakes his head. "That is such an old joke."

"Whatever, man. She can still get it."

I feel the burn. Not from the joke but from the whole week.

There is no part of my body that doesn't protest as I walk over to the racks and put the weights back in place.

The coaches informed us that there will be no practice tomorrow, so we can use the last Sunday before college officially begins to recharge. Which means the whole team's going to a bar after training. In my heart, I'm game. I just don't know how I'm going to get there and back without dropping dead. I need to stretch if I plan on surviving tonight.

"Cassiano."

I turn like a rusty robot toward the voice. Coach Green waves me over from the door. He's spent the whole week having random one-on-ones with everyone. No one in this bunch had the restraint to keep the conversations private, so I'm not freaking out as I follow him out of the gym.

He stays mum as we stroll down the hall adjacent to the gym. It's lined with offices on both sides, and he leads me to the one at the very end.

Coach doesn't sit in his chair. Instead, he leans against the desk and folds his arms. "I'm sure you've heard what these talks are about."

"Yes, sir." I hold my hands behind me.

He bobs his head. "So, who do you think is the right man for the job?"

And by that, he means who should be the captain of the team.

According to the chatter, most of the respondents pointed at themselves. Everyone here was either the captain of their high school team, the best player, or some story like this.

One week of sharing in the torture was enough to get to know everyone pretty well, but not in-depth. While I clicked early on with Conor and Nate, I can't really vouch for anyone else's aptitudes.

Nate's a bit of a wildcard. He's the kind of guy who does

his thing well, but not quite within the strategy that's been laid out for the play. It's gotten him flack more than once already.

Conor's the stark opposite. Level-headed and with iron-clad discipline. Problem is, he tends to play it a bit too safe on the ice. But that may be what the egos of this team need.

"My vote goes for Mahoney. He's got solid skills and is probably the most sensible of the bunch."

"Really?" Coach rubs his chin. "You're not putting your own name in the hat?"

I can't hide the grimace fast enough. Why does this feel like a trick question?

"Er, honestly, the only thing that matters is choosing someone who can turn us into a team. Not someone who's looking to stroke their own ego."

"I agree." Coach waves a hand toward the door. "That'll be all. Go stretch and make sure to get some rest this weekend."

"Yes, sir."

There's a sardonic glint in his eyes that tells me he knows what's what. There will be no rest for the Bolts.

I run a hand through my hair while tracing back my steps to the gym. Having the C on my jersey would certainly look good on my resume, but at the end of the day, what matters is winning. I can score with or without it.

And I'm sure Coach Green will make a smart decision and not put someone like Frankie Boucher as our captain. As a defenseman, he's top notch, but as a human being, I don't wish him on my worst enemies. He's the author of the worst heckling the Bolts have thrown to the Strikes this week. Not quite the example a team captain should put out.

It's precisely his buzz cut that I fixate on as I walk back into the gym. His back is turned to me, and there's a bunch of girls from the Strikes glaring up at him.

"What the..." The question dies in my throat as I take a

look around. No one's working out anymore. Instead, they're locked in yet another standoff. I sigh.

"Or what?" Boucher asks. "What are you gonna do if we don't give you any of the foam rollers?"

"I'm sure you're not wearing a cup right now, so you do the math."

At this point, I would recognize that voice in my sleep. It's none other than Tinker Bell herself.

I'm torn between telling Boucher to get lost and the inexplicable need to give Tinker Bell crap every time I see her. Except siding with Boucher in any way is a definite dick move.

"We're using them right now. Can't you see that?" Nate says with a scowl.

A different girl retorts. "Do they have your names written on them? All we're saying is that you should share them."

"We should do jack shit." Boucher looks around. "Am I right, guys?"

A chorus of grunts and mumbles agree with him.

I walk closer to the group of people, spotting rollers under the arms of Bolts and only one in possession of a Strike. The sparks of World War III are in everyone's faces. One more smart-ass quip could make it explode.

"Well, how many of the damn rollers do we have?" I jam my hands into the pockets of my joggers.

"Ten." Nate gives me a look as if the word tastes like vomit. "But that's not even enough for all of us."

By *us*, he obviously means the Bolts. Forget the Strikes.

St. Cloud spent millions of dollars on all new facilities, a whole hockey arena—complete with state-of-the-art screens and a concession stand taken out of a professional stadium—scholarships for all of us, and even an in-house PT. But they couldn't buy more than ten rollers?

Bro, I need a freaking nap.

"It can't be ten for you and none for us, meathead," Tinker Bell says. And that effectively unleashes the battle.

One of the Strikes rams into a Bolt, sending his roller tumbling to the floor. Three other people scramble to get it. You'd think this is an official game and the rollers are pucks. Although it looks more like we switched to rugby.

"Catch!"

By reflex, I lift my hands and catch a flying roller.

Immediately, four girls zero in on me.

I will never admit how my pulse spikes. While one-on-one, none of them would be able to even tickle me, but together, they may do some damage.

No wonder someone else tossed the problem my way. I glance around, trying to find the sucker who should be dealing with this instead of me. Everyone is in the middle of their own tug-of-war, though.

"Get back. I got him."

I look forward again as Tinker Bell pushes her teammates aside. Her big dark eyes train on me, and she blows a strand of hair away from her face.

"Wait—"

She doesn't.

She charges like a bull.

I freeze. I must've lost my last screws somewhere this week, because instead of throwing the foam roller away, I wait to see if she can even take me down. Not that I'll make it easy for her. I plant my feet wide and brace for impact.

It comes. Just not quite as I was expecting. Rather than slamming her shoulder into my solar plexus, she jumps. I lift the roller as high as I can.

The way her whole face scrunches up is about to make me laugh.

"Son of a—" At the last second, she decides not to insult

my mom, and I'm about to tease her. But then she takes a dump on predictability.

Because with one more jump, she cinches her arms around my neck and her legs around my waist. Her weight tips me forward. Just before she falls, I react to catch her—by her butt.

Her eyes find mine. The degree of anger in hers hasn't changed, but I remove my hand just in case. Tinker Bell grabs on to me tighter just as she reaches up. I've turned into a statue that can only feel the squeeze of her thighs around me, her stomach against my face. I feel a weight ease off my hand and know she has the roller, but I don't care. I can't think. I don't even know my damn name anymore.

With a grunt, she eases her legs off me but doesn't let go of my neck until her feet are on the floor. Which means I'm bent over to her eye level when she lets go.

There's a smirk on her face, and it snaps me out of the trance.

I grit my teeth. "You play dirty."

"All's fair in love and war." She shrugs. Her T-shirt is still bunched up around her waist where it pressed against my face.

"Don't make me play dirty, Tinker Bell." Since she's close enough, I lean down to whisper so only she can hear. "I promise you won't be able to take it."

She shoves me out of the way and walks out with her prize. And my dignity. The rest of her team eventually follows, and I'm not the only Bolt who stays pissed off after that.

# CHAPTER 4
## LUZ

"Dude, you just climbed Max Cassiano like a tree. What did it feel like?" JT Brewer asks. Her name is actually Justine, but one of the other girls almost died the first day when she called her Justine. I liked her spunk, so we've stuck ever since.

She nudges my side with her elbow, wagging her eyebrows.

The answer is *hard*. Not that I could possibly say that aloud and live to tell the tale.

But everything from his waist to the shoulder I used to prop myself up was solid as a rock. And just as strong. And I wasn't as upset as I should've been when his hand grabbed my butt so I wouldn't fall. Any other guy would've taken advantage of accidentally finding his whole hand splayed over my butt cheek, but he didn't. He pulled it away immediately, and that's what upset me. I liked it there.

That wasn't the most offensive part of the whole encounter, though. It was the fact that he has tiny freckles across the bridge of his nose. How dare—

I bang the foam roller against my head, trying to chase

away these thoughts. He's the enemy. I can't fraternize with a Bolt if I plan to make room for myself among the Strikes.

So, to answer JT's question, I shrug. "It just sort of happened, and it was too quick. I didn't pay attention."

"Yeah, right. And I'm Wayne Gretzky reincarnated."

I fight off a smile by biting my lips. "You do know he's still alive, right?"

"My point exactly." JT rolls her eyes.

I drop the roller on the floor of the locker room. Since I won the trophy from an opponent, I get first dibs. But just a few minutes of stretching my back with it won't be enough to ease the pain. My best friend ibuprofen is waiting for me after this. I wish the Bolts hadn't been such knuckleheads, making us fight for these things. If I could've started winding down earlier, then my muscles wouldn't be seized so tight at this point.

My groan echoes around the place as I work a few exercises with the roller. It catches a few stares, but I don't have a single neuron to spare on what people think when my brain is being bombarded by both pain and relief. Chronic pain is no joke.

"Is that from the roller or from Cassiano?" JT chuckles.

"He's all yours if you're so interested." My voice comes out like a croak. I'm slow as a turtle as I disengage the foam cylinder from under my body and throw it over to her. All I can do after that is lie flat like a starfish.

"Hmm, if he wasn't a Bolt, I'd consider it," JT says with a grin. Her myriad ear piercings glint under the stark white lights, easily visible because the sides of her head are shaved down.

I shake my head slightly. "Good, you're too cool for a clown like him."

"You're right. Men don't deserve me."

"Speaking of men," Chelsea White, a left winger, says with

a coy little smile. "Wanna go fish for some at O'Malley's tonight?"

She's the one who passed out beside me the first day, but only because she'd been struggling with a cold before bootcamp. On a normal day, she can bench-press me and you'd never think so. Out of anyone in this locker room, she's the one who could make it to a beauty pageant.

"What's O'Malley's?" I pull myself up to a sitting position to finish my stretching.

Chelsea sits with JT and me. "The main bar on campus, according to my roommate."

"Oh, cool. You talk to your roommate," I grumble to myself. Mine has zero interest in anything that comes out of my mouth. Which makes me think this socializing idea may not be so bad.

"I'm in." JT bumps her fist with Chelsea's. "If only because I don't have money to renew my Netflix subscription right now."

I'll lend her my password. Later. Tonight, I also want to see people outside of a screen.

"Great! I'll text you the meeting place and time later." She hops back to her feet and over to another group until the whole team is in the know.

JT rubs her hands. "Let the college life begin."

This week has felt surreal. Wrapped up only in intensive training, I haven't had time to look around campus—probably the way Chelsea's roommate found out about the bar—or even glance at the syllabus or the map of buildings to scout out where the library is or the cafeteria. But if there's a way to officially kick off college life, it truly is by hitting up the local bar.

Later, I head over to the bar with most of the team. A few of the girls are dressed to the nines, maybe hitting up a nightclub after. I kept it casual. And by casual, I mean I only changed my outfit like five times. In the end, I picked high-waisted shorts that make my butt look ah-may-zing. I tucked a T-shirt that has the *That's all Folks!* logo at the front into them and slipped on a pair of Converse. Some lip gloss and loose hair, and I look kinda cute.

JT drops an arm over my shoulders. "What's tonight's game plan, Rodriguez?"

"Hmm. Going with the flow? I honestly don't know what to expect here."

And I don't mean it just because it's officially my first college party of sorts.

St. Cloud is one of those Ivy League schools people sell a limb to be able to attend, unless applicants are old money. Their reputation has been built on almost two hundred years of academic achievements, including the stem cell treatment that helped restore my ability to walk six years ago. Never in my life would I have dreamed about attending this place. But here I am, all thanks to some alumni with enough cash to spare, and a dean who wants to put the school on the sports map.

The students at this college are famous for being uppity brainiacs, and the odds are high that that's the kind of people we'll encounter.

"Chill vibe. I dig." JT lets go of me to grab a flask someone sneaked in from who knows where and chugs.

She offers it, and I pass. I had to pop a couple of ibuprofen earlier aside from my usual chronic pain medication, and though the combination wouldn't be too dangerous, I really don't need the secondary effects. The fact that JT doesn't give me any crap about turning down booze puts her in my good books forever.

O'Malley's looks like a hole in the wall. It has the ambiance of an authentic Irish pub down pat, complete with the red brick walls and the rusty overhead sign. The fogged-up grid windowpanes add an extra touch of casual eeriness. Is it going to be full of grumpy old men, angry we're on their turf?

But then I walk in, and the place morphs. The inside is well lit and packed with high-top tables and a few booths crammed with people. There's an old-school jukebox in a corner, and just beyond are a couple of pool tables, a table hockey one, and a few dart boards. The bar is teeming with people waiting for drinks, and music and noise reverberate off the walls.

I whistle. "Okay, okay. Not bad."

Like ten of us cram around a high-top that typically fits four people. It catches a lot of eyes, and a few of them belong to Bolts.

"Ugh, why are they here?" JT sneers.

"It's only now clicking with me that we'll also have to see them around campus." A sad little sigh escapes from my lips. I refuse to let them ruin my night, though. "Anyway, want a drink?"

"A beer would be nice."

I give her a look. "We're still underage, you dork."

"Eh, had to shoot my shot."

"Leave that for the ice," I say while shaking my head. But it makes her chuckle.

The table isn't so busy now that people have migrated to the bar, to the games, or to the dance floor. I approve of the sound system, although the '80s music isn't my thing.

I wedge myself between some people chatting among themselves. In theory, it should make it easier for me to get the bartender's attention, but no. The competition's spread all across the bar.

"I'm really looking forward to modeling it on C++—"

"Nah, man. C++ is from the past. You have to try—"

I shake my head.

From the opposite side, someone says, "So, that's why the

intravenous alternative wasn't the most optimal, and it caused a reaction of—"

Welp, I have no idea what they're talking about. If I didn't feel out of place before, I sure do now.

"Excuse me!" I call for the bartender, but he's too far to hear over all the racket. I hoist myself up the bar just enough to really make him see me waving my arms. I'm rewarded with a *hold up* gesture.

Something brushes against my arm as I lower myself back to my feet. It turns out to be a guy who had the same idea and is waving for attention.

"Oh, sorry. Didn't mean to bump into you." He has to mostly scream so I can hear him. His eyebrows are scrunched up with worry.

"It's cool," I yell back with a shrug.

He's kinda cute, in an unassuming way. Dirty blond hair that's a bit too long, dark eyes, a wide smile. Maybe he likes what he sees, because he extends a hand. "I'm Brett. Freshman. You?"

"Luz. Also freshman." I shake his hand, and the bartender arrives right then. Dude radiates grumpiness for someone whose business is booming, so I forget all about Brett and place my order.

"Cool," Brett says, now that we're waiting for our drinks. "What's your major?"

"Biology major and economics minor," I respond. It's a weird combination, but my move after I retire from a *looong* hockey career is to open my own physical therapy clinic.

"We might have some classes together! I'm a finance major and econ minor."

"Here you go." The bartender drops two glasses of Coke on the counter and extends a hand. "Five bucks each."

"For soda?" My eyes bulge.

"No, for my bills," he says, deadpan.

Okay, fair.

I pull out a few bills from my back pocket and mourn their departure.

There's a crashing sound that grinds all the action to a halt for a moment. I sip on my drink as I glance toward the source. Two of the Bolts pick up a fallen dartboard, which is what must've made the noise. They're laughing loud enough to make me wonder if they're drunk, and just behind them is none other than the bane of my existence.

Max Cassiano's eyes find mine as though there aren't a hundred people between us. I want to look away. The last thing I need is for him to think I'm staring at him. But the second to last thing I need is for him to peg me as a coward. So I cock an eyebrow and pretend like I feel nothing. He sweeps his eyes aside, and I stagger in relief until my back hits the bar.

Wait, is he glaring at Brett?

"Ugh." Speaking of, the guy beside me grunts. "Those hockey jocks are a pest."

I mean, yes. But technically, I'm also a hockey jock.

"Oh yeah?"

"They walk all over the place like they own it."

"Totally." I give him my best serious business expression.

Brett eats it up and pops off. "Like, what's the point of having a sports team? It cheapens the school, you know? We're not into brute stuff around here."

Well, I guess that answers my earlier question. This is probably what I'll have to expect from other classmates.

I stifle a sigh. At least Brett gave me the courtesy of intel before I actually have to face the music.

"I see my friend calling me," I lie through my teeth. "But I'll catch you in class maybe?"

"Sure! Nice to meet you, Luz." He smiles as if he won something.

I walk away back to my *brutes*.

Pendejo.

# CHAPTER 5
# MAX

My roommate's a dick.

"Do you have to be up so stinking early?" Brett mumbles from underneath his blankets.

It's already been two hours since I left the dorm the first time. In that time, I caught morning training, showered, changed, and was on my way to my first lecture when I realized I left my iPad and a book behind.

I throw the things into my backpack, making as much noise as humanly possible. As far as I know, this shithead is also in this class. He's going to be late if he keeps yapping about how I disturb his sleep.

Not my problem. I slam the door shut on the way out without saying a peep.

Just a week of rooming with him tells me this semester is going to be miserable. Every damn day, he grouches about the fact that I have to get up at five for training. I'm this close to jamming his own pillow into his ears so he can have all the silence he wants.

The worst—or best?—part is that Brett took his scrawny self to the student affairs office to ask for a roommate change. I admit I'd been contemplating it and was pleased as punch that I didn't have to put in that effort, especially because training hell week turned my legs into Jell-O every day. Unfortunately, his request got denied. We're stuck together for a whole semester.

If they'd put us athletes in the same dorm rooms, all of this suffering would've been avoided. A-freaking-las.

On the bright side, the preseason starts in a few days, and between hockey and school, I don't expect to spend much time in my dorm room.

I hop on my bike. The campus is pretty walkable, not to mention it's scenic, like something straight out of a movie. Buildings made out of red bricks, old architecture type of columns, trees so old that some paths look like a forest. With the air still warm from the late summer, I don't expect to need my truck until the winter. And it's also a good way to keep my legs moving.

For a college so few can afford to attend, there are people in every corner. And all of them look at me, pedaling my way through, as if I'm some anomaly. I must have *hockey scholarship* tattooed on my forehead. Or maybe it's my size what gives me away. According to Brett and the hostile stares I'm getting, no one here gives a flying turd about sports.

I thought he was bullshitting, but then I approach the building and people outright point and stare. Like some high-school type of pettiness I never imagined from people in higher education. I guess the scene might change, but the characters remain the same.

After tying my bike to the rack, I walk in like I'm a trust-fund baby and own the place.

A trust-fund baby who is not above using a map to find his way around. I check my phone to make my way through the maze of hallways. Bending my pride over to look at a map isn't any worse than asking directions from people openly hostile to me, so here we are.

There are already a few guys in the classroom. I thought I was gonna be the most hype nerd here, but my chronic problem of never making it to the place first continues.

Their eyes follow me like hawks as I climb all the way to the back of the room and take a seat. My legs are crammed under the too-small table, and the chair's armrests are too low, adding to my annoyance. In this moment, I sort of admire Boucher for having no reservations about opening his mouth, even if what's going to spew out is garbage. But I'm just a lowly student athlete. I can't step out of line. Which is exactly how telling them to get the hell out of my sight would be seen as.

Whatever, this isn't the first time I've been forced to interact with people who don't like me, and it won't be the last. Soon enough, they'll forget I'm here.

Not even two minutes later, Tinker Bell walks in, and I forget where *I* am.

My brain short-circuits. She has her hair down like at the bar the other night. Without the hockey gear or the gym clothes, she looks like someone who belongs here. The group of guys turn their attention on her, but either she doesn't notice or she doesn't care.

She gets to the middle of the room and takes off the biggest backpack I've ever seen. In the process, she looks back and spots me. And freezes.

My eyebrows go up. It's fun to see she's still annoyed by my presence. One corner of my lips goes up, and she responds by turning around and sitting down.

Well, well, well. Maybe this class won't be such a bore after all.

"Phew," someone says as they slide into the room. Brett rushes in, taking a look around. He doesn't see me, but he zeroes in on Tinker Bell right away and heads her way.

I lean forward, but I'm only a couple of seats to the side of her and can't see her expression. Is she happy to see him? I didn't think she was impressed at O'Malley's, but you never know with girls.

Wait, I don't care. She's free to enjoy tasteless company all she wants.

I spend the next ten minutes taking out my iPad and random stuff, just to have something to do. More people stream in and sit haphazardly across the room. By the time the lecturer graces us with his presence, I've rearranged the junk on my desk like five times.

"Welcome to Intro to Entrepreneurship." I love how someone who is supposed to instill the excitement of being an entrepreneur sounds like he's about to nod off.

Hoo, boy. I start recording with my iPad. The plan is to listen to the lectures again while I train, but I also don't want to fall asleep while bench-pressing weights.

As the class progresses, I feel a strong urge to fling myself out the window just to feel something.

Tinker Bell brushes her hand down her long hair several times. She picks at invisible lint from her T-shirt and rummages through her backpack. Meanwhile, Brett alternates between watching the front and his neighbor. Especially when she plays with her hair. How come the dude hates me, a hockey player, but is mesmerized by her, a hockey player?

I tuck my tongue against my cheek, knowing the answer easily. Tinker Bell is hot. I figured it out on day one, when I caught her filling up bottles during training. She'd been in just a sports bra and padded leggings, and I suffer from really excellent eyesight. It's how I caught the scar down her back as she walked away.

I also suffer from superb tactile memory, and I can't forget how the curve of her butt felt in the palm of my hand.

Time to focus on the lecture.

"During this class, you will prepare a business plan you can take to the venture lab from our faculty."

Great, that's precisely why I picked this class. I won't be able to play hockey professionally all my life, and it'll be good to have a plan for what happens after. I want to open my own business, sort of like my parents did when they arrived in this country some forty years ago. I just don't know what my business should be about.

"And you will do this with a partner."

No one dares to voice their complaints yet, but it's in the rustle of papers, the groaning of seats, and the reluctant glances everyone casts around the room. I'm not looking forward to having to align my schedule with someone else's either.

"*And,*" the lecturer says with extra emphasis, "I have already decided on the pairings."

"What?" someone at the front explodes.

There's open annoyance now.

*Oh Lord. Please don't let me pair up with Brett Ferguson.* That would be too much calamity.

The lecturer starts reading the pairs aloud, and on the second round, he reads off Brett's name along with someone else's. I sag against the seat, and it creaks under the weight shift.

Tinker Bell glances back at me for the first time, as if the noise reminded her of my existence. It's at that moment that the lecturer calls out my name.

"Massimo Cassiano and Luz Rodriguez."

Well freaking well.

She whips back to the front. "But—"

The lecturer ignores her and finishes calling names. Meanwhile, Brett turns around to toss such a hostile look at me he reminds me of my relatives. And as if this were Thanksgiving and I were getting a lecture, I give him a shit-eating grin that is sure to increase his blood pressure.

The lecture ends, and as people trickle out, Tinker Bell marches right down to the podium like she's on a mission. I don't need super hearing to know what she's saying. I jog down the stairs, ignoring my roommate and all the stares.

"—work with someone else?"

"Well, I don't want to change partners," I say. Their attention shifts to me for a moment, and I shrug.

She'd fry me with her eyes if she glared any longer.

"Great," the lecturer says despite his voice making everything sound the opposite. "Because I chose these pairs for a reason."

The last couple of students leave, but not before taking one last look at the drama.

He jams his laptop back in its case and gives us a droll stare. "You two are the only student athletes in this class. I thought it would be easier for everybody to be paired with people at their level, don't you think?"

My jaw drops. So does Tinker Bell's.

"Thought so. See you next class." With that, he walks out of the classroom with all the dignity of someone who thinks he's in the right.

Tinker Bell splutters and turns around to face me, pointing at the door like words fail her. Finally, she lets out a very eloquent "what the hell?"

I run a hand through my hair. "Yeah, that just happened."

"Did we just get discriminated against?"

"That's… what it feels like."

She shoves my shoulder weakly. "And you didn't help my case, you jerk."

"Because I didn't want to." I put my hands in my jean pockets. "Here's an idea, Tinker Bell. Why don't you redirect all that hostility toward these people who think the two of us have a single brain cell combined?"

"Might be easier to just report them." Her lips pinch.

"Than to work with me?" I put a hand on my chest. "Whew, and here I thought you stopped hating me when you jumped me."

"Shh!" She looks around, but her shoulders relax when she finds the room is empty. "This is why I can't possibly work with you, you annoying, arrogant little—"

I cut her off before her rant can get more colorful. "Well, you're stuck with me, Tinker Bell."

"Ugh."

My cheek twitches. This is already my favorite class of the semester.

# CHAPTER 6
## LUZ

Today is our first game of the preseason. One of the
girls paces up and down the length of the locker room,
still in her skivvies. There's another one in a corner
who is praying the rosary, and in the quiet of my mind, I join
the prayers. Because I, too, am freaking out.

I sit on my bench, mostly dressed. One of my knees
bounces aggressively. If it would stop, I'd be able to put on
my wool socks. I run the palms of my hands up and down
my lap.

"Mija, *relax*," I mutter to myself.

It's not like it's my first game ever. And it's absolutely not
like I'm afraid of losing or getting hurt. Both things have
happened plenty of times, some more catastrophic than others.
So what gives? Why am I so nervous?

Beside me, JT takes deep breaths like a pregnant woman.
"I don't know why I can't just calm the hell down."

"Me neither." I shake my head. And again. "Why does it
feel so do or die?"

Chelsea's putting her auburn hair in a ponytail as she says,
"Probably because it is?"

JT and I look at her like she's suddenly talking about quantum physics.

"Think about it." She finishes her hair and sits back down on her bench, on my other side. "If we do a bad job, people are going to hate us even more than they already do."

And they hate us, aight. All week and in every one of my classes, I've heard people talking smack about the hockey players. They're rowdy, think they're hot shit, take up too much space, sweat too much, and generally don't seem to have a single coherent thought in their skulls. Obviously, they're talking about the Bolts. The problem is that the blanket statements are about *all* hockey players.

Until now, I haven't had the occasion to reveal to my classmates that I belong to that group. I guess they're not aware that there's also a female team. Or simply put, the Strikes are nothing like the Bolts.

But after tonight's game, there will be no hiding. For us, it's a home game. Which means that anyone who's bored on a Friday night can come watch. Our faces will show up on the screen above the ice while we're being introduced.

Plus, the women's team having a home game to break the ice—while the men's game is away—is a big cause for celebration. I heard Coach Young mention that there will be some pictures taken to commemorate the occasion.

Bottom line is that now everyone will know I'm a Strike. I should be jumping for joy, but instead, I'm nervous. I smack my cheeks. *Hard.* The slapping sound brings all activity to a halt, and all eyes settle on me.

"And who cares?" I say aloud, even though I'm talking to myself. "Who gives a damn if everyone in this school hates us? We didn't come here to be everyone's besties but to play hockey and to kick ass at it."

"Aw, yeah." JT slams her hand on her bare thigh and jumps to her feet. "Luz is right. Let's just do our thing."

Chelsea grabs my shoulder. When I look at her, she's smirking. "Besides, once they see how amazing we are on the ice, they won't be able to stop themselves from falling for us."

"That's right, baby!" Brittany Thomas, one of the forwards, tosses her dreadlocks over her shoulder. "And look at us, we are *fire*. Those nerds don't know what they're missing out on."

One by one, the whole team gets infected by that mood. Amid a chorus of yeahs and hollers, my knee stops bouncing. I put on my long wool socks and slide my feet into my skates. I even hum a song as I lace them up really tight. It takes me a moment to realize the song in my head is "We Are The Champions."

When I finish putting on all my pads—legs, top, and elbows —I realize I have a problem.

"Yo, where are the official jerseys?" I ask, peeping at the other stalls. Everyone has their practice jerseys hanging there instead of official ones with their last names and numbers.

JT blinks up at me real fast. "I forgot about that. Somehow, I thought we were gonna play with the practice ones."

"That's on me," Coach Young says, entering the room with the rest of her staff. Coach McDonald carries a big cardboard box in her arms. "The jerseys arrived last minute."

The training coach drops the box unceremoniously. Meanwhile, the head coach motions at us to stand in line. In various states of undress, the team stands before them.

Okay, my nerves have morphed into a different kind of fluttering in my veins. Excitement.

Coach Young crouches before the box. Time slows down as she flips the flaps open, one by one, and pulls out the first jersey. "Let's see… Leblanc."

"Here!" She gets the jersey flung at her face.

"White."

Chelsea braces for the throw. "Here."

Since she's next to me, I can look at the details up close. The base color is baby blue, with white and dark blue trim. There's a big lightning streak at the front in the dark blue color. The words *Thunder Strikes* are written in a vintage-looking font, with the name of the school at the top.

I exhale in relief. Thank heavens it's not some pink monstrosity.

"Hold up." I get closer. "Is that an A?"

Chelsea looks down, and sure enough, there's an A in the top corner.

"*Ooh.*"

That sound comes from Chelsea, from me, and from everyone else in the room.

"Rodriguez."

Before I can even look at the coach, she flings my jersey at my face with perfect precision. I can confirm the fabric is pretty tasty.

I pull some fluff off my tongue and check out my jersey. Number five. My last name is spelled correctly. Success.

While I'm doing my usual wiggling dance to pull it on, someone gasps with enough intensity to drain half the oxygen in the room. I freeze, but I don't need to look around long to find the cause of the shock. It's me. Everyone's staring at me.

"What—"

JT yanks my jersey all the way down and shouts. "All hail the captain!"

"The heck?" I finish my own question.

Stretching the fabric forward, I catch the C on my breast.

A pat on my back is strong enough that I lurch forward. That or I've suddenly grown weak.

"Not gonna question it this time?" Coach Young smirks at me, but not in a mean way. Her eyes glint.

"Uh, matter fact, I will. Why me?"

"Because of this." Coach Young takes another jersey, calls

the name, and makes another throw. "It's kind of annoying, but there's value in you questioning things. Just learn when to do it and when to stay mum."

"Uh… yes, ma'am."

"Besides," Coach McDonald adds with a little laugh, "it was kind of funny to see how you neutralized the Bolts' captain and stole the foam roller from him."

My eyes are probably wider than pucks.

"Wait. You saw that?" I shake my head hard. "Cassiano is their captain now?"

"Brewer," Coach calls and throws.

One second later, JT hoots. "Aw yeah, baby. Alternate captain!"

Well, we're certainly *a choice*. JT, who is extravagant. Chelsea, who is sly. And me. The most impulsive person on earth.

I wait until everyone is suited up and we're about to make the trip out to the ice. Deliberately, I slow down until I fall back with the coaches.

"Coach Young, I—don't get me wrong, this is a great honor. But I'm not sure I'm the right person for the job."

It's dark out here in the hallway, but her eyes can probably see right through my helmet and skull. I bet she can read all my insecurities, my fears, all the bravado I put out to hide them.

"I appreciate you bringing up this concern. One of the reasons I chose you is because you're not afraid to speak your mind." She pauses to take a pack of gum from her pocket. "You're part of the first-ever class of Strikes. The team needs to be memorable. You, Brewer, and White will make sure of that."

I cringe. "What if we make it memorable the wrong way?"

"Then the team crumbles, we get our budget cut even more, and maybe I'll lose my job." I can't believe she can say all that with a brilliant smile. She puts her hand on my shoulder pad. "So don't screw up, all right?"

"I—yes. I mean no, ma'am."

"Good. Now go give us our first W."

On that note, I march like a stiff robot to join the team. My heart pounds like I'm in the third period already, even though I'm stepping onto the ice for the first time.

The arena looks different lit only by strobe lights. I skate around, doing basic drills in a trance. The added responsibility feels like I just put on ten extra pounds in the span of minutes.

Well, I didn't come here to fool around. I came here to win. That hasn't changed. If anything, it's more important now. And the only way I can do that is by focusing on the game.

By the time the lights are on, I'm ready. I sing the anthem with a bit more passion than usual. Who would've thought a Venezuelan American girl would be the captain of her Division I hockey team? Not me.

Or that a girl who once lost her ability to walk would play again? Definitely not me. But I'm a tough girl. A little responsibility won't crack me.

I faceoff with a girl from the opposite team. She gives me a weird look, probably because the grin on my face is some villain type of shit.

The ref drops the puck, and it's showtime.

There is nothing more beautiful than the sound of sticks slamming against each other and against the ice. It's the soundtrack of my victory as I steal the puck and pass it over to Brit. I don't know if it's that we're all giddy about having just gotten jerseys and we're feeling like we're finally on a team, but we play like our moves have been choreographed.

Not even two minutes into the first period, and we have our first goal. I throw myself into the mass of bodies celebrating. We're gonna pulverize this team.

Play resumes, and I return to the bench for a line change. I spot something familiar in the scarce crowd. My brother's face. And my sister's. And her best friend's.

It's the latter who waves his arms at me and claps like a proud parent whose child just scored a buzzer beater. Very on brand for Brooklyn. Meanwhile, my siblings look disinterested to the naked eye. Aran, the middle kid, is probably watching our every move like a hawk. But Olivia, the youngest, couldn't care less about hockey and was probably dragged here by the other two.

My parents are MIA. I didn't expect these three to come to this game, let alone Mom and Dad. They don't even want me to touch a stick.

"Who's the kid who keeps waving, and how are his arms not falling off?" Chelsea squirts water into her mouth.

I sigh. "A family friend. The other two are my siblings."

"Aw, cute!"

Not.

Like the grown adult I am, I stick my tongue out at the three of them. They don't see my grin as I face forward again. I'll show Aran and Brooke how it's done. And I'll show everyone who said I could never play again that I, in fact, freaking can.

# CHAPTER 7
## MAX

"There's no *I* in *team*, and yet so many of you are whining that you weren't made team captain?" Coach Green shakes his head, hands on hips like a disappointed parent. "Instead of thinking long and hard about why you weren't selected?"

Damn. Coach doesn't have to go so hard.

I balance my weight from one foot to the other. Most of the grumbling hasn't been about me. But really about the fact that everyone wanted that C for themselves. Which means, great, we have a team made up of selfish pricks.

And then there's Boucher. He points at my face with his stick. "Are you sure you didn't pick him because he's some sort of celebrity?"

The hell? I reel back from the awkwardness that is taking way too much space in this locker room.

I'm not the more famous Cassiano. But the optics of having an opening game of Cassiano versus Cassiano are probably too good to pass up for St. Cloud, a school that still needs to find its place in the conference. Because, of freaking course, I have to faceoff with Leo tonight. Our opponent for this friendly game couldn't be any of the other ten teams, but the Bulldogs of Brighton College.

"So what?" I ask, annoyed to the point of barely holding back f-bombs. "The fact that a handful of people know my name won't make us win. Why don't you go out there and show everyone that you have the leadership skills for the job?"

Nate whistles. "Man, I got some baby cream for that burn if you need it."

"Why do you have baby cream?" Conor can't hold back his laughter.

"The jockstrap chafes the family jewels. Don't judge."

And those two are my alternate captains, ladies and gentlemen.

"That's right," Coach continues. "Just because you don't have a C on your jersey doesn't mean you shouldn't go out there and lead the charge. And that's what I want all you bunch of ninnies to do out there tonight. Is that clear?"

"Yes, sir."

Weakest chorus I've heard. This game is going to be a disaster.

Boucher slams past my shoulder on our way out to the ice, like a child. It's not like I was desperate for the C, but Frankie Boucher has less common sense than I thought if he thinks this attitude makes him more deserving of the role.

The arena is bathed in red flashing lights that make the ice look like it's bloody. Apt, because Leo's team isn't exactly known for playing clean. The stands are packed with Bulldogs fans who boo us the moment we enter. The Bulldogs circle the rink, stoking their fans to an even louder greeting.

I'll score at least one goal and shut them up.

One of the Bulldogs breaks formation suddenly, speeding up toward me like I have the puck and we're in mid-play. My lungs expand and contract with a heavy sigh.

Here we go.

"If it's none other than Maxi Pad!" Leo's obnoxious voice arrives before the spray of slush as he brakes. "Who the hell was fool enough to put a C on your chest?"

"Screw all the way off, Leo."

He laughs, knowing that sound is enough to sour my grapes. "Oh, this is gonna be epic. Can't believe I'll have the honor of crushing you on your college debut."

"The only thing that's gonna be crushed here is your ego." I skate by him, adding some emphasis as I say "*nephew*."

The way his expression changes makes me grin.

Leo is an outstanding player, and I can admit—only to myself—that I'm nowhere near a level where I can beat him yet. But it's like he's made it his life's quest to shit on me every chance he gets.

During Thanksgiving, Christmas, birthdays—including my own—and every time the whole Cassiano clan gathers, Leo has to go on and on about how he's the best in the game and I shouldn't even try. Just because he was born three years before me and found hockey first doesn't mean he can stake exclusivity over it. He even has my parents, his *grandparents*, convinced it's a waste for me to follow in his steps when they're so grand already.

Yeah, we're complicated. And the fact that I'm his uncle embarrasses the hell out of Leo.

Bunch of years ago, he was interviewed for *SPORTY* magazine, and when my name came up, he said I was his cousin. Like having an uncle younger than him would be some sort of mark against him. And ever since, it's the only leverage I have against him. I'm not above using it... a lot.

He keeps glaring at me as we sing the anthem. All I do is smile, even though I know the second play starts, he's going to come at me like a battering ram.

Leo bends forward in front of me. The ref stands between us, raising the puck. This is probably the most important faceoff of my life. I have to win, even if it costs all my teeth.

The puck drops with a slap.

My asshole nephew stabs at my arm with his stick, hitting a spot the pads don't cover. I still get the puck for the Bolts. He slams against me to slow me down.

"Good luck. You'll need it against me!" he shouts before skating away.

My arm throbs. Can't wait to return the favor.

Maybe Boucher and the others are right and I was a terrible pick for captain. Thanks to my nephew's bullshit, I sort of forgot that the Bolts are in shambles right now. It doesn't matter that I won the faceoff when no one's here to pick up the puck. Instead of starting on the offensive, the Bulldogs steal the puck from us and attack our goal.

The only reason they don't score is because of the providence. Our D is haphazard. Our goalie looks confused by the crowd in front of him.

It's gonna be a long game, huh?

A few minutes later, when my line changes and I sit at the bench, I can see on Coach Green's face that he agrees with me. This is torture.

"Defense! Look at the puck and not your own noses!" The veins in his neck protrude with the strength of his scream. Then he turns to me, and I brace for the demise of my eardrums. "Cassiano."

"Yes, sir?"

"Go out there and play dirty."

I blink rapidly. "Excuse me?"

"There's nothing friendly about this damn game." Coach bites on his bubble gum with enough force to pulverize it. "I don't care if it gets you in the penalty box. Go and do something that lights a fire under your teammate's asses."

I guess if the captain is supposed to be some sort of role

model for the team, that's what's needed right now to wake them up. Some assholery.

And I know just the way.

With a couple of instructions to my guys, I make a quick plan. I'm almost giddy when I'm back on the ice. One of the Bolts passes the puck over to me, and it's time to fool around.

I feint a pass to Conor. It acts as a siren call to Leo, who tries to intercept me. I may not be as good a skater as Tinker Bell, but I know a trick or two. I glide closer to the boards, baiting him. Sure enough, he picks up speed to smack right into me. I bend down and hit the puck to pass it. Leo rams into the board on his own a nanosecond before I get there. With the momentum I carry, I blow right into him at a low spot and make him crash down like a Jenga tower.

I can only chuckle as the booing intensifies. Leo glares up at me, but I skate away. The puck's still in play, and I don't have time for him.

Conor makes a shot on goal, but the Bulldogs' goalie deflects it. The puck slides to me like it's being served on a silver platter, and I shoot.

An instant before a boulder runs through me from behind.

The whistle pierces through the action. And not a buzzer. Which means I didn't score. Damn it.

"Take that, Maxi Pad." Leo rolls off me, giggling as if he scored some big win.

The ref signals a minor offense for number 21 of the Bulldogs. It sparks joy in me.

I figure being on a power play is better than what Coach Green had in mind, because he stopped screaming. At least for the duration of those two minutes. When it becomes clear we can't even score when we have one extra man on the ice, he resumes the yelling.

The rest of the game goes even worse. When it ends, I'm glad we only lost by two goals, despite not scoring any.

I sit in the locker room, drenched in sweat and water. Coach Green has enough juice to scream at us some more, despite the obvious fact that he's losing his voice.

"You all should be embarrassed!" He points around the locker room. "Do you wanna know what that looked like? Like a bunch of preschoolers trying out skates for the first time!"

Shit, I'm pissed off. Our little drama costs us this game. It might've been a friendly game, but the Bulldogs are at the top of the conference, and this sends a clear message that we're at the bottom.

Leo's face when the final buzzer rang is now engrained between the wrinkles of my brain. The self-satisfaction oozed from his pores, as if he expected no less than this result.

I bet my left butt cheek he's texting his dad right this second about what a loser I am, and that in the next few minutes, my brother will call me with one of his condescending speeches. Cossimo Jr. only pretends to act like my eldest brother in moments like this, when he can be all sanctimonious. Otherwise he ignores me, and I prefer it that way.

I rip off my jersey like it's the cause of all my problems. And yeah, maybe it's not too mature of me, but it feels good to throw my pads on the floor with all my might.

"Jeez, you're taking this hard." Conor divests himself of his uniform like a regular person. "It's only game one. We're only going to get better from here on out."

"I bet it's because of his cousin," Nate says, somewhat right on the money.

"Next time, we'll win," I grumble under my breath, peeling off my undershirt and slamming it on top of my pads.

"Anyway, while you process all of these emotions," Nate says in a light tone as he checks his phone, "how about we crash a party tonight?"

I give him a look taken straight out of my mother's book. A straight-up *what the hell are you thinking, son?* vibe.

"The Strikes won their game, and apparently, they're all gonna hang out at some house party." Since it's clear I still don't follow, he adds, "Let's go ruin their party." And he gives us all an unhinged smile.

"Bad idea. I'm in." Conor laughs.

I have so much anger corroding my gut that instead of behaving, I feel my lips lift in a grim little arc and say, "Let's go."

# CHAPTER 8
## LUZ

"Yeehaw!"

That may or may not have been me. I'm still reeling from our first win. Crammed in an Uber with half of the team shouting the lyrics of a pop anthem, there's no way I'm coming down from this high.

I don't even know whose house we're headed to. Someone said the word *party*, and I was in. My back throbs like a toothache, but a good time will take care of that better than any over-the-counter painkiller. At least if I'm having fun, it'll be easier to ignore the pain.

The lyrics artfully eviscerate trashy men, and someone screams, "Preach it, sister!" I bet the driver can't wait to drop us all off and be free.

Dude halts the van in front of a Victorian house teeming with people, inside and out. There are people sitting on the windowsills, chatting with others on the porch or front yard, and passing drinks to someone inside. The bass coming from the house makes the asphalt vibrate beneath my feet. I don't think my eardrums will come out unscathed from this. I still head over to the source of the noise. That's where the fun is.

I lock arms with Chelsea, who stumbles in her heels as if she isn't used to them. I foresee them being chucked out a window later tonight.

"Aight, ladies." JT stops before the whole group, blocking our way to the entrance. "We scored a big win. Now, let's rock this damn house tonight!"

I join in the chorus of hollers.

The second we walk in, every pair of eyes falls on us. Obviously, these Ivy League people have never seen a group of girls so hot in their lives.

I recognize the song playing on the speakers, and it gets my body alive. There's a bounce in my step as I make my way through the crowd, closer to the speakers. A few people dance with beer in hand, swaying side to side to the tempo.

Someone grabs my hand, and I'm relieved to find it's Brit. She gives me a grin that speaks volumes. *Let's show them how it's done.*

We let loose, just two girls who can follow a tune with their bodies. I know my skintight jeans are doing wonders for me as I shake my hips. The white crop top is certainly making a few eyes bulge.

Brit's a total knockout, though. In a black dress glued to her skin and a short skirt that shows off her mile-long legs, she has half the people in the room salivating. She'll have more than one suitor tonight.

Me? I'm literally thirsty.

"Want a drink?" I shout in her ear.

She shakes her head. "I'm good, boo!"

A couple of other Strikes have joined us on the dance floor, so it's not like I'll be leaving her alone to the wolves. After giving her a thumbs-up, I work my way through the throng of people to what I hope is the kitchen. Turns out I was right, but the counter has been taken over by a beer pong game, and there's no way to get through.

"Seeking booze? I got you, fam."

I have to laugh as JT pulls at my arm, somehow having read my mind and already having the solution. Best alternate captain a girl could ask for.

Latching on to her arm, I follow her through a narrow hallway by the staircase. The crowd's thicker here, but it's not because of the size of the space. No, sir. It's because here—in a bathroom—there's a whole freaking bathtub filled with ice and beer bottles.

"Qué carajo…"

Chelsea sits on the toilet lid, chugging a beer to the chants of two guys crammed in the space too. She finishes the bottle in record time, and everyone starts cheering as if the home team scored a goal.

"Oh, there you are." She wipes her face with the back of her hand when she spots us. "Want a beer?"

"Yes, please." JT opens her hand and Chelsea flings a bottle at her.

The other girl passes it to me, and I stare at it for a second too long, as if I could scan it for germs with my bare eyes. Well, I did see Chelsea grab it from the top of the tub. And it's fully capped, so at least the part that will be in contact with my lips is clean. I uncap it with my forearm, a little trick I picked up from my dad. One I'm sure he's not proud of.

"Dayum, girl!" JT watches as I toss the cap in the basket with precision. "That's a neat trick. Lemme try it." She gives up on the first try and ends up opening it like a civilized person —with the edge of the sink counter.

I take a swig of the cold beer and sag against the door-frame. More people come in and out, looking for a drink to fuel their mood. Someone shoves me pretty hard, and I'm about to get in their grill when I notice who it is.

It's the rudest of the Bolts.

"What's this?" He takes a look around in the bathroom,

zeroing in on Chelsea. "What are a bunch of little girls drinking alcohol for?"

"It's the only way I could possibly stand seeing your ugly face," Chelsea says in return, lifting a new bottle in a little toast.

I cackle like a maniac. Unfortunately, that catches his attention.

"What's so funny, you little b—"

"Don't even finish that sentence." The threatening tone in my voice isn't subtle. I cram myself into the bathroom to square up to him. As if that would intimidate a guy who has a full head on me.

"Or what?" The clown snorts. "You think you can possibly win against me? But you're so *tiny*."

His breath reeks of way more alcohol than I possibly could've had. Which gives me a brilliant idea. "Why don't we have a little drinking contest, then?" I bet he'll pass out with only a couple more beers, and that'll rid us of him for the rest of the night.

"Great idea." A deep voice comes from the door. I don't have to turn to see who it's coming from. Recognition passes through my body with a shiver. "Boucher, get out."

Boucher, the burly guy who wastes no time insulting the Strikes, scrunches up his face like a kid who's been told off. "No. She issued the challenge to *me*. I'm not about to wuss out of it."

But what if instead of drinking him down, I smash a bottle against his head? Would that make him stop talking? Surely it would be a service to all humankind.

I make the mistake of looking at Cassiano as he says, "Wouldn't a captain-to-captain challenge be more fun?" The way Cassiano's eyes glint tells me that, no, it wouldn't. At least not for me. But if I say that aloud, it'll be the same as putting my foot in my mouth.

So I shrug. "It doesn't matter who tries to take me on. I'll win anyway."

"Oh, snap!" One of the people I don't know pulls out two bottles from the tub, ready for the action.

"Are you sure?" JT asks in my ear, massaging my shoulders like a coach taking care of her boxer.

"Too late to back down," Chelsea confirms, grabbing a bottle from the guy who's been taking care of the stash. "We have to win no matter what."

I know. The problem is that Max Cassiano doesn't look anywhere near as tipsy as his buddy.

He doesn't look anything like his buddy, period. Cassiano is the kind of guy who turns heads, and I'm not immune to him when his attention is solely trained on me. He doesn't break eye contact as he opens the first bottle with his hand. A buzz is building up in my belly even before I take the first sip.

My party trick to open beer bottles makes his eyebrows go up. That's the last respite I get before someone counts down from three, and we start to drink.

Mierda. He's too fast. He keeps looking at me while he chugs like he's never drunk a drop in his life.

I struggle to keep up, but I won't call it quits. One bottle after another, I drink and drink, ignoring the way the bubbles burn my throat and the trickles escaping from my lips. There's beer between my boobs, but I take comfort in the fact that his gray T-shirt doesn't hide his spillage either. This goes on for who knows how long. What is time when you're trying to knock your opponent off his pedestal?

The walls of the bathroom feel closer. Or is it that the space between us has shrunken? Cassiano is way too close now. He catches me with his free hand as I sway. Which is annoying. It means he can still stand on his own two feet.

People still chant the word *chug* around us. I can't let my team down. On the plus side, I feel nothing as I take the first swig of a new bottle. How many have I drunk? How many has *he* drunk?

No importa. What matters here is that I have to be the last one standing.

"You don't look good, Tinker Bell," he says, wiping his face with an arm.

It takes me a couple of tries to find his real chest and poke it. "What you talking 'bout? I'm freaking hot."

"Hell yeah!" Is that JT? My girl.

Hold up, is he nodding or is the ground shaking?

"Sure, but let's just say I win and call it a night."

"*Never.*" I open and close my hand into the void, but a beer doesn't magically appear in it. "Another beer!"

Cassiano sighs.

Is he not even a little bit affected? Or are all those muscles of his a distillery?

I fixate on a thin line of beer descending from his jaw, all the way down the side of his neck. The trickle treks down his clavicle and disappears below his T-shirt. The second I wonder how far it goes, I start choking.

The convulsions are so strong I lose my balance, and this time, no one catches me as I go down. A shock of cold makes me yelp. I shake around, trying to get out of it. My lungs take a deep breath when I resurface.

The noise is unbearable. I almost want to go down again. People shout and laugh. It takes me another moment to realize why.

I fell into the damn tub.

My right hand comes up with a beer bottle. My crop top floats over a slush of ice and water.

Hold up. My back's never felt better.

"You okay?" JT grabs my arms, trying to pull me up. But I don't budge.

"Never better." My voice comes out in a slur. I narrow my

eyes at the Bolts' captain, who's still standing there like a statue. "By the way, you're cheating."

"What?"

"Beer keeps trickling down your mouth."

He snorts. "Yours too."

"Where's your proof?" I giggle, knowing that it's washed away in the gross tub water.

If he rolled his eyes any harder, they'd pop out of their sockets.

"The point is that I'm the last man standing, so I win."

A bunch of guys start cheering in a super obnoxious way. It becomes imperative that I stand up and show them that's not true.

Between JT and Chelsea, they help me get to my feet. But instead of the cheers I expect, someone whistles in a way that makes my skin crawl.

JT cringes. "Oh, crap. Girl, you're giving a show."

"What show?"

I glance down to where she points. My vision's blurry, and I seem to have four boobs. All of which are pretty clear, with my white top gone practically transparent.

# CHAPTER 9
# MAX

Tinker Bell is wild.

Not only is it a bad idea to take me on a drinking challenge, but now she's absolutely cracked up about the fact she fell into the tub. Her pink bra isn't hiding much from the onlookers, but it doesn't seem to faze her.

It's rattling me, though. Much more than the pool of beer in my stomach.

I turn around and push a couple of guys out of the room.

"Hey, man!"

"Show's over." I grunt, hoping they catch the drift. This may not bother her right now, but tomorrow morning might be a different story. I might've come here with the intention of raining on the Strikes' parade—and mission accomplished on that—but I'm not some perv.

"But—"

"Out."

I manage to shut the door, leaving the crowd outside. Both of her friends are trying to hide her from view, but they're tipsy too. The swaying doesn't provide a significant barrier between her and the onlookers.

"Any towels?" I glance around, trying to spot one. All I see is a soggy roll of toilet paper by the sink.

The one with all the piercings raises her hand. "I'll go find one."

She braves the door. The second it's open, people want to tumble inside to get a drink. It takes more work than I care to admit to close it again.

What are the odds the Strike will actually return with a towel? In a strange house, packed with people in various states of drunkenness, that'd be a feat harder than finding someone sober.

Meanwhile, Tinker Bell pushes her hair back with clumsy hands. It's stuck to her face and neck. Her cheeks and nose are red from the cold or the beer, but there are no makeup smudges.

A string of words I don't recognize tumble out of her mouth, and then she says, "My *phone*."

"Oh, it must be so dead," the other girl says, the one with reddish hair.

"*No.*"

I want to laugh. Except I keep getting distracted by the crop top and the way it's stuck to the curves and ridges of her chest like a second skin. It doesn't even hide the texture of her bra's lace.

Shit, I wouldn't have pegged Tinker Bell for a lace girl.

I shake my head hard enough to rattle my brain back in place. Can't start wondering if there's lace under her jeans.

I grab the hem of my T-shirt and pull it up. The air in the bathroom feels cold as ice against my skin, but Tinker Bell must be straight-up freezing.

"Excuse me" is all the warning I give. The two girls have turned into statues while I fiddle with my T-shirt until I'm grabbing it by the neck. I pull it over Tinker Bell's head.

She makes that sound when a lot of words want to tumble

out at the same time but her mouth can't keep up. Her protests are weak, and I manage to pull her arms through and lower the garment all the way. Looking down at herself makes her stagger.

I grab her by the shoulders. Moisture is already seeping through the fabric. But other than dark splotches, no one will see what they shouldn't.

Her friend clears her throat. "Uh…"

"You're naked," Tinker Bell says to my stomach.

"Technically," I say, not even trying to mask my amusement, "I'm only *half*-naked."

For a second, I fear she's about to lurch forward and puke her guts up. I brace, but all she does is squint at my abs.

"Damn, how many of you are there?"

Her friend bursts out laughing. "Oh, this is amazing."

"I think you should go home, Tinker Bell. You're very drunk."

"I am *not*." Her eyebrows crash, her nose wrinkles, and her bottom lip juts out.

I have to look away, because I'm this close to biting it.

"Er, anyway. Can you take her?"

"So you're willing to stay at this party looking like this?" The more sober girl draws a line up and down in the air with her finger.

This entire night hasn't been my best idea. I knew it was a dick move to play this game with a girl, but I didn't want to watch her take on Boucher. That wouldn't have gone well. Or it'd have gone even worse than this.

"I mean, what other choice do I have?"

"You could…" We both observe the other girl as she makes a too-long pause. "Take her home?"

"But it's so early!" Tinker Bell tries to shake her shoulders. All it accomplishes is that she crashes face first against my chest.

I freeze, hands up in the air.

Her friend gives me a condescending smile. "Tag, you're it."

Through gritted teeth, I say, "You do know I'm a virtual stranger, right?"

She shrugs. "You've already shown more chivalry than any other guy here. Besides, if something happens to her, I know exactly where to find you."

"Do you seriously think your captain would be happy with this?"

"Fine. I still think Luz could knee you in the cojones if you tried anything. Right, Captain?"

Tinker Bell hiccups. "Absolutely."

Doubt it, especially because she looks like she'd be trying to aim at two sets of cojones instead of one.

"Stay still," I order. She sways even more. While holding one of her arms, I turn around and pull her against me. It takes another try until she's positioned so I can pick her up. With one little bounce, I manage to tuck my hands under her thighs.

"I'll lead the way out," the other girl says. As if that were the toughest job.

But she opens the bathroom door, and the crunch does prove it a tough task. Progress is very slow through the house when we keep getting blocked by people who want to leer or make fun of us. Someone tries to take a picture, and I have to pause the trek to swipe their phone and delete it.

At last, we make it outside and I can breathe easier.

The other girl pulls up her phone and calls for an Uber. Meanwhile, Tinker Bell nuzzles her face against my neck and mumbles. "Hmm, pillow's hard."

I want to cry. And laugh. But I don't, because I have an audience.

Instead, I get a solid workout lowering both of us to the

sidewalk while we wait for the ride back to campus. Tinker Bell dozes off against my back, and either she's absolutely sopping wet, or she's drooling on my skin. I vow to never let her live this down. But first we have to survive the night.

It takes almost a full hour to get back to campus. Only when I'm about to reach the girls' dorms do I realize I have no idea which building or room she lives in.

"Hey." I shake her just a bit. "Tinker Bell, wake up."

"Stop calling me Bell. My name is Luz."

The other girl chuckles from a few steps behind.

"What's your room number?" I ask Tinker Bell.

I feel her stir. Her voice sounds more at my ear level when she asks, "Why do you want to know?"

"So I can drop you off and go on my merry way." My voice comes out in a whine. My shoulders burn from holding her weight for so long. At this point, all I want is to put her down so I can stretch.

"Well, I don't trust you." She collapses back on my shoulder.

I give the other girl a side-eye, as if saying *see?*

She mumbles something. I don't get it because her face is buried against the crook of my neck, and it's not like my skin can read her lips moving against it. I squeeze my eyes shut and take several deep breaths. This is all doing a number on my sanity.

"What's that?" My voice comes out choked and too deep, but all I get is a mumble.

Finally, the other Strike makes herself useful by checking something on her phone and saying, "The captain's room is one-three-two."

Oh, bless. That means she's on the first building, third floor, second door. That's the building we're closest to, and now that I have a clear goal, I make quick work up the stairs. I'm not even too winded when I finally stop at her door and let her down slowly.

Once she's safely inside, I'll retrieve my T-shirt and run on to my dorm, where I can take the longest cold shower known to man to wash away the sensations of her body against mine.

Tinker Bell has other plans, though. She slides down the door until she's sitting on the floor. Her head hangs like she's fallen asleep.

Turning to the other girl and ignoring the amusement all over her face, I say, "Okay, I think you got it from here."

"No way. I'm not strong enough to haul her inside and to her bed." She gives me a shrug, palms facing up in the universal what *can I do?* way.

I brush my hands down my face. Never would I have imagined myself to be so patient. Crouching down, I tilt her face up by her chin. "Tinker Bell, wake up. You can't sleep here."

With a groan, she cracks one eye open. "Cassiano? What are you doing here?"

A groan escapes my throat. I'm definitely paying for ruining her night.

Sighing, I ask, "Can you give me your key?"

"It's in my pocket."

"Your jeans have four pockets. Do you want me to stick my hand in all of them to find it?" The deadpan in my voice sparks her consciousness again.

"You right." Slowly, she tilts herself on her left side to rummage in her right back pocket. Out comes a dripping phone and a set of keys.

The other girl snatches the keys and opens the door. I hear her flip a switch, and light bathes the hallway. She declares, "Coast is clear."

Good thing no one else will have to suffer through this girl's mess, I suppose. "In you go," I tell Tinker Bell.

She extends her hands. Asking for help.

I snort. "You're kidding me."

"The floor keeps moving," she says with a very serious expression.

"Ugh."

I bend down, about to lift her up, when she grabs my arms and pulls me against her. Tinker Bell cinches her arms around my neck in a vise. If I was too self-conscious of her chest against my back the entire way here, it's an entirely different experience when she glues herself to my chest.

It's official. I am a saint.

Tinker Bell yawns. I need to stop wasting time standing here like a damn robot and put her to bed while she's still mostly cooperating. She hangs from my neck while I walk into the room. It's easy to tell which one is her bed. While one is dressed in all black bedding, the other one has a hockey jersey strewn on it, along with a couple of knee pads and what looks like a ball of dirty socks.

"In you go." I bend until her thighs touch the edge of the mattress. But she doesn't let go. She pulls until I lose my balance.

At the last second, I grab her head and pivot so at least she won't crash against the wall. I can't help the fact that my full weight falls on her.

Air escapes from her lungs. A curse from mine. The other girl whistles.

"Damn, you're heavy." Tinker Bell grunts.

I brace myself on all fours so as not to crush her. "Yeah. Let go of me."

She doesn't. If anything, her arms grab on tighter. Her eyes are at half-mast, trained straight on my face.

"Uh, Tinker Bell?"

"I'm cold."

I swallow with difficulty. "I bet. Let me just pull your blanket over you and—"

With strength I wouldn't think her capable of in her state, she pulls me flush against her. Tucking her face against my neck, she says, "You're so much warmer."

I can't move.

It doesn't matter that my arms are trembling, trying to hold my weight off her. Or that our legs are tangled in an awkward position where I feel way too much. Or that the dampness of her clothes is seeping through mine. My heart hammers in my ribcage. Any tipsiness I felt after chugging one beer after the next has been chased away by all of this.

I clear my throat, trying to untangle her arms from around me. But they're locked like steel, and now she's snoring softly against my shoulder.

Slowly, I twist as far as her grip will allow me, about to ask for help, when I find the other girl taking a picture of the scene. "Don't worry, it's not blackmail." As she tucks her phone back into her pocket, she says, "But if anything happens to her, I'll know who did it. Have a good night, though."

With that, she skips out of the room and shuts the door. Guess I'm not sleeping tonight, then.

# CHAPTER 10
## LUZ

Hmm, something smells good. I take a good, deep breath, expanding my nostrils as wide as they can go. It's not enough, so I bury my nose in the scent to capture it all. And whatever this is, it's also warm. The portions of my skin touching it are toasty, but everywhere else, I feel cold.

I burrow deeper into it. There's something soft under my hand. I splay it open and—no, hold on. The surface is soft, but beneath it has no yield at all. The fog in my brain dissipates just enough to let a single question shine through it. What the heck is this?

I run my hand across whatever this is. The softness is there, along with a little fuzz. My hand goes through a little bump, and then bigger ones. Ridges? Why are they contracting? There's a swooshing sound above me that fans air over my face. My hand stops at something cold.

My eyes snap open. The first thing I see is a bare chest.

Light streams from the window, so bright I have to squint against the pain. I count to three, with deep breaths in between. That beautiful smell is someone's skin, with traces of soap and something like sandalwood. I peek down at my trai-torous hand and find it on a belt buckle. If it'd kept going down—

I lift my hand abruptly.

Those ridges are abs. The most defined abs I've seen in my life, especially up close. The fuzz was the smattering of chest hair. I jump away until my back is glued to the wall.

Max Cassiano has both hands under his head. His eyebrows are cocked, and I can't interpret the expression on his face. Amusement? Anger? Annoyance?

"I was afraid you'd keep going."

The way I gasp is enough to suck half the oxygen from the room.

"Qué—no. How? *Why?*"

He remains silent for a moment, just staring at me through narrowed eyes.

That's annoyance, all right. Did I fondle him the whole night? I've been known to get a bit handsy when I'm drunk, but I've never woken up in bed with a semi-naked guy. Espe-cially not someone whose muscles are a work of art. In this position, it's clear how tiny his waist is. His biceps bulge as testimony to many a hard workout session. His hair is tousled with sleep, and there's a layer of scruff on his face.

I can't blame my sleepy self for wanting to cop a feel. But at the same time, if this situation were reversed, I would be well on my way to committing murder.

When I open my mouth to beg for forgiveness, he inter-rupts. "You got way too drunk at the party and fell in the tub. Bad idea, because your top got fully transparent. So, I put on my T-shirt on you."

I look down at myself. Sure enough, I'm swimming in a damp, gray T-shirt. That explains why he's showing off his goods.

Clearing my throat, I say, "Yeah, well. I couldn't back down from the challenge."

"Then," Max continues, as though this is a conversation about the weather. "I had to carry you on my back all the way here—"

"What?"

"Okay, we took an Uber. But I still had to do all the lifting." He moves his head to get a better look up at me. "By the way, Tinker Bell, you're a lot heavier than you look."

"I'll have you know it's all muscle."

"Yeah, I know. I could feel it."

My eyes are wide. "What is that supposed to mean?"

"If that wasn't enough," he says, adding a snort for punctuation. "When I finally tried to put you to bed, you wouldn't let me go."

Oh, no. I squeeze the fabric of his T-shirt against my chest. Tension shrinks me like a raisin. In a careful but terrified whisper, I ask, "What did I do to you last night?"

Once, during a party in high school, I got so drunk that I grabbed my two friends and turned them into my very own pillows. No matter how hard they tried to go back out to have fun, I squeezed them against me until they gave up. It helped that they're two skinny girls.

Cassiano is anything but small, and yet here he is, glaring at me.

"Let's just say I couldn't sleep a wink."

"I will never live this down, will I?" Something that sounds like a mix between a whine and a groan escapes from me.

The corner of his lips quirks. "How did you read my mind?"

The door opens with no warning, and I die. For like a millisecond.

Dressed all in black, with combat boots, studded belt, and a lip piercing, is none other than my roommate.

My knee-jerk reaction is to kick Cassiano out of my bed. As if that would erase from her mind what she just saw and whatever conclusions that picture may lead her to.

There's a groan from the floor, and I scoot to the edge of the bed. He's so big he takes up all the space between the beds. The landing zone—his butt—is massaged by his hand, giving me ample view of the broad back I apparently clung to all night. I wish I remembered how it felt against me.

No! Qué estoy pensando?

I shake my head hard enough to give myself a headache.

"It's not what you're thinking!" I squeak out to my roommate.

Her blue eyes settle on the fallen guy, and for the first time in two weeks and a half, she says a single word.

"*Nice.*"

I freeze. So does Max.

She walks in, picks up a book from her desk, and stuffs it into her messenger bag. With that, she turns around and closes the door behind her.

My heart pounds so hard the drumming leaves no energy for my lungs to take in air. I try to take a few deep breaths, but it doesn't work. Flashes of heat and cold travel up and down my body. The contents of my stomach spin like a top. My head throbs in tune with my pulse.

Meanwhile, the boy sits up on the floor, running his hands through his hair and messing it further. Is it as soft as his skin?

Oh, crap. I've gone and lost it.

I need to get his scent off me. It's addling my brain and not letting me *think*. I take his T-shirt off in one motion, ball it up, and throw it at the back of his head.

Slowly, Max plucks the garment off himself and turns back to me.

He chokes on his own saliva.

Weirdo.

Pounding his chest, he manages to say, "Boobs."

"What?" Of course I have boobs. What is he talking about?

I look down. A shriek tears from my throat.

I'm in my bra. Tangled with the gray of his T-shirt is the white of my crop top. That obviously didn't stay in its place.

"Please, lightning strike me!" I cry as I grab my pillow and hug it against my chest.

The door opens again. My roommate takes another look at the scene, marches up to her desk, and swaps out the book she grabbed earlier for a different one. She pauses at the door once more, her eyes swinging between me and our, uh, guest.

She says, "Have fun."

I can only breathe again when she shuts the door firmly.

Max Cassiano explodes into laughter. It bends him over, having robbed him of the poise needed to sit straight. Damn it, he has a really pretty laugh. Deep, all the way from his belly, and as free as a kid's. Too bad it's at my expense.

There's a dirty jersey on my bed, so I put it on while he rolls onto his side, laughing. I jump off the bed and grab my pillow, then pelt him with it.

"Stop. Freaking. Laughing!"

He's too weak to fend off the attacks and just lets me pummel him. I pound his chest a couple more times, but the fight has left my body, taking my soul with it. I fall, sitting on the edge of the mat.

"I am socially dead, am I not?" My voice is thin and airy. "Everyone and their mom must have seen what a mess I was yesterday. And now my roommate thinks we did something."

"Who cares what she thinks?" His body is still racked by chuckles as he separates our clothes. He returns the favor by pelting my face with my top, but I don't even react. "What matters here is that you learn your lesson and never challenge me again."

"You cheated." I kick his thigh, but it only stubs my toe.

"Did I?" The question is muffled as he works his T-shirt over his head, his arms into the holes, and—goodbye, abs.

"Well, yeah. You kept dribbling beer all over yourself."

"So did you, Tinker Bell." One of his knees is up, and he places his elbow on top. There's something sly in his eyes as he glances up at me. "In fact, I remember beer making your clothes stick to your—"

My stomach roils with nausea, a.k.a. the consequences of my actions want to make themselves visible. "Anyway," I say, swallowing with difficulty. "Thank you for all your help, but it's time you go. I have a hangover to nurse, and you're not helping."

He gets up, but not at the speed I wish. It's like he knows the best revenge for my offenses is to stick around and annoy me. The reminder of his body under my hand is still too fresh. I need to go back to thinking about him as some conceited fool and not as a boy I want to make out with. Or more.

He brushes off his butt. "Fine, but don't forget you owe me. And I'll collect when you least expect it."

"Crap."

"Oh, and make sure to put your phone in rice." Max gives me one last little smirk before he walks out.

I collapse face down on my bed. If the impending hangover doesn't do me in, Massimo Cassiano will be the death of me. And frankly, I'll deserve what's coming to me.

# CHAPTER 11
## MAX

will die. No, I *am* dying. Coach's intent is to cause mass casualties. I hope to be the first one to go. That way the torture can just freaking *end*.

But no, I have to go and be a competitive bastard. I wish this were the moment when I learned to give up, except somehow, I'm still holding on. By a thread. My entire body trembles like a leaf. The arch of my back threatens to collapse several times. There's a pool of sweat on the mat beneath me. Every muscle in my body stopped burning a while ago and now just feels cold. Like I'm turning into a marble statue, frozen in a plank forever.

The worst part is that the mirror is right in front of me. I can see veins bulging in my neck and temples. My face is so red that, in any other circumstance, I'd call 911. I will my reflection to hang on. There's no way I'll be the first one to drop.

All around me, the rest of the team is trapped in the same struggle. Coach Green paces up and down the line of players.

"I can't prevent you all from being reckless, but at least don't get caught," he says in a grumble. This is all thanks to

Boucher, whose video of him doing a keg stand at Friday's party reached the staff.

The culprit himself is the first to collapse with a thud. Somehow, he still has the energy to open his big yap, though. "The Strikes were also drinking. Why are we the only ones getting punished?"

Coach barks, "Because they didn't get caught!"

Yeah, thanks to me forcing people to delete the videos of Tinker Bell passed out on my back and also chasing one Strike who took an incriminating picture and getting her to delete it too. And this is what I get. Ten minutes in a plank position.

Finally, the whistle goes off. Some of the guys let go, but I have to go be that dipshit who slowly, calmly, eases back to his knees and takes deep breaths as if he could've kept going for the world record.

Bile rushes up my throat, and I swallow it back down like a champ.

Next to me, Nate sounds dizzy as he whispers, "Okay, but we're hitting O'Malley's this Friday, right?"

"How can you think about partying after this?" Conor shakes his head. Again, probably feeling as dizzy as I am.

"It's not like they'll sell us booze at the bar."

"I have class," I croak out without following the string of their conversation. "But how am I going to get there?"

I look down at my thighs. It might be my imagination, but they look thicker than usual. Like inert tree trunks.

"Same." Conor groans like an old man while he struggles to get on his feet.

It takes me a good while to follow his example. And a few more seconds to balance myself. Still longer until I'm able to put one foot before the other. Last week, I had about twenty minutes to spare before Intro to Entrepreneurship. Today, I'll be lucky if I make it twenty seconds before the lecturer.

A frigid shower helps ease my muscles, turning me into

something resembling a normal human. I get the point Coach was trying to make. We were immature, especially coming off losing a significant game. So would I do it again, given the choice?

Absolutely freaking yes.

It's not like I'll forget the way Tinker Bell felt me up any time soon.

I shake my head to myself as I bike over to the business school buildings. That whole episode was a glitch in the matrix. She wasn't herself, and I don't think I was either. I should've left the second she fell asleep, even if meant walking across campus half-naked. But I didn't want to. I kept waiting for the moment she woke up so I could see the look on her face when she figured out what she'd done. Giving Tinker Bell crap is an unexpected source of fuel for me.

Speaking of, I spot her right away as I walk into the classroom. She sits in the middle, wearing a T-shirt with sunflowers printed on it. She must be the sun, though, and the rest of the guys in class her sunflowers. They keep sneaking glances at her as if they can't look away. Especially her seat mate.

"Stinking Brett," I mutter under my breath.

My roommate is the only one who dares to sit next to the hottest girl in class. Not even other girls approach her.

I climb up the stairs with purpose. And would you look at that? My body no longer hurts. Her dark eyes meet mine for a second before she looks back at Brett, who's speaking who knows what nonsense to her.

I sit directly behind them. If they feel me, they pay me no heed and continue their conversation.

"—so annoying, strutting around like a rooster who thinks the whole world is his henhouse."

"Oh, absolutely." She tucks her chin in her raised hand. "He's *so* annoying."

Why do I have a feeling they're talking about me?

"You're telling me," Brett says, grunting. "I'm unlucky enough to be his roommate."

Definitely about me, then. And not even caring that I might overhear.

I take out my stuff from my backpack and put it on the desk with a lot more force than necessary. But a couple of girls bound up the stairs, making a racket at the same time, drowning out my tantrum.

"Poor you." Tinker Bell's voice sounds weird, but I can't tell why. "Those hockey guys are an eyesore, huh?"

Wait—

"I just don't get why the school started a hockey program." He shrugs, confidently opening his mouth once more to say, "This just isn't their world, you know? St. Cloud produces great intellectuals, the next world leaders, big-shot CEOs, etc. Not… jocks."

Does he not know that the girl he's trying so desperately to impress is one of those jocks?

I press a hand against my mouth to hold back laughter.

So it wasn't that she was riveted by the hot takes about me. She's baiting him until he finds out she's the captain of the St. Cloud Thunder Strikes.

Brett must've interpreted her silence as an invitation to fill it, because he continues. "If they're all like my roommate, they probably don't have a single brain cell combined. All he does is train. When does he study? Or does he think the school's not gonna flunk him since he wears a uniform with its name?"

I roll my eyes so hard it makes me dizzy for a moment. That's when I can't keep myself quiet anymore.

"Funny, I think the one without a single brain cell here isn't me."

Brett jumps so high he almost smacks against the ceiling. Meanwhile, Tinker Bell turns around with a grim smile.

"You know what? For once, I think I agree with you," she says.

"What?" Brett's forehead scrunches up, the picture of confusion.

I tilt my head, eyes solely on my class partner. "Were you never planning on telling him?"

Tinker Bell takes a deep breath and releases it slowly. "I was trying to find the right moment, but he wouldn't shut up."

"Excuse me—"

"Listen up, you snob," Tinker Bell says. "I just wanted to get some dirt on your roommate, not to hear you spout shit about hockey players like it's your life's mission to be a jerk."

I choke on my own saliva.

Brett's gone pale as a ghost. "I—what?"

"She's a jock too, you fool." I jerk a thumb at her. "She's the captain of the women's hockey team."

"Yeah, do I reek of sweat too?" She makes it a point to sniff her armpits. "I had a grueling practice this morning that I can only put up with thanks to not having a single thought in my skull."

"I didn't mean—" Red rises up Brett's neck and settles in his face. "You're okay—he's the one who—"

"Oh?" I lean over the desk, as if that got me any closer to Brett. "So you mean only the male players are the gross ones? Or just me?"

Someone starts chuckling. The two girls from earlier are close enough that they've caught on to the whole conversation and can't hide their amusement. I can't blame them. Never have I seen someone put their foot in their mouth in real time like this.

"Whatever!" Brett grabs all his things in his arms and gets up with a huff. "Enjoy each other's company, you little shits."

I wave at him as he makes his way down to the front row. Where he sits firmly facing forward.

"Was that mean?" Tinker Bell mumbles.

"I forgive you. But next time you want dirt on me, just ask me."

"Not to you." She tosses a frown at me over her shoulder. "To him."

"Hmm. Well, he was the one painting us with the stereotypical brush."

"Everyone on campus seems to think so."

I scratch the top of my head. It's true. Brett's just the most outspoken person I've encountered, willing to share his feelings about the hockey program to anyone who'll listen.

With a big sweep of my arm, I dump everything into my open backpack. I hang it from my shoulder, and, using the desk as a pivot with my hand, I leap over the row of desks to land beside Tinker Bell.

I pull up the chair beside her and sit down. "That's why we have to show them all that we're more than just our looks."

She presses her lips into a thin line. "Damn it, I hate that you're right."

"I, for one, am really looking forward to working with you on this project." I take my sweet time taking my iPad and other things back out. "Especially knowing you owe me big time."

"I am *not* going to do your part of the assignment, if that's what you're hinting at."

"Oh, that's not what I mean. At all." My smile has the effect of increasing the intensity of her frown. "I wouldn't want to deprive you of my company. Especially not when—unlike Brett there—you said I smell *so good* and feel *so warm* against you."

She pinches my thigh with enough strength to make me yowl.

"I did not say any of those things!"

"Yeah, you did." Even through the throbbing ache, I chuckle. "More than once."

She wouldn't let me go because I was warm, and she cuddled up against me all night like she'd never heard of a blanket. And then, in the morning, while her hand ran up and down my body, she mumbled against my neck how good I smelled. And some other interesting tidbits I choose to keep to myself because I don't look forward to her stabbing me with her pen.

Tinker Bell lowers the intended weapon and drops it back onto her desk. "One more word, Cassiano…"

"And what?"

A strand of her long hair falls over her face as she tilts it to glare at me. "Honestly, I don't know. But you won't like it."

I chuckle.

This is really bad news, because during the rest of the class, I can't focus on what the lecturer drones on about. My attention keeps going to the girl beside me and how hard she's trying to pretend I'm not here.

# CHAPTER 12
## LUZ

No one says college is easy, but they also don't have to deal with a Max Cassiano. It's not my fault he looks like a dream come true, especially up close. Who wouldn't feel something while sitting right beside him during an entire class?

So, obviously, I'm itching to run as far as my legs can carry me the second the lecture is done. Not seeing him up close and personal for an entire week might just be the balm I need to heal after this weekend. This is the only class we share, so all I'll have to do is avoid him during practice. Shouldn't be that hard, with the alternating schedules the Strikes and Bolts have. And also with the open hostility between both teams.

But the lecturer ruins all my plans.

"You'll give your presentations the week after Thanksgiving. It sounds far away, but time is a construct that never works in your favor. So get to working right away."

Well, he doesn't have to be a ray of sunshine like this.

Max nudges me with his elbow, and I make the mistake of looking at him directly.

"Are you free sometime this afternoon?"

I'm conscious of the fact that there are words coming out of his mouth, but none of them register. The light from the windows hits his eyes directly, and I discover the most curious thing. I thought they were as true blue as our uniforms, but they're lighter than that. Like pools of clear water from the Caribbean beaches my parents used to take us to when we were kids.

"Tinker Bell?"

The automatic gnashing of my teeth after hearing the nickname snaps me back to reality.

"Sorry, I was thinking of three different ways to kill you, so I didn't catch any of that."

"Oh yeah?" When he smiles, an almost imperceptible dimple appears in his left cheek. Only that one. What irritates me most about it is that I've only seen it appear when he's making fun of me. "What are they?"

I shush him and look back at the front. "You'll have to discover them yourself. And class isn't over. Stop distracting me."

"You do know that if you kill me with the first method, I won't get to discover the other two, right?"

I press my lips into a tight line. The traitors want to stretch into a smile. Somehow, I've gone from being annoyed that he always has a comeback to finding it amusing. This boy is dangerous.

And I'm not the only one with the same idea. A couple of girls sitting in the row below have spent the entire class sneaking peeks at the insufferably hot guy. At least they're blessed with not having seen him without a shirt. I haven't recovered from that sight yet.

The second the lecturer finishes class, Max grabs the back of my chair so I can't push it and get up.

"Schedule, now."

I sigh. "Can't we just, like, work separately?"

"When?" He starts nodding the second I don't have an obvious response ready. "Uh-huh. Between class and training, we have only the time we make for this boring assignment."

"You're starting to sound like the lecturer."

"Maybe he was right." Max shrugs. "So, are you free or not?"

*Let us not pretend like this is an invitation for a date,* I tell my heart as it accelerates.

"Fine," I grumble, checking my schedule on my phone. While our classmates trickle out, Cassiano and I look at the pockets of free time in our schedules and only find two matches. One is this afternoon, like he suggested earlier.

"Great. Then I'll see you later at the library, Tinker Bell."

My things don't deserve the punishment they're getting as I jam them into my bag with violence. "When will you stop calling me by that ridiculous name?"

Max shrugs on his backpack. A strand of his black hair falls over his forehead. The dimple makes an appearance again, and I brace.

"When you stop being so damn cute, Tinker Bell."

I suck air between my teeth. The best I can do for myself is to wait until he's out of the room to exit. I no longer have the capacity to put up with him without melting like a candle. How am I going to survive today's study session?

I turn into a bundle of nerves the rest of the day. It's even hard to eat lunch. Chelsea notes it right away when I sit at the cafeteria with the girls, just poking my food around the plate.

"What's with you?" she asks.

JT peeks at my plate. "If you're not gonna eat it, can I have it?"

I take a couple more bites and push the plate off to her. I check the time while she polishes off the food. One hour and twenty-four minutes before my study date with the enemy.

No, *not* a date.

Why did I have to wear these clothes today? My sunflower T-shirt looked cute and cheery this morning, the ripped jeans fun. I feel like a rag doll now. But if I change, it'll look like I made too much effort for something that is totally casual and means nothing.

Which is absolutely the reason why I arrive at the library early, seeking a spot where I can lounge for a bit and look busy. But Max beat me to the punch.

I find him alone at a corner table, close to the windows. He's wearing noise-canceling headphones and scribbles on a notepad with a pen. I hide behind a bookshelf because I'm not ready to face him yet. That was the whole point of arriving early, so I'd have a quiet moment to psych myself up to face him.

Why is life so unfair? He has the most basic, nondescript outfit in the world. A black T-shirt and blue jeans. And yet he looks like he walked out of a catalog. Actually, no—he looks way better than professional models. They're too skinny for my taste.

Max Cassiano? Just my taste.

The sleeves of the T-shirt hug his arms right at the curve between his deltoids, triceps, and biceps. I love that spot. His is so defined it makes my tongue turn into knots. The fabric stretches from the neck to his shoulders, because they're so wide.

And that jaw… it deserves sonnets.

I sigh, collapsing against the bookshelf and grabbing a couple of books so I don't make a fool of myself by swooning to the floor.

"Wow, he must be one of the hockey players," a girl's voice drifts from the other side of the shelf. For a second, I think she's talking to me, but a different girl responds.

"Right? That's not the body of an average student."

Correcto, mis amigas. This guy busts his ass every day.

The first girl makes a sound as if a sigh and a grunt had a child. "Damn, if the rest of the team looks like him, I might just become a fan."

"Me too. Just looking at him is making me feel things."

"Wait till you see him up close," I say in a too low murmur they don't hear.

But pause to stare at Cassiano some more. I rise on my tiptoes to do the same. He's looking around, as if trying to find someone. My heart trips over itself. Me? Is he looking for me?

Of damn course. We're supposed to meet here for homework.

There's a small thud, and one of the girls picks up the conversation again. "There's no way he's single, right?"

"We should just ask him," says the other one. "What do we have to lose?"

I bite my lower lip. Until now, I haven't asked myself these questions. I have no business finding their answers.

First of all, he's super annoying. Second, he's the captain of the enemy. Therefore, my biggest enemy. Third, I agree. There's no way he doesn't have five girlfriends at the same time. Fourth, even if he's single, it doesn't mean he'll be interested in dating *me* when he can have the attention of any girl on campus.

Fifth, and this is the most important one, I don't have time for boys. What I do have is limited to hockey, and I don't just mean schedule-wise. I can only play for a few more years before my chronic pain becomes too unbearable. I'll be lucky if I'm still on the team my senior year. I can't waste that precious time on some guy who can discard me and move on to the next girl as easily as changing sticks.

With a deep breath, I use the girls as cover to close in on the table. True to their word, they approached Max, and he's now talking with them. And now that I see them out in the open, they're cute. At least one of them should stand a chance.

"Nope, I'm married," Max says, so clear it turns a few heads.

I stop in my tracks and blink. Hard.

He's married?

"Oh." The first girl tucks her hair behind her ears and nudges her friend. "Okay. Well, sorry about that."

"Yeah, sorry."

"No problem." He gives them a tight little smile. "Bye."

The two girls scramble away, leaving me without anywhere to hide. And because I also suffer from chronic big mouth, I open it and say, "You're *married*? But you're, like, eighteen. And you're not even wearing a ring."

"Which they didn't notice because they don't have your dynamic sight." He motions at the chair in front of him, and I plop my butt down on it. Max leans forward and whispers, "I'm married to hockey."

"Oh." I frown at the mix of annoyance and relief roiling in my gut. "You weirdo."

He turns off his headphones and sets them down, giving me his full attention. "Aren't you the same?"

I busy myself by taking my laptop and a few other trinkets from my bag.

"Sure. Fully committed, until death do us part sooner or later. Hopefully later."

"Exactly. Having to take so much time out of training for schoolwork is almost like cheating already."

My eyebrows go up. He seems to mean it.

"Oh." I tilt my head. "So you actually want to go pro?"

"Don't you?" Cassiano blinks at me, as if confused. "Go pro or die trying?"

For the second time today, he sucks the air out of my lungs. But this time for an entirely different reason.

He reels back when he sees the change in my demeanor. The memories of almost dying while trying rush back, and a switch flips on, sending my nerves into overdrive. The flare of stress-induced pain along with the arrogance of someone who doesn't even fathom it turns my whole demeanor from curious into sour grapes.

Cálmate, I tell myself. He doesn't know I almost *did* die trying.

"Let's just get to work," I snap, and for the entire session, I'm unable to look up from my laptop screen.

# CHAPTER 13
## MAX

You know when there's something in the back of your mind that's bothering you, but you don't know what it is?

That niggling feeling doesn't leave me the entire week. I train on and off the ice, go to class, study, eat, and even shower, trying to pinpoint it. I work my brain so hard that I become unable to use my mouth. In fact, I miss a couple of *yes, sirs* to Coach Green during practice that earn me extra skating time.

The eureka moment only occurs when I'm sitting at O'Malley's with the Bolts. I'm scarfing down a burger when the Strikes walk in and my eyes settle on their captain. It's as if a voice in my head says *her. It's because of her.*

"If my roommate teases me about our loss one more time," Nate says, balling up a dirty napkin and throwing it onto his empty plate with violence, "I'll get kicked off the team because I'll wring his neck."

"You too?" Conor shakes his head. "It's like we were all paired with roommates who hate hockey."

"Not hockey." I speak without tearing my eyes away from

Tinker Bell, who hasn't noticed me yet. "They hate everything sports. It's not intellectual enough."

Nate rolls his eyes. "Obviously they don't understand the game."

Not only is it packed with rules, but the strategies are full of nuance. We have to consider the skills and condition of each player, juxtaposed with the performance of the opposite team. All this on top of being a contact sport where the action is very, very fast, and decisions have to be made in fractions of a second.

See? I even know the word *juxtaposed*. I have more neurons than Brett gives me credit for.

It's not him who had me annoyed the whole week, though. I've barely seen him since class on Monday. That last bit can be said about Tinker Bell too. Aside from our library study session, we've barely crossed paths at the facilities. But I can trace the beginnings of my funk back to that moment, when her expression shifted from easy-going to an impenetrable fortress.

Yeah, my original goal with setting up the session was to make some progress on our project. I'm not in the business of neglecting my studies, no matter how much I want my future to be all about hockey. Having to work with her, though, is like a cherry on top. I'm certain I'd be much less enthusiastic about that class in general if, say, I had to pair up with Brett. Or any of the other snobs looking down their noses at me.

Tinker Bell knows where I'm coming from because she's there too. And talking with her almost has the same dynamic as playing a hockey game. There's always a faceoff, every quip is a goal scored on the other's net, and my heart rate is always high.

Not during that study session, though.

"Ah, so that's why," I muse aloud, off tune with the conversation. The guys turn to me.

"What's why?"

"Never mind. Got distracted." And my burger is not going to eat itself, so I focus on that.

Unfortunately, Nate traces my line of sight and lands on a table full of Strikes.

"Well, no wonder your face changed."

"Did it?" I ask with a mouthful of burger.

Nate snorts. "Yeah, it was like you went through the four stages of grief."

"I'm pretty sure it's five stages," Conor says while dumping so much ketchup on his fries they're more sauce than solids.

Nate waves a hand. "You get what I mean. It's just that between the rest of school and the Strikes hating our guts, it's enough to make a man lose his appetite."

Something neither of us does, considering we all polish off massive plates of burgers and fries.

To make a point, I ask, "Should we get pie?"

"Oh yeah." Conor rubs his stomach. "That'll hit the spot."

"You guys suck." But even as he says this, Nate laughs.

"That's probably why the Strikes hate us." I take a good swig of my Coke.

Aside from the incidents during the bootcamp week, every little thing has turned into an opportunity to antagonize one another. The Strikes have bragged nonstop about having the opening game at home, while we had it away. They've tried to hog the program's PT. And I've even heard them complaining that our equipment is better.

The Bolts aren't innocent either.

With Boucher as the leader, the heckling has gotten bad enough that Coach had to sit us down to explain the difference between good-natured ribbing and something that can get us a formal complaint. Twice already, when it was time for us to leave the gym and suit up for the ice, a few of the guys loitered to cut the Strikes' time with the equipment. That was my first real chance to go full captain on their asses. But rather than thanking me, the Strikes gave me death stares as if I were just as bad.

Is that it? Did Tinker Bell realize she was getting too chummy with someone she should hate with all her guts? Is that why she got so cold?

As if sensing my eyes, she tears herself from her conversation and looks at me. It doesn't even last a second. She even makes a point of turning her nose up.

I slam the plastic glass of soda a bit too hard against the table.

I want to see her turn that pointy little nose up at me up close and personal.

Nate turns back around again. "But you know what? They're not much better."

I lean forward, closer to them. "What if we settle this once and for all?"

"Oh? Color me intrigued." Nate rests his chin on a raised hand, ready for gossip.

Meanwhile, Conor narrows his eyes. I'm not sure if he's interested or about to launch into a plea for sanity and pacifism.

"Calm your tits," I tell him. "I'm not advocating for violence. I am, after all, a responsible man."

"*Sure*, Cassiano." His voice is droll. "You're the paragon of responsibility."

I gasp in an exaggerated way. "What have I done to deserve this sarcasm?"

"Oh, I don't know. What about challenging the Strikes captain to a drinking game and further deepening the rift between the two teams?"

Oops. I forgot to add that little episode to the tally.

"What did you want me to do? Leave her defenseless against Boucher?"

"That's a good point," Nate says, nodding to himself. "That would've ended so much worse."

"What, pray tell, is your great idea now, oh captain?"

"So glad you asked, Mahoney." I chuckle at the way he glares. "My proposal is a good ole round of pool."

"Oh." Nate leans back. "I was expecting something spicier."

"Like what?" I cock an eyebrow.

His cheeks get suspiciously dark.

"*Oh*, does someone have the hots for a Strike?"

"Never." Nate enunciates the last *r* in a way only a Spanish speaker can.

"Methinks the gentleman doth protest too much," Conor says in a singsong voice. "Which one is it, Garcia?"

It better not be Tinker Bell.

I force myself to take several deep breaths. It's not like she's mine. Everyone's free to have the hots for her. In fact, not having the hots for her is what's ridiculous. And she's free to take her pick of suitors. Nate would be a good candidate. He's half Mexican, and though he's a bit eccentric, he's a good guy.

*But I'm better.*

Or am I? I would be, if I wasn't about to turn into a Neanderthal all on my own.

"*Uh.*" He clears his throat. "That girl just catches my eye. I'm not saying I'm love or anything—"

"Which one, man?" I ask with a tad more bite than necessary.

Nate glances over his shoulder once more. "The one in the red top."

Red top? I glance at the Strikes' table again and—

Hallelujah! Tinker Bell is wearing the school colors, black and blue.

"Brit Thomas, huh?" Conor waggles his eyebrows.

"Shut up."

Fortunately, I get to live with my own embarrassment in secret. They don't need to know that I'm so relieved it's almost as if my soul returned to my body from a long trip.

"Let's go, we're going antagonizing." I get up from my chair.

"Wait, we're really doing this?" Conor asks.

"Aw, yeah." Nate pumps a fist.

Brett's right. Collectively, right now, the three of us have only one brain cell.

The first one who spots our approach is the captain of the Strikes. The easy smile falls off her face, and is immediately replaced by weariness. In contrast, my mood lifts higher and higher the more steps I take.

Nate beats me to the punch. He leans on their table and says, "Evening, señoritas."

A round of scoffing greets him. I, too, want to laugh at him. But I'd never do that to my buddy. At least not in front of his crush. But after this, I plan to make his ears bleed.

Tinker Bell sits in a corner, on the side of the table closest to us. Slowly, she looks up at me. Funny how I'm no longer annoyed, huh?

"What are you bunch of fools doing here?" JT Brewer says in greeting.

With a smile, I say, "I was just thinking—"

"Breaking news, ladies and gents," Tinker Bell murmurs loud enough that I can hear her, despite the noise all around the bar.

"That this silly rivalry we have going on is bad for the reputation of the hockey program," I finish saying, as if there were no interruption. "So we should settle things with a friendly game."

"Why would we?" The girl who was part of the bathroom saga snorts. What was her name again? Something White.

"Unless you're too scared." Conor shrugs.

Honestly, I didn't expect that low blow from him. But it's exactly what gets the Strikes to leave their seats.

"What are you plotting, Cassiano?" Tinker Bell stands a hairsbreadth from me, glaring with enough force to make another man tumble backward.

If I tell her what I'm planning, though, she won't play.

"Aren't you tired of all of this?" I tilt my head, trying to look like the picture of innocence. "We waste so much energy hating each other instead of focusing on what matters."

"So what do you suggest?" she asks, taking a step back so that when she folds her arms, she doesn't have to touch me.

The too-long pause on my end isn't because I want to rile her up, although it seems to be working that way, judging by how her jaw tightens. It's just that I'm having another eureka moment here.

I want to play *just* with her.

*Cassiano*, I tell myself in a voice that sounds too much like my dad's. *You're supposed to be married to hockey.*

This isn't good, and I know it. Tinker Bell distracts me too much. I spend half of Intro to Entrepreneurship glancing at her. When I'm on the ice or at the gym, I expect to catch a glimpse of her every ten minutes. I have no right to make fun of Nate when I'm suffering the same ailment.

The rational approach would be to ignore her. Or, since I can't do that because of our project, then it would be wise to not seek her out. But I've spent the whole week with a thundercloud hanging over me, and the second she glanced up at me, the sky cleared.

"You and me," I say, wishing my voice didn't come out so thick. "A game of pool."

"Pool?" Her eyebrows go up, as if she expected something different.

I bite my lower lip but can't hold back my smile. "Winner grants the other a wish."

"That is so childish," one of her friends, Brit Thomas, I think, says.

"Oh yeah?" I hear Nate ask. "Then why don't you play a round with me?"

Atta boy, shoot your shot too.

Tinker Bell tucks a strand of hair behind her ear. "So, like, if I win, I can get you to rein in your buddies forever?"

"If that's what you wish, yup." I put my hands in my pockets. A halo's probably appearing over my head.

Her eyes narrow. "If the point is peace between our teams, then why does it sound like you have a different wish?"

I lean closer to her and whisper right in her ear. "Win and find out, Tinker Bell."

"That makes no sense." She pushes me away. "I would only find out if I lose."

"So, are you in, or are you gonna balk?"

She's too easy to rile up. Color rises up her throat, and she explodes with a volcanic "You're so gonna lose, Cassiano."

For all I know, she's a world champion in pool, and I'm gonna eat my words. Even if that's the case, I'll still get what I want. To spend some time with her.

A couple of minutes later, we manage to clear both tables. Nate and Brit Thomas take one. I stand across the other table, running chalk over the tip of a cue, being glared at.

Conor, brave man that he is, looks at the other two Strikes and says, "What about we play darts? And between two pool games and one of darts, the team that wins two of the three earns eternal glory and respect."

"Deal. Let's go," Brewer responds.

"You heard them," Tinker Bell says, loading up the rack with the last ball. "Eternal glory and respect are at stake."

Yeah, so is my sanity.

"Do the honors," I say, letting her take the first crack.

"Oh, you'll regret this." For the first time, her lips draw up in a smile. "I'll take the stripes. You're solids."

"Sure."

I'm liquid, more like.

She's in another one of those tops that are too short, like the manufacturer got tired of sewing it halfway through. It rises up when she leans over the short end of the table. Even though I'm not standing right behind her, I can see the outline of a very narrow waist tapering to wide hips, the defined muscles working as she hits the balls, the thin scar running down her back.

Lord have mercy, for I am a weak, weak man.

With all the strength I have, I tear my eyes away from her and back to the table. It was a solid hit. Not the kind an amateur makes. I may be in trouble in more ways than one.

More than strength, the key to pool is precision, and that falters significantly every time she leans over the table. It takes me a couple of fails to really get my head in the game. A bigger prize than just sneaking peeks awaits if I win.

The race starts to get tight. For every ball she pockets, I follow suit. I catch chatter from the others—mostly consisting of insults—but Tinker Bell and I are so focused on winning that we don't even stop to give each other crap.

And then the moment arrives. Sink or swim. We have one ball each, plus the eight ball, and it's my turn.

"Aren't you gonna tell me what you want?" she asks while I position my cue over the green. An obvious attempt to distract me.

I measure the angle of the strike very slowly, running the cue over my finger like a caress and decidedly not looking at her. "Afraid I'm gonna win?"

She scoffs. "Of course not."

I strike the ball and pocket it. Her sharp intake of breath does not go unnoticed.

That's when I make the potential error of looking up. Tinker Bell leans over the table, both hands holding up her weight over the edge. Her hair falls over her shoulders like this is some sort of pictorial. The frown on her face is supposed to make her look intimidating, but it doesn't.

I decide then what I want from her when I win. It hadn't quite coalesced in my head until this moment.

"Let me win first, Tinker Bell."

"The pressure can yet get to you, you know?"

No. I'll win this game even if it's the last thing I ever do.

I lean over the table again. From the corner of my eye, I catch a glimpse of her abdomen contracting as if she's holding her breath. I hit the eight ball. My heart beats so fast my smart-watch beeps on my wrist. The ball makes a careful trip toward the nearest pot. I will it to sink. A bead of sweat trickles down the middle of my back. And then—

It sinks in.

"Yes!" I pump my fist in the air. The shout catches the attention of people nearby.

"You won, Cassiano?" Conor asks, frozen before throwing a dart.

"Yeah, baby." I smile up at Tinker Bell.

If looks could kill…

"Nuh-uh." I wag my index finger at her. "Don't you go and say I cheated. It was a fair game."

She folds her arms tight enough to cut off circulation. "What do you want from me, Cassiano?"

Slowly, I set the cue on the table and walk around it until I stop right before her. We're far enough away from the others that I don't need to whisper.

"Aside from eternal glory and respect," I say in what I recognize is a very obnoxious way, "what I want from you is…"

Through gritted teeth, she says, "If you keep stalling, all you're gonna earn is a kick in the—"

Okay, okay. If the roles were reversed, I'd be wanting to sock me in the face too.

"Nothing terrible," I assure her. "All I want is a kiss—and not right now, but when I say so."

Tinker Bell's eyes widen. She takes a step back. "A what?"

"You heard me. Be on the lookout." To make matters worse, I wink and leave her to join Conor's dart game, as if I haven't just dropped a nuclear bomb on Tinker Bell. As if my smartwatch wasn't going into overdrive.

# CHAPTER 14
## LUZ

I am—in a succinct word—*screwed*.

It's been two days since the pool game. I'm in the middle of the season opener, and I can't stop thinking about Max Cassiano.

My leg bounces while I watch the action from the bench. Our goalie just made a save worth a prize, but we need to put more numbers on the scoreboard. We're tied in the third period, and all I've contributed is one assist.

The team's been giving it their all, despite being matched with one of the top contenders for the season. And here I am, wondering when Cassiano is going to kiss me.

Earlier today, I crossed paths with him during dryland training. I was in the middle of a stick-handling drill when he strutted in with his coach to speak with mine. Our eyes met for a brief moment and…

The insufferable guy smirked. Made the whole dimple appear and all. As if he knew all I could think about was that he was walking around with my next kiss.

I've never felt rage quite like at that moment. Who cares that the girls won their respective games and that, in theory, it means the Strikes reign supreme in the hockey program. I lost against Cassiano. Again. And now I'll have to put up with him kissing me.

"Line one, go!" Coach Young calls for me and the two other girls.

We swap over with the third line. I hit the ice with viciousness. JT passes the puck to me. I handle it through the skates of an opposing player. It riles her up, and when she comes, I'm ready. I let her ram against my side and, taking strength from who knows where, I tuck my shoulder against her body and push her down on her ass. Before her legs tangle with mine, I leap over them and skate away.

The squalid home crowd rises in sound volume. Among them, I know, are my siblings and my sister's best friend. The only one who would contribute to the noise is not the one I'm related to.

Sure enough, when I skate by them, Brooklyn screams. "Go, Luz! Sink one in!"

I pass the puck back to a teammate. Chelsea? I don't know. It's a baby blue jersey and not a green one. The opponent can probably read my intentions, because two defense players come to intercept me. I pivot around one of them, leaving them in the dust. My teammate passes the puck back.

I imagine the goalie from the other team as Max's smug face. The slapshot is so hard it takes several seconds before the buzzer goes off.

I throw my hands up in the air. One by one, my teammates slam against me.

"That was wild!"

"Go, Captain!"

Look at that. Maybe I should let Cassiano piss me off before games more often.

"Stop it," I mutter to myself as I head over to watch the

next faceoff. The fact that I keep thinking about him, even in these circumstances, is a big problem.

Somehow, we manage to cling to the one-point lead until the final buzzer. Which means the winning goal was mine. It should feel fan-freaking-tastic. But as I skate around the ice to thank the few people who showed up for our game, I'm angry.

I only played solid hockey for the last fifteen minutes of the game. If I'd had my head screwed on right, the win might not have been so narrow. As the captain, I'm supposed to set an example for the rest of the team, and today I was a mess.

Before heading back to the locker room with the rest of the team, I brake before my family to get their impressions.

"That was amazing." Brooklyn has both hands over his chest. "This was way more exciting than watching a pro game."

"Why are you trying to suck up to Luz so hard?" Olivia asks, deadpan. "Do you have a crush on her or something?"

The way Brooklyn's face lights up like a streetlight might imply so. It almost makes me laugh.

"Sorry, kid. You should like someone your own age."

"No, I—"

"That was pretty bad." Aran stands up and jams his hands into the pockets of his bomber jacket.

Brooklyn's attention snaps to him. "What? Did you not see that incredible goal?"

"Sure." My brother shrugs. "But everything before that was embarrassing."

"Tell me how you really feel, why don't you." I glare at him for a moment, smacking the ice with my stick. "But you're right. Damn it."

"Just do better next time."

I feel the urge to tell him to stick it where the sun doesn't shine, which is a syndrome most people develop when dealing with Aran. The thing about him, though, is that he's incapable of telling a white lie, even if it means soothing someone else's feelings. And I knew this was precisely what I would get when I stopped by. I needed confirmation from someone else that I did actually suck before that goal got to my head.

"Get home safe, pequeños," I tell them.

Brooklyn glances from me to my brother. "But—"

"Yeah, see you next time." Aran nods and turns to scoot away between the rows of seats.

While Olivia pulls at her friend, she says, "Go shower, Luz. I can smell you from here."

How is it possible to love my siblings and hate them at the same time?

I roll my eyes and skate away. Brooklyn's voice fades in the background as I trod through the corridor and away from the arena.

Coach Young's voice echoes through the locker room as I walk in. "—good effort, but we're going to need more consistency. Today we just caught the opponent off guard, and we can't rely on beginner's luck if we want to make it through the season. Is that clear?"

"Yes, ma'am," we all respond.

"And you," she says the moment she spots me. "We'll have a word later."

"Yes, ma'am." I have to swallow a self-pitying sigh. No doubt she'll say the same thing Aran did, but probably in harsher terms.

"Why's Coach not jumping for joy?" JT pulls her jersey off and tosses it onto the floor. "We won. Shouldn't we be celebrating?"

"Correction," I say as I drop onto my bench. "We *barely* won."

"Still a W, bruh."

I take off my helmet and slam it into the bottom of my stall. Then I stay still for a moment, stewing. Our next game's in a week. I can't continue to living like I did this week without it affecting my performance again.

The only way to pluck this out of my mind is to pay my debt, because it's the anticipation that's killing me. Knowing I agreed to kiss Max Cassiano. Wondering if he's going to pop out of nowhere and demand I make out with him in front of everyone. I have to get past this right away.

And he's training right next door.

Energy rushes back into my limbs. I lift up the jersey so I can unbuckle the top pads and drop them on the floor like they burn me. I work through the buckle of my pants like it's the enemy, leaving the leggings on underneath. My hands fumble with the skate laces until I'm able to chuck them off. Standing, I roll down the wool socks and drop the shin guards to the floor.

I put on the sweaty jersey again. It hangs to my upper thighs. That's fine. I won't be flashing anyone.

"Uh, where are you going like that, Luz?" someone asks me.

"I'll be back in a few minutes," I say back.

Halfway through the gym, I notice I'm wearing compression socks and no shoes. Too late to turn back, though. I lift up my chin and march on.

When I push through the gym doors, the nearest Bolts stop what they're doing and stare at me. Especially my feet. My back throbs to the tune of my rapid heartbeat, but I ignore it. Everything will feel so much better once the mission is complete.

A couple of the Bolts' coaches eye me with trepidation as I walk across the floor. As if a single girl could really cause significant damage to twenty men.

Soon, it becomes clear who my target is. One of Cassiano's buddies takes one look at me and says something I can't quite catch. The Bolts' captain is in the middle of a series of pull-ups, wearing headphones, a backward cap, and no shirt.

Of course. This couldn't be easy, huh? He couldn't have been wearing a parka.

His back is to me, which means I get the full display of shoulder, arm, and back muscles working as he pulls his body weight up and down. Actually, more than his body weight. There are training weights tied around his ankles.

Ugh. Por qué tiene que estar tan bueno?

I stop behind him for a second, taking a bracing breath.

"Bro," his buddy says, pointing at me.

Max stops, glances back. I catch his eyes widen for a moment before he eases himself down the bar. He rips the headphones off.

"What are you doing here, Tinker Bell?"

*Making a fool of myself, obviously.*

*No, Luz. You got this.*

"We need to have a word."

Coach Green appears beside me. "Is everything okay here?"

When I face him, I'm wearing my sweetest, most polite expression ever. "Everything's fine, Coach. Just need to have a word with Cassiano, captain to captain."

The distrust in his expression—in everyone's—is a bit insulting. Not gonna lie.

"Is that so?"

I smile even sweeter as I look up at said captain. "In private."

To his credit, Max takes stock of all the Peeping Toms and nods.

"One sec." He crouches down to take off the weights from his ankles and drops the headphones on a nearby bench. I note that he doesn't pick up the T-shirt strewn on it, but I don't remark on it. "Lead the way, Tinker Bell."

Let's see if he learns how to use my name after this.

My braid swings as I turn. I don't know if the sweat trickling down my skin is because I just finished a game or because of what I'm about to do. I walk us out of the gym, through the hallway, and into the empty equipment room. And lock the door.

"Did you know you're not wearing shoes?"

I turn to face him and fold my arms. "And did you know you're not wearing a shirt?"

As if he forgot, Cassiano runs a hand across his abs and looks down. "Oh, yeah. Be right back."

But I block the door.

His eyebrows shoot up. "Tinker Bell?"

What is more nerve racking? Facing a tough opponent in the way before the net? Or working up the courage to kiss a guy?

Absolutely this. But Luz Maria Rodriguez is not a coward.

"We're going to settle it right now," I say, sounding a lot more composed than I feel.

"What… are we…"

"Oh, please. Stop playing a fool, Cassiano."

He takes off his cap, runs a hand through his damp hair, and puts it back on again. All throughout, he blinks like a goldfish. "I'm not playing. I'm really confused right now."

Can't believe he's going to make me say it.

"The bet," I grit out.

"Oh." It takes him one more moment to really process. "*Oh.*"

I push him against a rack packed with helmets, gloves, and pads of all sizes. I leave my hand against his chest. The skin is slick with sweat and so hot to the touch it almost feels like he's running a fever. Beneath, his heart thumps fast. Could be from the workout or from me. And I hope it's the latter.

"Ready?" I ask, as if this were a race.

His Adam's apple bobs. He shakes his head. "I mean, yeah."

I'm annoyed that he looks skeptical, as if he can't quite believe I'll go through with kissing him. I grab his arms and wrap them around my waist. Rising onto my tiptoes, I drape mine around his neck and pull him down.

Cassiano sucks in air the second before his lips crash against mine. Finally, he gets with the program. His hold around me tightens just enough to make my body arch against his. I splay a hand against his nape, threading my fingers through his hair. They push the cap off his head, and I hear it fall to the floor.

His lips are so soft against mine. What a contrast to the rest of his body. I feel one of his hands cradle the back of my head. It helps me angle so I can press closer, so I can close my lips around his bottom one and suck just a little bit. It tears a groan from him that makes his chest vibrate. I do it again, this time running my tongue across right after. Cassiano opens his mouth wide, and I pull him closer. The friction between our tongues sends fire down my body and melts my legs. Only his arm around my waist keeps me from falling.

I run a hand down his neck, across the expanse of his pectoral, until I feel his heart hammering against my hand again. He has to be feeling how hard mine's racing too.

I'm in way over my head, but I only realize this while I'm kissing him. I should never have accepted this bet. Screw eternal glory and respect. I was safer away from him. I was better off without knowing what kissing Max Cassiano was like.

It takes herculean effort to tear myself away. Our lips make a sucking sound that echoes across the equipment room. Cassiano groans and drops his head against my shoulder.

I blink stars from my eyes, fixing them on the ceiling. It's as if I just woke up from a dream I shouldn't even be having.

Pushing myself away from him, I say, "There, I've paid my dues." My voice sounds warped even to my own ears. In fact, everything looks different now.

The Thunder Bolts' captain sags against the shelf. His hair's a matted mess from my fingers pulling at it. He lifts his face up enough to glance at me from under his eyebrows. That must be the glare he gives his opponents in the heat of the game. It makes my breath catch.

Slowly, Max pulls himself to stand to his full weight. He towers over me.

"These weren't the terms of the prize," he says, his voice rough like gravel against my skin. "I said *I* would kiss you *when I said so*."

"Well." I stretch myself to my tallest height, as if that could intimidate him. "What matters is the kiss. Now that's done, and so is the bet."

"No." He takes one step forward. It's enough to push me against the opposite rack. Cassiano braces one arm against it and leans down. "It's when I say so."

"Then… say so."

My eyes are locked on his. Though they're usually bright with amusement, they're so very dark right now. I can't tell if it's because he's angry or what. But I'm not scared. He's braced against the shelf on the side opposite to the door, leaving me room to walk away if I wanted to.

*If* I wanted to. Running away won't get him out of my system.

"I'm going to kiss you," Cassiano says, his voice low like a whisper, "right now."

I have to bite my lips to keep from screaming *sí, por favor*.

Somehow, I manage to keep my cool as he lifts me up and wraps my thighs around his waist. And even when he stares at me, as if daring me to crack. I brace against his shoulders and wait.

I expect another desperate clash of lips. Instead, he tortures me by placing a slow, soft kiss on one corner of my lips. Then on the opposite corner. From there, he leaves a hot trail to the center of my lips. I squeeze my eyes tight, trying to rein in the urge to sigh.

One of his hands travels up my hip, under the hem of my jersey. The pads of his fingers find the skin of my side and keep traveling up, sliding to my back. His lips make languid strokes against mine. His hand finds my scar, and it tears a guttural noise from me. I've never liked anyone touching it, but it feels amazing as he strokes his way up my back.

He smiles against my lips. "Do you like that?"

"Absolutely not. Do it again."

Cassiano's chest vibrates with a chuckle. He sneaks his hand under the back of my sports bra, and the strength leaves my body. Humming, he kisses me again, this time coercing my mouth open right away. I don't even try to fight it. By this point, I recognize that he won the bet. He won it fair and square.

I grab his hair as his mouth explores mine carefully. Almost as if he didn't want the kiss to end. But it has to, before someone tries to come in. Before I give him more than he bargained for.

With a little groan, I hold his head with both hands and pull away. I open my eyes, but his remain shut for a moment longer. His throat works down a heavy swallow. His swollen lips part to release a little sigh. And then he opens those blue eyes of his.

Max is so beautiful. It hurts to look at him from this close. Especially knowing it can't happen again.

"Damn," he manages to croak out.

It takes me another second to be able to speak.

What comes out of my mouth is "are we done?"

Something flashes through his eyes. His brows crash like thunder.

His hold under my thighs shifts, and he slides me down his body until I'm on my feet. He steps back to pick up his cap and put it on. "Yeah, Luz. We're done."

Before I can say anything, he turns around and leaves.

I collapse against the shelf, sliding down until I sit on the floor. Every piece of fabric against my skin feels like a brand. My heart is about to leap out of my throat. I touch a finger against my throbbing lips.

"Oh no. What have I done?"

This is way, way worse than how things were before.

# CHAPTER 15
## MAX

don't know whether I'm more pissed off at Tinker Bell or at myself.

After closing the equipment room door behind me, I lean against it for a second. The surface feels like ice against my bare skin, which, in contrast, could be used for frying an egg. I run a hand down my face.

First, I need to make sure no one sees me right now, or people will guess too quickly that this wasn't just a captain-to-captain chat.

The anger churning in my gut works like a bucket of cold water. I get to the men's locker and sit down on my bench until I can breathe easy again.

I really had myself convinced that a little kiss wouldn't change anything. That it would just be fun and games, and I'd move past the curiosity that scratches at my subconscious every time I see her. Except I'm like a kid who says he'll have just a small bite of the chocolate bar before dinner and now wants to eat the whole thing in one sitting.

My plan all along has been to focus on hockey first and schoolwork second. Nothing else. Girls are a distraction, and

I'm one of those fools who tends to get too wrapped around their pinky fingers if I'm not careful. Now I know that Tinker Bell's the most dangerous girl I've ever met.

One more second, and I'd have lost control.

I dig my elbows into my thighs and bend over, hiding my face in my hands. She fits perfectly against me. I wish I could've explored how long her scar is and let my hand travel lower—purposefully grab her curves. And she kisses like it'll be the last time every time, with zero reservations.

That's the problem. It's obvious she kissed me to get it out of the way. Like it was a transaction. I inflicted this punishment on myself.

What a clown.

A few more minutes of stewing pass before I'm able to return to the gym. All I can do is go through the motions after this. I'm useless for the rest of the day.

I find the place empty, which must mean training's over and everyone must be in the conference room. I put on my performance shirt and grab my things to join them. The coaches are reviewing a video from a game last year that features the team we'll face tomorrow. Fortunately, no one pays me any mind when I sit in the very back row.

Unfortunately, nothing sticks in my head. It's empty.

Before I'm able to leave the conference room, Coach Green slides up to me. "So, what did she want?"

To absolutely screw me over.

What I say instead is "Just to hash out some details about sharing the facilities."

Yeah, we shared the facilities of our mouths.

"Oh yeah?" If suspicious was a person, Coach Green would be it.

"Uh, Coach." I clear my throat because my voice sounds foreign. "If you don't mind, I have to go shower. I have plans tonight."

What they may be is yet to be seen.

He gives me one more look. "Fine. See you tomorrow. Don't do anything that will get you in trouble today."

Too late.

Like a sheep, I follow my teammates to the showers. At my stall, I turn the water as cold as it can get. It sprays on the guy beside me, who turns out to be Boucher.

"Jeez, dude. Are you trying to freeze over?"

"Yes." I grunt. I need to turn into an icicle so every cell in my body forgets what it feels like to have Luz Rodriguez pressed up against me, devouring my mouth like it's dessert.

A few minutes later, I'm getting dressed, and Garcia tries to invite me to another party. But all my brain can process is one leg through one hole, the other leg through the other hole. One arm through one hole, the other through the other.

The ritual of getting dressed is interrupted by a buzzing in my pants. I must've left my cell phone in the pocket.

I pull out the device. The words on the screen take another moment to break through my subconscious. Then I grimace so hard I turn into a raisin. Just when I thought today couldn't turn any more tragic.

I press the green button, and the second I place the phone against my ear, my mom screams. "Massimo Cassiano! Are you planning on never seeing your mother again?"

"Hey, Ma—"

"Don't give me that, boy." What am I even giving? But she doesn't let me guess before she continues. "Leo has already dropped by twice since the start of the semester. Twice! And his college is farther than yours."

The guys nearby give me looks. They can probably hear every single word with how loud she talks.

Hanging up on her mid-conversation is not an option, unless I want to die at eighteen years old. The only way to cut this short is to give her what she wants.

"Fine, I'm coming over."

"Right now?"

"Yeah, see you in half an hour." Better to rip off the Band-Aid today, while I already feel like stepped-on gum.

She harrumphs. "Va bene."

The call ends just like that. I stare off into the distance.

"Your mom?" Mahoney asks.

I mutter as I finish getting dressed. "Yeah, it was good knowing you all."

There are several reasons why I haven't gone home. And as I shut my locker and bid a good night to my teammates, I regret living so close to it. I should've taken the partial scholarship offer at a west coast college instead of coming to St. Cloud. The debt to distance ratio would've been worth it.

Too soon, I find my beat-up pickup truck in the dorm's parking lot. The fenders are rusty on the edges, and she looks slightly unhinged, like her latest owner. This truck used to be Dad's, back when he needed to pick up crates of fresh vegetables from local markets. Since he now gets them delivered to the restaurant, the black 1989 Dodge Ram became mine.

The door hinges squeak as I open it. A puff of dust flies up as I dump my sports bag on the passenger seat. The whole frame sags when I climb into the driver's seat. I close the door, and the bang echoes around the empty cabin.

I lower my forehead to the steering wheel and stay there for a moment. Eighteen minutes. That's how long it takes to drive home. I need the rest of the half hour for myself.

Tomorrow I'll be okay. I'll focus the entire day on the game. Then on Sunday, I'll study my cheeks off. And when Monday comes, and I see Tinker Bell in class again, I'll...

Have to figure that out on the fly.

Sighing, I turn on the truck. The radio plays some classic Bon Jovi, and I leave it. I have no willpower to wrangle the stubborn piece of crap that only dials every two stations and only takes cassettes. At least there's a silver lining. My mom's food is the best this town has to offer.

I sing along in a deadpan to the part about being halfway there, despite only leaving the parking lot.

This town is fairly small. The only outsiders are the college kids who come from all over the world to get the best education. But once you leave the college area, it's pretty clear the rest of the town has nothing to show for it. A few businesses, some shops, a street with restaurants smack in the city center. That's where I head.

Romano's is my family's restaurant. It's the best Italian food in town. Even though my family originally hails from Palermo, but whatever. Americans wouldn't have recognized the name of our hometown, so Romano's it was.

Being a Friday night, the place is packed with customers, and I have to park a block away. The weather is starting to cool down at this time of year. The night breeze helps me chill my steaming head just a bit.

I walk into the chaos of the restaurant, ready to face whatever this will turn into. Lily, wife to my second brother, Alessandro, is the first one to spot me. She stops in the middle of taking a table's order and screams toward the kitchen.

"Alessandra, Massimo is here!"

Half of the customers turn to look at me—the half unused to all the shouting that happens in this place.

Mom barges out of the kitchen, the revolving doors banging against the wall. Her hair's in a tight bun, always, and covered with a net. The apron tied around her waist is pristine.

Alessandra Cassiano has zero tolerance for imperfection, which is why I've always been such a problem.

"Sit down." Her command is all the greeting I get.

A table for two by the register is already set up with a water pitcher, plates and silverware, and a basket of bread with olive oil and Parmigiano-Reggiano. My grumbling stomach will not say no to that, so I sit down.

"Your father's out doing a delivery," she says, hovering by the table. There's a crease between her eyebrows as she looks down at me. "You're in the bone, ragazzo. Are you skipping your meals?"

I mumble. "Pretty sure I've been eating more than usual."

But also working out like a machine.

"Alessandro," Mom calls out to my second brother, who must be in the kitchen. "Is the lasagna ready?"

"Almost!" he shouts back.

Mom turns around and heads back in, grumbling in colorful Italian.

I don't even know why they bother putting on music in the background. Between a staff where every person has megaphones for lungs and loud chatter from the customers, it's impossible to relax in this place.

"You really do look scrawny," Lily says while she walks by. Also her form of greeting.

My family's love language is food. And thinly veiled insults.

I tear a chunk of bread, dip it in olive oil and balsamic vinegar, and sprinkle it with cheese. It tastes like a little piece of heaven in the middle of this hell day.

The banging doors tell me Mom's coming back out. A moment later, a steaming plate of lasagna is set in front of me. She always makes me the same, thinking it's my favorite. In fact, it's Alessio's, my third brother. I'm a simple spaghetti and meatballs kind of guy.

To my surprise, she sits across from me. I freeze on my way to taking the first bite. Mom looks like she wants to say something but doesn't know how. Very unlike her.

"Everything okay?" I ask.

"I heard from Leo that your team is not good."

I could kill him.

I stuff my mouth with food so I don't say that aloud.

"Why don't you just focus on school, like your father and I said?" She glances around at her kingdom. "Help out at the restaurant like your brothers."

"But it's okay if Leo plays hockey?"

Her lips set in a tight line. "Well, he's good at it."

"And I'm not." I don't stop eating, because this isn't the first time I've been lured with food into this exact conversation.

"I didn't say that."

I take a sip of water. "Why don't you come watch me play, then?"

"It's all the same." Mom waves a hand. "Stick waving, punching. Everything moves too fast. I get dizzy. It's boring."

"How do you know if you've never seen a game?" But I have a very strong feeling I know the answer already.

She confirms it, saying, "I saw Leo play last week. It was enough."

This time my stomach closes shop. I set the silverware down and wipe my hands with a napkin.

Alessio is the only member of the family who has watched my games since I was a kid. The rest couldn't care less. But now that he's moved out of state—and Dad's still pissed about that—I have no one in my corner. Not even my own mother.

"So you'll go watch your grandson's game, but not your son's."

She reels back, as if realizing only from my mouth what her own words mean.

"Massimo, don't be such a *child.*"

I give her a stupefied look. "But I am one. *Your* child, to be precise. Who, by the way, is three years younger than the grandson you keep fawning over."

"I do not fawn!" Her shout turns heads, but in a second, the customers go back to eating.

I toss the balled-up napkin onto the table and stand. "Tell Alessandro thanks for the food."

"Massimo, stop this second."

I don't. She won't leave the restaurant during peak hours, so she doesn't come after me.

And isn't that the theme of my life? I'm the unexpected error they still don't know what to do with. Mom was forty-eight when she had me, way past what everyone thought possible. My three brothers were all adults. In fact, Cossimo Jr. had already had Leo, my parents' first grandchild.

That's why I'm always the last in line. Getting reminded of that today, of all days, is like pouring a pound of salt on a paper cut.

I climb back into the truck and collapse against the seat. I run my hands through my hair and pull at it. A weird laugh bubbles from my chest.

In a way, I should be thankful to Mom for the reminder. Showing my nephew up is what I need to focus on, not trying to find someone to give a damn about me. Life's shown me time and again that that's just not gonna happen.

I fasten my seat belt and set the truck in motion toward a franchise pizza place.

# CHAPTER 16
## LUZ

For two nights, my dreams replay the kiss between Max Cassiano and me.

The first night, the dreams took things further, and I woke up covered in sweat and gasping for air. The bedsheets felt like a vise around me, but kicking them away didn't help. The second night, the scene turned into a nightmare, where we were discovered by both Strikes and Bolts. Insults and mockery rained on us until Max decided he was better off pushing me away.

Mondays always suck, but even more when you have to see the guy you've developed a teeny-tiny crush on in class. And more so when all you should be doing is avoiding him.

My plan was to get to class late so I wouldn't have to sit near him. Unfortunately, training's done early, and I have nowhere else to release all this nervous energy, since the rest of the team are heading to their own classes or back to sleep.

I skate as slowly as possible through campus on my Mars-blades. I pause to put on the cardigan I strapped around my waist. Pause again to do up its buttons. Someone asks me for directions, and I give them the most detailed outline of the planet. I make a detour to get juice from a vending machine, and take my sweet time drinking it before I resume the trek.

It's still fifteen minutes too early when I make it to the classroom. Even after taking forever to change into sneakers and put the inline skates in my bag. Max's roommate evades my eyes as I find my seat. Serves him right for being such a judgmental prick.

Max is nowhere to be found yet.

I tense up even more. The seats around me are empty. He could walk in at any minute and head right over.

Then what? How am I going to face him? Or, more to the point, how am I going to face him and pretend that nothing's changed? Because, in theory, nothing has. We're two barely-acquaintances who are the captains of teams that hate each other.

And he terrifies me.

Somehow, with his *Tinker Bell this* and *Tinker Bell that*, with his easy smiles and the twinkle in his eyes, he disarmed me. I didn't ask him to. In fact, I didn't even flirt with him. But he still sneaked his way past my defenses.

What could he do if I just opened the doors and let him waltz in?

He would take over.

A shiver runs down my spine, and I burrow deeper into my cardigan. I didn't fight my parents so hard to keep playing hockey in college just to get sidetracked by a hot guy. But I know in my heart of hearts that Max Cassiano could take that number one spot. I can't let him.

I keep a discreet watch of the front door until the lecturer arrives. As class starts, I take a look around but still don't spot him. It's almost ten minutes in when he makes his way through the back door and sits in the very back row, far away from me.

He spends the entire period with his attention on the lecture. Not a single time does he glance my way.

I do sneak several looks at him at different intervals. He's as stoic as a soldier throughout. When the class ends, he picks up his things and bolts out of the room.

We have a standing study session at the library every Monday afternoon until we're done with the project, so it's not like I'm off the hook. But I also can't call him to cancel, because I don't have his freaking number. I'll just have to show up.

My cortisol levels are on high all day. For the first time I can remember, I'm unable to eat any lunch. My stomach is in knots when I walk into the library, but I don't find him anywhere.

I sit at the same table as before. Maybe five minutes pass, and he still doesn't arrive, so I figure I should busy myself with other coursework. While I'm setting up, someone tries to sit across from me, and I tell them the spot's taken. Obviously by a ghost. But the guy agrees to sit somewhere else.

There's a sudden shift in the noise volume. Someone gasps, and I turn. The cause strides across the library, blue eyes trained on me.

A nearby girl whispers to a friend. "Wow, who is *that*?"

Trouble, that's who.

Every muscle in my body is coiled tight, as if expecting a defense player from another team to ram into me. Instead, Max pulls up the chair across from me and sits down.

"Sorry I'm late."

That's it. No other explanation.

The amount of focus he uses as he takes out a few things from his backpack compares to a faceoff before a game.

The girls nearby who tracked his progress from the entrance glare at me as if I'm public enemy number one. Every one of his girlfriends probably had to live with this. Not that I'm his girlfriend. Nor do I want to be. Nor would I be, if I wanted.

Maybe I should say I have cramps and just go take a nap. I sure feel exhausted already.

"I was reviewing what we worked on last time," Max says while firing up his iPad. "But I think we need more reference material. Everything reads more like wishful thinking than data-driven fact."

Funny, that's exactly how I feel about him right now.

I clear my throat. "Okay, that's a good point. Why don't you look for papers online while I check out business books?"

Despite bracing myself the entire day for this, I'm still not ready for when his eyes meet mine.

My brain's a little shit. It plucks the memory of his eyes at half-mast from the back of my mind, of how he looked up at me while my legs were wrapped around his hips, one of his hands grabbing my thigh and the other one traveling up the skin of my back.

The intensity of his eyes right now is just like that. It's as if he's remembering too. My clothes feel simultaneously too hot and too cold.

With a shaky breath I can't hide, I get up from my seat. "Yeah. So. Be back when I find something."

I hope to find nothing but a black hole I can disappear into.

This is too much. I'm out of my depth here. I've flirted with guys before, kissed a few, but none of them felt like this. Like each one could've been the brink of disaster.

I hide in the economics and business section of the library. It's not far enough from him, but at least there's an AC vent pointed directly at my steaming face.

Here's the thing: after this class ends, I'll only see glimpses of him in the sports facilities. We may run into each other at a few parties, but the more time that passes, the more I'll get busy with hockey and school. The odds that he gets a girl-friend will get higher as well. The time from now until then will suck, as if every day is Monday, but I've survived much worse.

"Yo puedo," I tell myself, pumping my fists a little.

The first step is to actually follow his lead and work. My heart rate starts calming the heck down while I check out the spines on the nearest shelf. What the hell am I even doing here?

I run a hand through my hair, clearing it away from my face. Right, business plan stuff. The basics for how to make a business case to pitch to investors. Something that is actually helpful since sooner or later—hopefully later—I'll be looking for capital to open my own business.

With that reminder, I finally start paying attention. I find a couple of books I can check out and put them on the carpet for later. I browse through the shelves, find a thick tome that looks promising, and put it on the pile. Rinse and repeat a couple more times until I find a book that looks exactly like what we need.

I try to reach for it, but it's on a shelf too high for me. There isn't a step stool in this aisle, but what if I use the pile of books on the floor?

Coach Young would murder me if I got injured this way, though. I stretch myself all the way, and the tip of my finger graces the spine, nowhere near where I can get a decent grasp. A jolt of pain shoots from my back up to my brain, and I freeze. This is a bad idea. I need to find a step stool.

A shadow descends over me. A hand above me easily plucks the book from its place. I recognize the sleeve of a denim shirt. When I turn around, Max Cassiano will be standing in front of me.

I take a deep breath, which doesn't help at all with the way my nose soaks up the warm sandalwood scent in the air around me.

When I turn around, he offers me the book in silence. I use

it as a shield between us, and as much as I wish to run away, I can't. His eyes have me rooted to the spot.

"We need to talk," he finally says.

I give a weak smile. "Nothing good ever comes after that sentence."

"Can we just forget what happened?" Max bites his lip while running a hand through his hair, both of which I now know to be silky soft. "I shouldn't have made the bet in the first place, especially not without giving you a chance to not accept it. That was a dick move, and I'm sorry."

I… shit. I hadn't thought about that.

But he's right. I walked into it blind. If it had been any other guy, if I hadn't already had a bit of a thing for him before the pool game, I'd be fuming. Absolutely ready to rampage. In fact, I'd have reneged on the whole thing, damn my pride or the supposed eternal glory for my team.

Pretending to be angry would be a lie, though. Saying I'm not would be an admission that I wanted to kiss him all along. I don't want to do either.

I stare at him, unable to pry my mouth open and spew out a single word.

"Look." He cringes and takes a step back. "It's obviously made everything weird between us, and we still have to work on this project together. So can we just pretend it never happened?"

Oh, but *it* happened, all right. I can pretend, yeah, but I'll never forget.

He must've seen me sneaking glances at him in class. He definitely saw me freak out when he arrived at the library. I'm not known for my poker face. Right now, I am the definition of weird. Because of him.

Accepting his proposal is the easiest path. The best. The only option. The one that leads exactly to the plan I created for myself: keep my head in the game and in school, gradually drift apart from this guy.

The fact that he's offering it himself, as a sort of olive branch, is a blessing in disguise. It means I don't have to lie to him. He's doing it all for me.

"Okay," I say, tucking my hair behind my ear. "You're right. I'm sure you also can't afford distractions this early in the season. And it's not like it was a big deal."

"Right."

"So we're good." I shrug.

A muscle in his jaw ticks. "Let's just get to work so we can finish early."

A.k.a. so he doesn't have to see me for long.

"Fine."

But before I'm able to move my limbs again, he grabs the pile of books I collected and walks away. Like some damn gentleman.

Getting over Max Cassiano isn't going to be easy.

# CHAPTER 17
## MAX

feel like I'm walking underwater while I drag myself to the gym. The janitor is the only one in the building before me, and he gives me a weird look.

In front of me, the window at the front of the facility shows the beginnings of dawn. The sky is a haze of blues and purples, cut by the first rays of a yawning sun. I should still be in bed, but between my roommate's snoring and the whirring of my brain, that was impossible.

After stopping by a treadmill, I unzip my windbreaker and drop it into my sports bag. Normally, I'd put on a pair of head-phones and listen to my lectures again, but today I don't need the noise. The point is to shut my brain up. So it stops running through every conversation with Tinker Bell, analyzing every minuscule expression on her face.

I hop onto the machine and start at a quick walk, gradually increasing the incline and the pace until all I hear is the heavy thuds of my strides, the breath rushing in and out of my chest.

Why can't I be like other dudes who just shrug these things off and move on to the next girl? I can't stop thinking about her. The more I try, the more her face keeps appearing in my mind. At this point, I may have to ask Boucher to bash me over the head with a stick. Just to see if a concussion makes me think about something else.

I almost kissed her at the library—after psyching myself up for days about how kissing her had been wrong. The grand speech I'd prepared melted down like butter under too much heat as I looked at her. Maybe it was the isolation. She'd been browsing for books in a quiet section when I found her. Only books would've witnessed had I kissed her again.

But Tinker Bell hugged the book I picked for her to her chest, as if she needed a barrier between us. That's what snapped me awake.

She's not interested in me. If anything, she doesn't seem to like me very much. Annoyance oozes off her every time I show up. I should've read the signs instead of mucking everything up like this. I pick up the pace until it's a punishing rhythm no less than I deserve. It's clear from our conversation yesterday at the library that she agrees I was out of line. And that it should never happen again.

If I'm being honest with myself, it's a blessing in disguise. Hockey has to be my number one priority in college. It's what will get me out of this town, away from my family and on to a successful life. When I have something to show for myself is when I'll be able to consider dating.

Definitely not right now. I'm still a nobody on my way to nowhere, and not just because I'm running on a treadmill. I have to take the L and carry on. So I like a girl who doesn't vibe with me, so what? I won't die from that.

Gradually, I reduce the speed and incline and spend a couple of minutes regaining my breath. I pant like a horse that has galloped to the ends of the earth. By this point, the sky is more yellow than blue on the horizon. When I step off the treadmill, I've worked up a good enough sweat. I grab my bag, about to head to the mats, when I notice two abnormalities.

The first one is Tinker Bell, and she's already on the mats. I get a flashback to the first day of bootcamp, when she beat me to the ice and my first words to her were almost Boucher-level. No wonder she can't stand me.

Our eyes meet through the mirror, and she looks away. My chest squeezes. I have to take a deep breath so the constriction eases.

The second thing I notice is a couple of guys using some of the weight machines. But they're not Bolts. They're also not in any of my classes. There's about half an hour until the gym floods with Bolts, and both the Strikes' captain and these guys are gonna get the boot. But for now, they can do whatever they want.

I change course to the rowing machines. They face directly into the other machines and not to the mats. I try to develop tunnel vision as I set everything up to my height, focusing on the straps around my sneakers as if my life depends on it, before I start rowing.

An excited whisper draws my attention up, though.

One of the guys nudges the other, wide eyes trained on the front where I know Tinker Bell is doing leg training.

I don't stop pulling at the handle as I look. Tinker Bell is in a baggy T-shirt and leggings. Nothing eye-popping. There's an elastic band around her calves that I know gives a good burn while crab-walking in a crouch like she is.

And then she does a sumo squat.

As she lowers herself, the T-shirt molds around her waist, and the curve of her butt is on full display. The two snoops look like an old cartoon. All they're missing are the wagging tongues.

I stop rowing so abruptly my seat makes a loud clanging sound when it slams against the stopper. It makes everyone turn to me.

Slowly, I unstrap my feet and get up. The only reason I'm

not rushing to throttle them is because I know it would get me suspended from the team. But in my mind, I do more than ram into them.

"What do you think you're doing?" My voice comes out in a growl as I approach.

One of the jerks looks away, as if that automatically makes him innocent.

The other one has the nerve to open his mouth and spew out some shit. "What the hell is your problem, man?"

"My problem," I say through gritted teeth, "is you two creeping on a girl who is working out and thinking that's okay."

"I—W-We're not creepers!"

"Yeah, you are. And you'll only stay alive if you beat it."

One of them points an accusing finger at me. "Who do you think you are? You don't own this place."

Just before I say that neither do they, Tinker Bell's voice sounds from behind me.

"He might as well. We're the captains of the hockey teams, and you're in our territory." I feel her walk up beside me. "If we say you should leave, then you scram as fast as your creeping asses can."

"You—" The guy's face grows red at an alarming rate. "You bit—"

Tinker Bell tenses.

Before he even finishes his sentence, I throw their bags at them. Hard. Enough that they stumble on their feet. "*Out.*"

"What's happening here?" Coach Green strides into the gym. Going by the thunder on his face, he probably heard the shouting.

"These two are just leaving." Tinker Bell pauses, then adds, "Right now."

One of the creeps hugs his bag against himself but stands straight, as if he has justice on his side. "Aren't these St.

Cloud's facilities? We're St. Cloud students. You can't just tell us to come and go as you please."

I get in his grill. It makes him shrink even smaller than he already is. "Do you want me to report you for sexual harassment? Because I'm really thinking I should."

That drains the blood from his face. His buddy, who talked back less, starts pulling at him until the little shit gets the hint. I follow them until I make sure they're out of the facility. If I ever see them again, I may not want to hold back.

When I walk back into the room, Tinker Bell has her arms wrapped around her as if she needs a hug.

I stop. And remind myself it shouldn't come from me.

Coach takes a look at me. "What the hell was that?"

"The two creeps were leering at Rodriguez," I say, using her last name for the first time.

Coach scratches his head. "I'll ask about getting signs on the doors saying access is restricted."

"That might not be enough." She's trying to look tough, but she keeps worrying her lower lip.

"Well, try not to work out alone," Coach says with a sigh. "And maybe wear baggier clothes."

I freeze. I don't even have to look at her to know how fast her blood pressure is rising.

She takes a deep breath. "That is not the issue here. The problem is—"

"Are you okay? That's what matters," I ask at the exact same time. It makes her pause right before telling Coach Green to shove it.

The older man doesn't notice anything amiss and speaks. "Cool yourself, Rodriguez. Coach Young and I will take steps so this doesn't happen again. And Cassiano? Well done."

"I—yes. Thanks."

"I'll be in my office until practice starts." He eyes the two of us for a moment. "Don't overwork yourselves while I'm gone."

The heck is that supposed to mean?

And why is she glaring at me like I'm the enemy?

She waits until Coach is out the doors to poke my chest hard enough to bruise. "What the hell was that, Cassiano?"

"What?" I rub at the sore spot.

"You interrupted me. As if you didn't want to hear what I was just about to say."

"It's not that." I frown. "I know you're angry, but Coach isn't the right target."

"And who are you to decide that?"

I reel back. "I was just trying to help."

"Well, don't," she snaps. Her eyes crackle with anger. "I didn't ask you to. I was ignoring those creeps for a reason. Now I'll have to be on my toes because they may seek me out for payback. But do you feel good that you *helped*?"

The way she spits out that last word lands like a slap on the face.

"I-I'm sorry. I didn't think—"

"Yeah, you didn't. Men never do." After one last glare that could melt steel, she pushes past me and marches right out of the gym.

I don't know what to say, so I squeeze my jaws tight and stand there like the world's biggest screwup. One thing is certain: I can't possibly make this girl hate me more.

# CHAPTER 18
## LUZ

"Mierda."

I turn into a statue just before dropping onto the ice. Max Cassiano is on the opposite goal, practicing his shots with military precision. A memory appears from the back of my mind of a news article I read a couple of years ago. It mentioned him along with the term sharpshooter, featuring a picture of Max in the middle of an incredible slapshot the opposing goalie had no chance of stopping. It broke a middle school record or something.

Back then, I got annoyed at all the fanfare. Where were the news articles about girls breaking hockey records?

Even worse, the bylines about my miracle recovery appeared in the health section and numerous medical journals. Not a peep in the sports section, though.

But that wasn't Max's fault. That was good ole institutionalized sexism. Just like how what happened with those creeps wasn't either. I looked for him all week to apologize for overreacting, and no dice.

It could've been a coincidence. Both teams have been

getting ready for major games tomorrow. Except it almost felt like he was avoiding me. Once I caught him changing tack abruptly the second he saw me heading over. On top of that, we haven't texted since we exchanged phone numbers for the school project. But this week I sent him a couple of messages asking to talk, and the jerk left me on read.

Now, here he is. Suddenly. With no escape.

That's probably because he hasn't spotted me, though. There's still a pile of pucks beside him, so he takes one and fires it like a cannon at the goal. Rinse and repeat without glancing back.

I make as much noise as possible when I drop onto the ice, even going as far as banging my stick against the boards. The noise catches him in the middle of picking up a puck. He turns over his shoulder and…

Well, I wish my opponents grew as pale upon my sight as he does.

"Hi." I skate over until I stop at a reasonable distance. "Stop looking at the exit, and let's talk."

Those ridiculous blue eyes of his shift back to me. He clears his throat. "I didn't think there was anything left to say."

"Oh, now I know you're being a brat."

"Whatever." He shoots the puck to a passer. Once it bounces back, he makes a tight swing with his stick and bags it where the goalie's third hole would be.

I take one of the pucks from the pile and skate around the goal with it. Max watches me until I disappear behind him. He repeats his exercise while I skate all the way to center ice. My original goal was to do some skating drills until I grew tired enough to sleep. Between jittery nerves about tomorrow's game and this weird air with the Bolts' captain, it's been impossible to sleep.

Pretending I'm on a breakaway, I go from zero to max

speed in a short burst. I'm better at skating than puck-handling, so I put more thought into the latter. Max doesn't get out of the way even though he sees me coming. As if he's the goalie, I shoot around him and bag it in the net.

"That's right, baby!" I raise my hands as I glide around the net. "Cut the check."

He snorts.

"Your career as a goalie is over, Cassiano."

"Look, I've been here for a while already. I'll just leave the equipment here for you and go."

I brake in his way. His hair is tousled, and a strand curves down his forehead. His cheeks are flushed from exercise, and there's a sheen of sweat on his skin. Like me, he's just in training clothes and skates, no pads. But he still looks enormous.

And yet it's clear he'd rather be anywhere but here, facing a five-foot six girl.

"I get it. Right now, you would probably rather watch an open-heart surgery than look at my face."

He recoils. "That's not it—"

"Well, thank goodness. I may not be fit for a beauty pageant, but I don't look that bad."

"Tinker Bell." There's a growl in his voice that sends tingles down my spine. Pleasant ones. "What do you want?"

"To apologize, you fool." I have to take a deep breath when I, myself, recognize that's not the right way to go about it. "That's what I've been trying to say all week, but you've been avoiding me."

Max snags one glove between his elbow and his side. With his freed hand, he musses his hair even more. "I haven't been avoiding you. I've just been busy."

"Oh yeah? Busy enough to walk the other way?"

Even though his eyebrows plunge in a mighty intimi-dating way, the increasing redness of his face gives him away.

"That—It's because I remembered I had something else to do."

"And what was that?" I lift a puck with the blade of my stick and bounce it in the air. "What was that very important thing?"

Max's chest expands dramatically as it takes in air before draining it all the way. "What was it that you wanted to apologize for?"

On the one hand, I want to give him crap like he used to give me. But on the other hand, I know that would lead to me finding him even cuter than I already do. And that would be too much for my heart.

So, I say, "I lashed out at you, even though it wasn't you I was mad at. So I'm sorry about that."

If not for the occasional blink, I might have confused him for a museum art piece instead of a living, breathing human. His expression is as serious as if he were in an exam, tasked with a problem that he alone is responsible for solving. Max tucks his tongue against his cheek.

Finally, he speaks. "No, you were right. I should've checked with you first. I was focused only on me and what I felt was right or wrong. Did those guys ever show up around you again?"

Not to be dramatic, but someone is playing pin the tail on the donkey with my heart right now. And I know exactly what's stabbing at my heart repeatedly: his kindness.

The weight of this realization weakens my knees, and I drop to a crouch, trying to make myself smaller and tucking my chin against my chest so he doesn't see my face. All the heat of my body has traveled there in a second.

I see him kneel on the ice from the corner of my eye. Vaguely, I remember once vowing to make him kneel before me. But the feeling was completely different back then.

"Tinker Bell? You okay?"

No, I am not okay.

However, I lift one hand. "Give me a second. I'm trying to not embarrass myself."

"Okay?"

I've created a picture of Max Cassiano in my mind, but that isn't who he is. From his interviews, I figured that a boy who was so talented and good looking had to be a conceited turd. And when I met him—right on this ice—I took his teasing as a confirmation that my assumptions were correct.

But he's been a damn gentleman. Taking the clothes off his back so I wouldn't keep flashing everyone, carrying me on his back, shaking his annoying roommate off me, and scattering those creeps. Even after he tricked me into kissing him, he never touched me anywhere I didn't let him.

He recognizes when he's wrong. Gives me space. Even now, when I'm having an emotional crisis, he doesn't push. He just waits.

Max is a genuinely good guy. Not one of those who pretends to be nice as a veneer to hide all their ugly intentions. No, he's just sweet.

Me gusta. Max Cassiano me gusta.

Knowing this changes nothing. We already agreed it's best we go on our merry ways. The sane part of me says I should focus only on hockey for as long as I have with it. And school's no joke. I'm nervous about midterms. Max is simply so huge that even an unrequited crush would take up all the space in my life.

"Thank you for your concern. And no, they didn't appear again." I suck in air like the Little Mermaid coming to the surface and look up at him. "So does that mean you accept my apology?"

"Were you really that concerned that I wouldn't?" Max blinks fast.

"What can I say? I have a flair for the dramatic."

"I see." He leans back on his haunches. "If it makes you feel better, sure. But there's really nothing to apologize for."

What I really want to do is push him onto the ice and kiss him until the cold seeps through our clothes and until the kiss grows too hot to be in public. If I stare at him for a moment longer, I think I may betray myself.

I get back on my feet. "Anyway, why were you out here training on your own?"

He moves slower as he pushes back up to stand. I head over to the goal and sweep a few of the pucks out. My heart pounds as if I've been skating at full speed for ten minutes.

"Same as you, I assume." His deep voice is somewhere behind me, not close enough to give me a heart failure. "I couldn't sleep."

"Big games tomorrow, huh?"

We're both playing squads that are considered contenders for the conference title. It's the last time we'll have games at the same time on the same night. Which means I could maybe sneak into a Thunder Bolts game to observe their captain in action. Purely for research.

"You'll do great," I say as I take out the last pucks. "I don't know about the rest of the Bolts, but you're off the charts…"

The words die in my throat as I turn. He's right in front of me, as close as he was at the library. Except this time I'm trapped between him and a hockey goal.

"Uh, Cassiano—"

"How do you know?" His voice is a low rumble. "That I'll do great."

Well, I—crap. Right now I don't even know my own name. Someone should tell him that his eyes are weapons of mass brain destruction.

I lick my lips, and his attention goes there.

No, I need to bring this back to friendly territory.

"Oh, you're a big deal in the hockey world, Cassiano." I

shove him away in what I hope is a friendly way. It gives me a few extra inches of space to breathe. "You might not have known me before bootcamp, but I knew about you. Your face's been plastered on all the up-and-coming-talent lists for years."

"A shame."

I tilt my head. "What?"

"That I didn't know about you before." Max lets out a little snort. "Especially after I put my foot in my mouth from the get-go."

"Your only mistake is that you keep calling me Tinker Bell."

For the first time in days, Max cracks a smile. The spark returns to his eyes, and it does bad things for my pulse.

"But it fits you so well."

"Don't make me punch you in the nose just when we're starting to make up."

Max bites his lip, probably holding back laughter. "So, what are we now? Friends?"

"I guess." I shrug, as if it doesn't both disappoint me and make me feel exhilarated. "Friends know each other's actual names, though."

"Funny you should say that. You keep calling me Cassiano, even though that's my *last* name."

"Oh, should I call you Massimo, then?"

If he could cringe any further, he would disappear into himself like a black hole. "Ugh, no. That's what my parents call me."

"Ha! Massimo it is, then." Since his head is lowered almost to my level, I reach forward and rub his head as if he's a kid. "That's a good lad."

He only puts up with the attack for a second. Before I know it, his hand captures my wrist, and with a jerk, he pulls me up against him.

My mouth parts and out comes an "oh."

See, the thing is that friends don't look at other friends like this. Like they're one second away from crossing that line.

It doesn't help that his lips are a masterpiece. I know the bow of his top lip fits like a glove against both of mine. His bottom lip is full and soft, and it's easy to picture myself running my tongue across it.

When I raise my eyes to find his, I almost feel consumed by fire. He has to be thinking the same thing I am. Otherwise he wouldn't be looking at me like *that*. He'd be pushing me away.

"Oh, someone's here?"

At the new voice, Max and I scramble away from each other. My legs tangle in the air. If not for my great reflexes, I would have fallen on my butt.

Chelsea skates onto the ice.

"H-Hey, Chels!" My voice comes out so squeaky even the Bolts captain gives me a weird look. I clear my throat. "Uh, what brings you here?"

"Did you forget? Winning a bet for eternal glory means we get the ice at night for the foreseeable future," my alternate captain says with a smile that, from anyone else, would precede a cascade of mockery. She doesn't add anything further, though.

Max picks up his fallen stick without looking either of us in the eye. "Right. Well, I was just wrapping up for the night. Have at it."

I don't know whether he's a coward or the sharpest tool in the shed, because he takes his delectable behind away. Why didn't I come up with that excuse first?

"What was all that about?" Chelsea asks, eyebrows up.

"Nothing. He really was just leaving." I'm glad my voice sounds totally normal now. "Wanna practice passing?"

"*Sure.*"

In the elongation of the word, it is clear she doesn't believe me for squat. But it could've been worse. I could've been found getting cozy with the enemy by Brit or JT instead. That I wouldn't be able to live down.

I have to be more careful now. Not just for the sake of peace between the Strikes and the Bolts, but also for my own. One more look from Massimo Cassiano like *that*, and I might just let him score in my net.

# CHAPTER 19
## MAX

"Dude, what the heck is wrong with you?"

"I don't know," I answer Nate, knowing full well what *the heck* is wrong with me. "Anyway, tell them to hold the bus for me."

He gives me an annoyed look. "You're not that special, captain of the entire freaking team. But fine."

I unbuckle myself and get up from my seat. "Careful. I'm gonna start thinking you have a crush on me or something."

"Just go get your panties, dipshit."

I toss him an air kiss that only darkens the expression on his face. Nate's pissed because I interrupted his rant. He's nervous that among the team we'll face tonight is one of his high school rivals. Poor guy probably wanted reassurance from me, and instead, I burst out, saying I forgot to pack my underwear.

As I hop off the bus, I promise myself that I'll listen in full and give Nate the exact list of reasons why he's the best defenseman I've played with and why I'm glad he's the one watching my six.

If I told him why I forgot my underwear in the first place,

he would pick me up and throw me out the window of the moving bus.

I distinctly remember having to sit down on my bed earlier today, my heart pounding so fast it almost made me run to the hospital. Nerves weren't the reason. At least not because of the game. I spent the whole night awake with random palpitations every time I remembered how close I'd been to pulling Tinker Bell against me last night and having my way with her right there on the ice.

We'd have melted the whole thing down, the way my imagination went. You can't blame a guy for getting dizzy at the rapid rush of blood to a single area of his body, huh? Good thing that whole episode happened with no witnesses.

Coach Green and I cross paths as I climb off the bus. "Where the hell do you think you're going?"

"Uh, so, you're not gonna believe this, but I forgot to pack underwear."

Coach presses his mouth tight into a very unimpressed expression. I, too, know I'm destroying my hard-earned reputation right now.

"Fine, if you're not back in ten minutes, we're leaving without you."

"Yes, sir." Fortunately for me, my dorm is a sneeze away from this parking lot.

A bunch of wolf whistling explodes behind me, and while I jog away, I take a glance back to find half of the Thunder Bolts hanging out of the windows.

"Go get your thong, princess!"

"What's wrong with going commando? It reduces friction."

Too many of them crack up at that, leaving me no choice but to stop and flip them the bird.

I stumble on my own feet and don't crash onto my butt by sheer luck. Because right behind our bus is the women's team bus. And on the curb, their coach and a few of the Strikes stare at me, probably thinking I'm swinging free even though I currently am not. Among them is Tinker Bell.

Turning around, I decide I'm not gonna talk Nate up when I return. I'm going to murder him instead.

Some dude taking out his laundry gives me a once-over as I walk into the dorm building. Guess they're still not used to seeing burly dudes in a full suit yet. I wish I'd brought my bag with me, because now I'll have to stuff my boxers into my pocket, and I don't want to deal with the mockery.

I push the door to my dorm room open. Inside, Brett leaps on his chair in fright.

"You can keep watching your naughty videos, bro," I say while I check out the mess on my bed. Papers, books, a balled-up towel and—voilà. I grab the boxers and stuff them into my pocket. "I'm out."

"I was not watching porn!" He points at the screen of his laptop. An Excel sheet full of numbers is apparently what had him so engrossed. "I'm not some jock who can only think with his pants."

I was just about to walk out the door, but that stops me. "What is your problem, man?"

"You're all the same." How this went from a passing comment from me to him getting in my grill, I have no idea. But here he is, angry, as if I've punched him with no warning. "All you do is look down on guys like me and think you're the kings of the world. You're all freaking bullies."

Is my brain still addled by my hormones? Why do I feel like this guy's having a conversation with himself?

"So you're saying I bullied you just now?" The incredulity in my voice is obvious.

"N-No." He glares at me, though, in contradiction to that answer. "But it's just your attitude—"

"That is so not the same." I square up to him, taking a step closer. "In fact, with the number of insults you hurl at me and my friends, I could argue that the bully here is you."

I must've touched a nerve, because it makes him shout. "I am *not* a bully!"

"Neither am I. Maybe you'd know that if you stopped being such a judgy prick for a second and get to know me." At his stunned silence, I add, "Look, I honestly don't know what I've done to make you hate my guts, but you should know I couldn't possibly care less what you think about me. Keep hating me for all I care. I don't have time for this."

I whirl around, expecting more insults to fly as I jog down the stairs. All is quiet, though. Except in my mind.

At this rate, I'm going to be a disaster on skates tonight. I'll have to spend the bus ride listening to hard rock to get me in the right mindset.

I pick up the pace across the gardens and back to the parking lot. Soon it becomes clear I don't need to rush. The whole bus has drained of people and a crowd made out of both teams loiters on the curb.

As I approach, someone bandies out the word *discrimination*, and that's how I find out it's not for some kumbaya.

"What's happening?" I ask Conor, the nearest Bolt I find.

"It's a mess, man. The Strikes started complaining that their bus is old and they want to take ours instead." He sighs.

"What?"

"I'm going to ask you to calm down your team," Coach Green says to Coach Young.

The woman's eyes blaze with ferocity, but somehow she keeps it in check. I've seen Dad asking Mom to calm down, and let's just say the exact opposite happens.

Of course, that's when Frankie Boucher opens his yap. "Yeah, you ladies need to stay nice and quiet."

I make the mistake of glancing over the divide and meet Tinker Bell's eyes. It's pretty clear to me that if I open my mouth right now, I will be dismembered. If only in her mind.

"We are calm, Glen." Coach Young's voice could freeze the ocean. "It's your boys who took a comment we made and turned it into a scene."

That sounds about right. I can picture Boucher doing just that and riling up all these clowns. I run a hand down my face.

You know what? None of this shit would've happened if I'd just accepted going commando after tonight's game. It wouldn't have killed me. All this drama might.

"Why don't you tell *them* to calm down instead?" the Thunder Strikes captain asks, folding her arms. "Or is it my fault again that men can't behave themselves?"

And that's when I put two and two together. She must have been the author of the comment. Boucher must've heard it, either because he wasn't on the bus or because the windows were still open after they heckled me. The feeling that this whole thing is my fault grows into a boulder I can no longer shoulder. There's only one way to drop the weight.

"I apologize on behalf of my team."

My voice parts the crowd like they're the Red Sea. Among the sea of surprised faces, chief is Coach Green's. It's like the thought of just saying sorry never crossed his mind. I get that he's a tough guy who treats us all like we're soldiers, but this is ridiculous.

So I say exactly that, with my whole chest. "This is ridiculous. We're all wasting time here, even though we both have games we can't be late to."

Tinker Bell does that thing when words stumble on each other before they spill from her mouth. "It's not ridiculous. Our away game is farther than yours. Why do we have to ride the smaller, crappier bus?"

"Because we're bigger, princess." Boucher throws his hands up in the air. "How can you expect us to squeeze into that minivan?"

Volume rises up on both sides again. I press a hand against the sudden throbbing in my temple. The fact that Luz Rodriguez looks at me as if I'm the bitterest enemy doesn't make me feel any better. Here I thought we'd made peace yesterday, but this isn't just about the buses. It's about the fact that we're going to forfeit both games if we keep this up.

"Coach." I sidle up to him. "Way over ten minutes have passed since our departure time."

"Well, what do you want me to do?" He frowns as if he isn't the adult here. "I feel like I'm walking on landmines with everything I say. This is why my wife's threatening to divorce me."

And Coach Young doesn't look any more willing to talk. If anything, I think she's holding it together by a thread.

I'm the Bolts' captain. There must be something I can do.

Abruptly, I whistle over the noise. When I get the attention of both teams, I say, "I'm sure no one wants to forfeit their game. So how about we solve this by flipping a coin?"

Taking the silence as consent, I fish around my pockets, take out the boxers by accident, and jam them back in. It makes someone snort, and I glare at the offender. Of course, it had to be Tinker Bell. This night can't possibly get any more humiliating.

Finally, I find a coin and show it to everyone.

"Strikes, you're heads, and we're tails," I say. Someone whistles at some hidden meaning there, and I ignore it.

"Fine."

I flip the coin. Without looking away from the opposite captain, I catch it in one hand and slap it against the other one. Then I show it to her.

Her pretty face scrunches up. "Tails."

You'd think the Bolts just won the conference cup with all their cheering. But while I get dragged back onto the big, new bus, I have a niggling feeling I just drove the final nail into my own coffin. Forget kissing Luz Rodriguez again. After this, she might not even want to be my friend.

# CHAPTER 20
## LUZ

steam with so much anger even the window beside me fogs up.

"Why are you still like this?" Brit nudges me with her shoulder. "We won! You should be happy."

"For real." JT kneels backward on her seat in the row in front of ours. "Hell, maybe we should even thank the Bolts. Their obnoxiousness sure lit a fire under our asses."

We pulverized the other team tonight. Based on the talk in the locker room, I wasn't the only one who imagined we were facing off with the Bolts instead. Those poor girls from West Bank College stood no chance against our collective ire.

What my friends don't know, though, is that my current hissy fit isn't because of the Bolts. Or their captain. But because of myself.

I sink farther into my seat and fold my arms, well aware that I screwed up again.

Sometimes—not often, but right now is one such occasion—I wish I was a sweet and dainty girl. Someone who isn't constantly burning with the need to prove herself. What I guess is called having a soft temperament.

Worse still, I *know* I'm not always right. But I also know I'm not always wrong. And that's the side I *always* bet on—that I may be right.

Tonight, Max won again. He cleverly sidestepped the conversation about why one team consistently gets the fancy bus, which is what made me blow up in the first place. Maybe he agrees that the Bolts should keep it because they have bigger bodies and more tender butt cheeks, but the fact remains that it wasn't the time or the place to have that discussion. And apparently he was the only one who could see that.

Clearly, he's made of better stuff than me. A captain should be able to keep their head cool and guide their team through the difficulties. He did that. I didn't. I was ready to pour more fuel on the fire.

Once more, I showed Max Cassiano my worst side. That's why I'm fuming right now.

"For real. Maybe they have their uses after all," Brittany says with a laugh.

In front of her, Chelsea rises up slightly and wiggles around until she's also facing us. Her smile puts me on edge. "And the most useful of all was their captain, huh?"

I narrow my eyes but say nothing. She's been tossing around innocuous comments like this since she found Max and me alone on the ice last night. Obviously, she's fishing for information I'm not going to provide.

"Hate to admit it, but if not for him, we'd have missed the game." JT cringes until her shoulders are as high as her ears. "Gratitude toward a Bolt got me feeling like I need to shower again, but with bleach this time."

Brit shudders. "Ugh, same. He's kinda hot, though. Unlike Boucher."

A murmur of assent echoes around them.

Until they catch me giving them the most exaggerated look.

*Kinda hot?* Kinda hot is putting a piece of pizza in the

microwave for three minutes. Hot as hell is the oven that baked the pizza. Max is the oven. And I can't stop dreaming about him, even though I know he's going to burn me.

I run a hand down my face, exasperated that even my thoughts about him are getting out of hand.

"Geez, chill." JT lifts her hands up as a barrier between us. "No one here is going to go fraternizing with the enemy. Okay, Captain?"

I sink as far into my seat as I can.

Coach McDonald stands between the front seats, grabbing the backrests. "Listen up, Strikes."

"Yes, ma'am," we all respond at once.

Normally, Coach Young is the one who makes all the announcements. She lost her voice after screaming her throat raw tonight. I don't know whether she was that pleased with our seven goals, or if she was offloading stress after the confrontation with the Bolts.

"We're almost at St. Cloud. Coach Young has decided to hold the post-game debrief tomorrow morning before practice, so be there fifteen minutes early."

"Yes, ma'am."

"For now, just head straight home and get some rest."

That is the happiest *yes, ma'am* I've shouted back in a while.

The girls start making plans about going to O'Malley's, but after my blunder today, I'm feeling really obedient, and I head to my dorm.

Music drifts out of the building as I approach. Energy drains from my body with every step. Perhaps being alone to stew in my misery isn't the best idea. I could change out of my letterman jacket and slacks into something cuter and hit the bar with the others.

As I climb up the stairs to the third floor, I have to pause for two people blocking the way. They're making out with all their might and don't notice me right away. One of them finally spots me and pulls her partner closer, away from my path.

"Sorry."

"Don't be sorry," I say with a sigh. "I'm just jealous."

I leave their laughter behind as I keep climbing up. That's really what I wish I was doing. Making out with Max in some dimly lit corner. I wonder if he's at O'Malley's. And if I could pull off sneaking him out without anyone noticing.

I push open my bedroom door with a shoulder. Shock of all shocks, my roommate sits on her bed typing on her laptop. She lifts her eyes to me for a fraction of a second and then keeps tapping at her keyboard.

First, I drop my bag at the foot of my bed. Then I drop myself onto my bed, face down.

"Did you lose?"

I almost have a heart attack at the sound of her voice. Rolling my head, I make sure she can see the raw shock in my face.

"You know, I wasn't sure if I'd hallucinated your voice the one time Max was here, or if you could really speak."

She shrugs infinitesimally. "I can. I just choose not to."

"Fair." I huff to get my hair away from my face. It doesn't work, so I leave it there. "What changed now?"

A moment passes that almost convinces me she won't speak again. But then she does. "Your entrance was very dramatic, and I'm bored."

"Why aren't you out partying like usual?"

Just because she's a goth through and through doesn't mean she lacks a social life. In fact, that's one of the reasons we don't talk much. I'm always with the team, and she's always with her friends. I saw them just once at O'Malley's, a whole bunch of people in all black. They walked in, saw the scene, and walked right out. Never saw them again. No idea what their usual haunts are.

"I broke up with my boyfriend," she says in a deadpan that betrays zero feelings.

"Huh, so the heartbreak makes you talk?" I think that's a glare. Maybe I should stop teasing. "And no, we won."

The murderous intent she radiates eases off. "Then what's your damage?"

"Boy problems too."

I roll onto my back and squint at the light from the lamp. The sigh I release is so big it drains my chest.

"I wouldn't have thought a girl like you would have boy problems."

"What's that supposed to mean?"

She motions at me. "You're hot."

"Thanks. So are you." Since she scrunches up her face in denial, I add, "No, seriously. In a sort of *I will punch your throat while The Cure plays in the background* type of way."

Her eyebrows fly. "You know The Cure?"

"I know a lot of things. I'm not some stereotype." I fold my arms in mock anger, until I remember that sometimes I can't find two brain cells to rub together and produce a spark of rational thought. "Scratch that. I'm not as smart as I pretend."

She sets her laptop aside. "Like I said, I'm bored. Let's do that roommate bonding you've so clearly wanted."

"You knew?"

She snorts through her nose. "It was obvious. I just used to ignore you."

But there's no bite to her words, so I jump to sit at the edge of my bed. "How good are you at keeping secrets?"

"Moderate." The admission is fresh but concerning. "I don't run in your circles, though. The risk is small."

I nod while I mull it over. "Okay, but just so you know, if any of this spills to the public, I know where you live."

"And I know just how big your biceps are. Proceed."

"You're very weird, but I like you, Lynn Davis." It feels weird to use her name for the first time just now. To strike the point, I stretch out my hand. "Nice to meet you. I'm Luz Rodriguez, your roommate this semester."

For a second, she glances at it as if it's gross, but she ends up shaking it. "Sure, now tell me all your secrets, Luz Rodriguez, before I keep entertaining the murderous thoughts in my head." She motions at me to begin the tale, and I'm only too happy to oblige.

"Okay, so…" It already feels like a weight is lifting from my shoulders as I start. "You know I'm the captain of the Thunder Strikes, the women's hockey team, right?"

"Now I do."

I snort a little. "Yeah, and that there's a men's team called the Thunder Bolts. It's packed full of Neanderthals."

"Oh, that I do know. There's a douche named Boucher in one of my classes. Hate that guy."

"Ugh, everyone does. I feel bad for you." I cringe, remembering how the crap spilling out of his mouth made me lose my cool today. Max must be a saint to put up with him. Or he ignores him altogether. "He's solely responsible for our collective bad reputation."

"I hope he's not your boy problem." Lynn cocks an eyebrow.

I gag, and it's not even fully exaggerated. "He's a problem, but not *mine*."

"Whew."

It's funny to hear it in such a monotone.

"The problem boy is their captain."

Her eyes pop, and she interrupts. "*Oh*. Yeah, I also know of him. He's the semi-naked guy, huh?"

"Yeah."

I sigh. She sighs. We sigh. This is what we call bonding, all right.

"But the actual problem is that he's a freaking cinnamon roll."

"I am literally not seeing a problem right now."

"He's the captain of the Bolts. The enemy of the Strikes. For which I'm the captain."

Slowly, her mouth opens into a perfect O shape. "Ah. It's an enemies-to-lovers type of thing."

"Except we're forced to stick to the enemies part. The teams would flip a gasket if we started dating."

"What's the big deal?" She shrugs, hands up as if this were the simplest issue. "Just bang him in secret. Or date him in secret, whatever."

I bark a laugh.

Lynn's lips tremble, but she keeps the straight face. "I mean, I would definitely bang him in secret and in public if he wanted, but that's just me."

"It's not that simple." I wipe tears from my face. "A guy like him could get his pick of girls. Cuter and nicer than me. And after what I did today, he probably hates me."

"Oh?" She rests her chin on her hand, elbow on her knee.

I spill all the beans I've been holding. The Strikes are my friends, and they'd lap a tale like this up—if it didn't involve a Thunder Bolt. And my high school friends are so busy, we rarely have time to text more than a few words at a time. That's why I've had to keep all of this hush-hush. It's killing me.

I give Lynn the highlights and lowlights, not even bothering to make myself look good in the story. I've been a mess, and I know it.

"Listen," she says at the end. "If I've learned something about guys, it's that they're simple. Just ask him if he wants something with you or not. And if he does, then keep it all a secret. It's no one else's business who you get with."

True. And if the teams don't know… then World War III won't start, and no one's game will be affected.

"Thanks, Lynn."

"And if it doesn't work out, I'll take him."

I give her a sweet smile. "Sorry, but I intend to make it work."

# CHAPTER 21
## MAX

The text from Tinker Bell catches me on my way back to my dorm after the game. I have my settings so I only get the notifications and who they're from, but not the content of the texts. I learned the lesson the hard way once, after Leo caught the contents of a text from my ex and mocked me about it for days.

So I stand in the middle of the courtyard, staring at the screen. The decision was made before the beginning of time. I'll read any text she sends me. Whether I have the backbone to reply is a different matter.

She… intimidates the hell out of me. A fact none of my boys can ever, ever find out about. I want to impress her. Be someone she can respect. And I keep putting my foot in my mouth, to the point that I know the taste as well as my mom's marinara.

Sighing, I swipe the text open.

**SPARKS**

On a scale from 1 to 100, how much do you hate me now?

I double-check to make sure it's her, indeed. I saved her contact as Sparks because everyone knows I call her Tinker Bell. And there were definitely sparks when we made out.

Of all the things I might've expected, though, this isn't one. I scratch my head and consider how to answer.

ME

100...

She sends back the wide-eyed emoji. My lips pull back in the kind of smile that riles her up.

ME

...percent don't hate you at all

Why?

The three dots on her side appear and disappear a couple of times. I resume walking to the dorm, keeping one eye on the ground and one on the screen.

Whatever this is about, it takes her a while to figure out the wording. I make it into my room. Brett's still at his desk, studying. He glances once at me, his mouth a downturned U that tells me he's still throwing a hissy fit after our earlier conversation. I turn my back on him and open my closet.

My phone pings. I grab it, despite the fact that one of my arms is out of my suit jacket and the other one is still jammed in.

SPARKS

It's just... I feel like I was justified, but I botched the approach. And you kinda took the brunt of it at the end and I'm sorry

I reread that several times over. I put my phone down on a shelf, take the jacket off, and hang it. Then I come back to the phone. The words *I'm sorry* from Tinker Bell are still there.

She's a pretty commanding type of person, and seeing as how long it took her to type out the words, this feels like something that was hard for her to say. Especially for a second time.

ME

Thank you *wide-eyed emoji*

But this is like with the creeps at the gym

It's not about me

You were def justified

Sorry for coming across like a villain

SPARKS

Why can't the rest of the Bolts be more like you?

ME

The world's not ready for so many perfect men

SPARKS

I take everything back

"What are you giggling about?" my roommate asks, his voice sounding grumpy.

I snort. "Puh-lease. I don't giggle. I exude a manly chuckle."

"You straight-up sound like a five-year-old girl giggling."

The glare I toss over my shoulder goes unnoticed, since he's still busy clacking away at his keyboard.

After tonight's win, the team wanted to hit up O'Malley's to celebrate with burgers and darts, but I bowed out with the excuse of studying. Which is valid. Exams won't ace themselves.

Instead, I spend the whole night texting with Tinker Bell. And the next day.

When Monday rolls around, we sit together in Intro to Entrepreneurship. I had a smart moment earlier where I set my watch to not beep if my heart rate exceeds a certain level, which probably saves me from the embarrassment of her realizing how much she affects me.

Sometime during the lecture, I'm biting the end of my pencil when I feel something. I turn my face slightly and catch Tinker Bell staring up at me. She doesn't even turn away or act like I have something on my face.

Naw, she's not like that. Her eyes, black like onyx, stare into mine with such blatant openness it's me who feels heat travel up my neck. What if those impossibly deep eyes have the power to stare into my soul? What if she can see that I'm going wild about her?

The only way I know to deal with this is by joking. I grin and pull the pen out of my mouth to ask, "Jealous of the pen?"

Her eyes flicker to it for a second, then to my lips. The same heat burning me up from the inside settles on her cheeks. Like maybe she hadn't noticed she was staring.

"Get your mind out of the gutter, Cassiano."

It wasn't even in the gutter until that moment. But after that, I keep imagining all the parts of her body I would love to nibble softly.

A couple of days later, I'm going even crazier.

We don't have any other classes together, and with the tension between the Bolts and the Strikes, it's impossible to even catch a glimpse of her at the gym. My addiction to peeking around in hopes of seeing her gets even worse. I almost murder Conor once while he's bench-pressing and I'm supposed to spot for him.

"Damn, Cassiano!" he shouts while he and I struggle to pull the weights back up safely. "You almost killed me, bro."

"Yeah, you've been weird today," Nate adds from the adjacent machine. "Or I should say, more than usual."

"Sorry, sorry. I don't know where my mind is."

On a Latina who makes the air crackle with electricity, that's where.

"Go sit." Conor frowns up at me before shifting his attention. "Garcia, be my spotter."

I'm not above admitting my wrongs, so I do as I'm told and sit for a moment.

This isn't good. I'm supposed to be married to hockey.

As if my body has a mind of its own, I pull my cell phone from the pocket of my joggers and click the iMessage app. She's at the very top.

"Don't do this, Max," I tell myself. But I click on her texts anyway.

The thing is… it's my birthday this Thursday. And the one gift I want is her company. The problem is we're not dating. We said we'd be friends, and that's what we are now. And Mom basically commanded I show up at the restaurant because she's making tiramisu for me. Dismissing tiramisu would get me disowned and excommunicated. Bringing Tinker Bell over—especially since *we're not freaking dating*—would make absolutely zero sense.

And yet my fingers start to type.

ME

Are you busy this…

I delete that. If she says she's busy this Thursday, I'm going to look really pitiful saying *oh, okay* and going off to nurse my broken heart.

Like in hockey, I should be direct. In your face. Decisive.

ME

It's my birthday this Thursday. Wanna hang?

If I could cringe any harder, I'd turn into a pebble. I delete that second part.

*Wanna hang?* Can I be any less cool?

ME

It's my birthday this Thursday and...

"What?"

I startle at the sudden question.

Nate and Conor are sitting on either side of me. Somehow. Without me noticing them.

"Who's Sparks?" Nate motions at my phone with his chin.

"Dude, it's your birthday?" Conor's eyes are wide. "This calls for a huge party."

"Wait, I—" I mean to say I'm making plans already, but then I look down at my phone and...

Great, I hit Send on the incomplete text by accident.

"My roommate is the little brother of that guy who threw the house party we went to at the beginning of the semester," Nate says, already jumping for his phone. "I'm sure those guys won't say no to arranging something."

"No, I—" The expectant looks they give me tell me that this isn't about me. This is about them having a reason to get drunk. "Fine, just make it Friday after the game. I have to go home on Thursday."

I congratulate myself on my quick thinking there. While they start making preparations right in front of me, I check my phone again and find that Tinker Bell sent me a single question mark. It could mean *and?* As in, she doesn't see how that should pertain to her. Or it could mean I should finish the damn sentence.

I hope for the second one.

ME

And I would like to see you

Send.

I wait for exactly one hour to get a response. Or at least that's how it feels like.

SPARKS

Sure

What do you have in mind?

"Yes!" I jump from my seat, pumping a fist in the air.

"Right?" Nate probably thinks I'm celebrating whatever he said. "Those chicks are hot, so if none of them are into the birthday boy, I'll be next in line."

I frown down at him. "The hell are you talking about?"

"Chicks." His eyes are as wide as they can go. "We'll invite so many chicks. Get you laid. Get us laid. It's gonna be grand."

I glance over at Conor, who is nodding like there's nothing to see here.

How can I tell them I don't want *chicks*? I just want one. A very specific one. One I don't even know for sure is really interested in me. Sure, she practically ate my mouth when we made out. But that doesn't necessarily mean she wants the rest of me. Not when I myself, *of my own volition*, went and told her to forget that all happened. And she agreed.

I head back to my dorm after training's over, unable to break that to them. They still think that, in three days, I'll be looking for the chance to hook up among the attendees of my so-called birthday party and thank them for it.

I crash on my bed, facing the ceiling. Damn it, I have it real bad. I always knew I was a whipped fool with my ex, but even that wasn't *this* bad. At least in that relationship, I was whipped after we officially became an item. Tinker Bell has me wrapped around her pinky finger already, and we haven't even gone on one date.

"What's wrong with you now?"

I jump sky high. "Where the hell did you come from?"

My roommate's sitting on his bed, a textbook on his lap and a scowl on his face. "I've been here the whole time, dolt."

"Oh." I can't even deny it. I am a dolt. I respond in a mumble. "What's wrong with me, you ask? I have to attend a party for my birthday that I don't want, with girls I'm not interested in instead of the one I'm into."

"Wow. I wasn't sure before, but I definitely hate you now." The deadpan in his voice and expression make me laugh. "And you're really agonizing about this like it's a terrible thing?"

"Yeah." I sigh with my whole chest.

"What if I disguise myself as you?" He shrugs. "I wanna meet girls."

"Wait." I shift on my side to prop up my head. "Why are you being… friendly, or whatever the hell this is?"

He frowns down at his book. "I wanted to see if what you said was true."

"Huh?"

He glares, as if I should've read his mind. "That you're not an asshole if I get to know you."

I can't help it when my jaw drops a bit. "Miracles do happen, huh?"

"Shut up."

"How about this? Come to the party, meet the team, and see that everyone's just as obsessed with meeting girls as you. You might end up with friends and a date. Who knows."

Brett watches me in silence for a moment. "You sure?"

"Yup."

"No hard feelings?"

I shrug. "None, unless you keep projecting weird shit I haven't done onto me."

Brett sighs and adds nothing further. I guess that's as far as apologies go. Fine by me. I'm not expecting to become the dude's BFF.

My phone pings, and because I haven't dropped it, I lift it

right away. It's another text from Tinker Bell, picking up the previous conversation.

SPARKS

I can bring a piñata

I don't even care that my roommate may think I've lost the plot. Her text makes me freaking giggle like a five-year-old.

ME

No need for that

But my mom is making tiramisu

If you want

Is it too much, too soon? Probably. I freak out three seconds after hitting Send.

SPARKS

So like

Meeting your family?

"Aurghhhaaah."

"So you do speak caveman," Brett murmurs.

I spring to a sitting position. My heart pounds even faster as the three dots appear on the screen. She's typing something even before I can think of how to not sound overbearing. I have to clean this up fast.

ME

I mean not necessarily

I just have to drop by for tiramisu, but I can pick you up after that

SPARKS

It'd be cool to meet them

See where the next Sidney Crosby comes from

ME

Isn't it too soon? We're not even dating

It's a big gamble, but I hit Send. Her three dots appear right away, but I still feel like I'm in free fall as I read her response.

SPARKS

Then let's make it a date

I do a double take. Another. I get closer to the screen. The word *date* is still firmly on it.

Tinker Bell wants to make a date out of this. With me. In three days. I'm getting the birthday gift I wanted.

I jump to my feet and hug Brett.

"What the—"

"*Heck* yeah." I push him away, but I grin like a fool. "It's a date. I have a date."

# CHAPTER 22
# LUZ

*have a date with Max Cassiano tonight.*

I have a freaking date. With the captain of the men's hockey team. Who is supposed to be my enemy. Because his team is full of turds on skates. Except for him. He's…

Like a dream.

"Hey, Cap. Snap out of it."

I shake my head hard. Somehow, while standing in line to run skating drills, I've circled back to the thought that's been doing a whole routine in my head all day. There's only one girl in front of me waiting her turn. If not for JT's voice behind me, I'd have embarrassed myself here. Coach Young blows the whistle, and the girl before me takes off.

"Thanks. You saved my behind," I say over my shoulder.

"What's got your panties in a twist?" The question comes from Chelsea, two spots down the line.

"Uhh…"

But I can't tell them. Their wide eyes, eager for gossip, would turn thunderous the second they found out who I'm crushing on.

Saved by the whistle. Except I still make a late start.

Unwilling to be reprimanded by Coach, I push with all the power my legs have. Which is significant. I'm the best skater on the team for good reason. I weave in and out through the cones, using edge work that deserves a medal. My back pinches and pulls. I might need to up my usual medication dose if I don't want to wince every five seconds during the date.

I almost crash against the boards when I round the ice behind the net. Not because of all the speed I pulled, but because I thought of the D-word again. That's gonna be the second ding from Coach, so I better get it together for the last drill. I shoot the puck I've been carrying throughout the drill and bag it in the net, a perfect wraparound.

"Damn." JT shakes her head at me as I return to the line, but then the whistle echoes around the arena, and it's her turn.

I get high fives as I skate to the back of the line. The coach might give us all the minutia of where we suck, but we Strikes like to encourage each other. There's a little pang in my chest. I wish they could encourage me to date the guy I like, but…

After a few more seconds, JT slides down the line to get her high fives and get behind me.

"What's your secret?"

My heart stops. "Huh?"

"To skate like that." She nudges me. "And I hope this isn't offensive, but, like, someone with a big scar like yours probably went through some shit, and look at you."

Well, if my chest could swell any larger, I'd turn into a blowfish. This is much better than what I thought she meant by *secret.*

"It's because all she does is skate, skate, skate." Chelsea joins us again, and we smack her glove with ours. "Every time I try to sneak in some late practice, she's already here tearing up the ice."

I shrug. "Skating's my biggest joy, especially after what gave me the big scar, as JT put it."

"Oh, I wanna hear that story."

"Me too." Chelsea pokes her head out from around JT's shoulder. "I've been curious."

"Me three." Brit slides down the line, skating like a flamingo.

"I mean, it's not like I'm shy about it. My story's all over the internet."

I'm met with a chorus of "*ohh*."

"How about we go get dinner at a nice place tonight and then tell each other our life stories?" Brit's eyes shine at the prospect.

JT nods. "Sure. It's not like I have a date or anything."

"Who could possibly have time for dating?" Chelsea sighs so hard her shoulders sag. "All we do is train, study, class, train…"

A flash of heat travels up my body and settles in my face. "Ha ha, yeah. Who has time for dating?"

Me. I have time. Or more like I want to make time. Before Max realizes he has really bad taste in girls and finds someone less fighty. Someone sweeter. Maybe blond. I don't know.

"Anyway, I'm always down for girl bonding time, but today's kind of—"

Chelsea's eyes are about to pop out. "Wait, don't tell me you have a date tonight."

As if the D-word had magical qualities, the entire line of varsity Strikes turns around to me, completely losing formation.

"Someone has a date?"

"With whom?"

"Ugh, what does it feel like?"

"But with *whom*?"

"Ladies!" The strident whistling can only come from Coach Young. "Is this a training session or a pajama party? Get your butts back to work now."

While everyone at the front of the line focuses back on the drill, the back still has its attention on me.

"Well?" JT's face could be a meme, all wide eyes, pinched lips, and obvious amusement. But I can't appreciate it when I'm soaking through my uniform in sweat, my heart beating faster than during the training drills.

I'm about to get caught in a lie, unless I lie even bigger.

"No, no. Chill, everyone. I don't have a date."

"Then join us for dinner!" Brit claps her gloves excitedly.

Oh. Um. The point isn't to make them think I'm free. How can I escape this?

I wave a glove in the air, trying to act cool. "I just have a ton of coursework to catch up on, and like, exams are coming up and all."

"Screw homework. Am I right?"

Not a single person in line contradicts JT. I don't have the heart to either. If one could attend college and get the whole experience without the crippling mountain of debt, the unreasonable assignment deadlines, or the overbearing professors whose entire identities are built around berating students and being condescending to them, and without exams—it would be perfect.

"C'mon. One little girls' night out won't hurt your grades." Chelsea winks, and once more, I wonder if she knows something more.

Their nagging becomes more and more relentless as the training session progresses. They back me up against a corner I can only get out of if I say I have firm plans and what they are. Which I also can't do.

Later, half-naked in the locker room, I send Max a text.

ME

Uhh, change of plans

PAPIRRI

*Eyes emoji*

ME

The girls are sus

I launch into the tale of the events that transpired during training and how I got cornered into a girls' night out tonight. Every so often, I glance around, but the girls must be tired and icky from training, because they're more focused on hopping into the showers than on giving me more crap.

PAPIRRI

Um we can reschedule

ME

NO WE CANNOT

We can't reschedule your birthday

PAPIRRI

Ehh, it's not actually a special occasion

I look at my phone as if it's grown a head all of a sudden, just as I would to him if he were standing in front of me telling me his birthday's no biggie. This must be a guy thing, downplaying any important emotion to not be seen as *emotional*.

ME

No, no

We'll make it work

I'll just go get early dinner with them

And have tiramisu later with you

How about that?

It sounds a little bit like a euphemism for something else. Hopefully he doesn't read it that way.

But if he does, would it be so bad? I mean, there's a reason I saved his contact as papirri, Venezuelan slang for a man who is really, really freaking hot.

My phone pings again with his response.

> **PAPIRRI**
>
> That works
>
> Just text me the address, and I'll pick you up

Somehow, in the span of the couple of minutes of rapid back-and-forth texting, the girls' idea of a chill night out has changed a bit. As I hop into the shower to scrub every corner clean, I hear them talking about maybe hitting the club after dinner. But that's great. It gives me an excuse to leave early. I can always say I got diarrhea from dinner, and a girl can't dance with a leaky butt.

Except, life has its own plans. They only become apparent as I walk up to the restaurant the girls chose, and I look up at the sign. Really look at it.

Romano's. Isn't that what Max said his parents' restaurant was called when we texted?

"I heard this is the best Italian restaurant in town. I'm so excited to try it out," Brit says while opening the door. As someone from out of town, this would be new to her.

Not to me. My family and I have been coming here for ages. When Max said it was his family's business, I felt silly. As if I should've known every detail about his life already. He's been pretty famous for years, but usually his cousin Leo is the one who gets the most coverage. And I couldn't recall a single mention of Romano's in articles about them.

To be sure, I text him under the table.

Oh. I give him a heads-up so he knows that's where I am with the girls, but for some reason, that text doesn't get through. Or he's busy with something and he's not reading it.

"Who you texting?" JT asks across the table from me.

Or rather, she shouts. Between opera music in the background and the fact that patrons at every table seem to think they're on their own, it's impossible to even hear my own thoughts here.

"No one," I respond at a high decibel, despite checking my phone again. Still no answer.

"Here are the menus." A middle-aged man shows up beside our table out of the blue, dumping well-worn menus encased in stained plastic on our table. "I'll be back later."

From experience, I know it will take him a good while to remember we exist. But as he moves on to another nearby table, I try to sneak in a good look. The man wears a shirt with sleeves rolled all the way up to his elbows. An apron that has seen better days is tied around a thick waist. He has the same dark hair with the slightest wave that Max has. Could this be his dad?

"Dude, where's the bread?" JT also stares at the man, as if willing him to read her mind. "I need bread. Right yesterday."

"Me too. You can't hear it, but my stomach's rumbling." Chelsea rubs the flat plane of her stomach. On cue, mine roars like a lion.

I open the menu, and not a second later, the waiter shouts. "My son!"

If I were a better actress, I'd glue my eyes to the pictures of delicious plates on the menu. But no. I whirl around and—

That's not Max Cassiano. Instead, his cousin Leo walks through the door. A few customers must be regulars, because they recognize him, and he makes detours to greet people here and there like some sort of celebrity.

"Wait a second," Brit whispers as much as someone can in all this chaos. "Is that who I think it is?"

The other two shift their attention from the menus to the guy.

"Oh shit. It's the Bulldog Cassiano." Chelsea makes a face as if she's smelled something gross.

"Ugh." JT winces. "I don't know what's worse, a Bulldog Cassiano or a Bolt Cassiano."

"This one," I say firmly. When they give me funny looks, I add, "At least the other one's in our school, you know?"

Vague murmurs of agreement.

Brit speaks while looking at her menu again. "I guess. And if he weren't an obnoxious Bolt, I'd find him a little hot too," she says, echoing a similar conversation we had not long ago.

"A little? Try a lotta." Chelsea snorts. "I still can't get over how he carried you on his shirtless freaking back, looking like some Greek Olympian carved from marble. Didn't you feel *anything* that time?"

I'm not entirely sure if she means in my heart or in my loins, but either admission would be too problematic to share.

"I was too drunk." I bury my face in the menu.

"Sit here, boy!" The waiter sounds very close by. From the corner of my eye, I catch Leo Cassiano sitting at the table right by my side.

He glances at us and smirks. "Oh, I like this table."

"Get lost, Bulldog," JT tells him with a sweet smile that looks pretty metal on her.

The waiter glares at her. I debate whether to kick her under the table, but pass. Something about Leo Cassiano rubs me the wrong way. It's like when I first met Max and felt the constant need to prove myself to him, except worse. Max doesn't have an ounce of the creepiness this guy oozes from his pores.

"You must be friends with Max, then." He chuckles in a way that makes me want to punch his face.

"Let's just ignore him." There's such an edge in my tone that at once, the girls put their full focus on the menu.

"Anyway," the waiter says to his son. "You here for Maxi's birthday?"

My ear perks up.

"Nah, I'm just here for Nonna's tiramisu. Who cares about that loser?"

I force myself to take a deep breath. Only then do I notice I've been strangling the menu.

"Speaking of, here comes my little brother," the waiter says with a grunt.

Because I'm nosy, I glance over my shoulder and... in comes Max.

Huh? Little brother?

His eyes meet mine right away. Either he saw me from outside, despite having my back to the door, or he has a radar as attuned to me as I have for him.

But then a customer catches his attention, and while he greets that table, I mull the words over again. If the waiter is Max's brother, not father, and in turn, the man is Leo Cassiano's dad...

"Well, this is dramatic," JT says, watching the action and reading my mind. "Who would've expected this plot twist, huh?"

# CHAPTER 23
## MAX

'm a simple man. I don't want the party the guys are planning to allegedly celebrate my birthday. All I want is to go out with Tinker Bell, share a piece of the best tiramisu in the world, and then kiss it off her lips. That's all.

Obviously, I can't even get that much.

The moment I walk into the restaurant, it becomes clear I'm in much more danger than expected. I thought I'd just come here to get a hefty piece of Mom's specialty dessert, then go to a nearby bookstore to hang out until Tinker Bell texted me where to pick her up.

Except I saw her text after I parked the pickup a few blocks away, saying the Strikes' choice of venue was precisely my parents' place. I figured I'd have to bust out my best acting skills during the transaction with Mom. But on the plus side, I already knew where to pick Tinker Bell up. We'd just have to figure out the logistics via text.

The worst I expected was the other girls heckling me. Not for my damn nephew to join them.

"What are you doing here?" I ask as I walk up to him and Cossimo Jr.

My nephew puts his hand on his chest, as if offended by the harsh tone of my question.

"Is that the way you talk to family?" My brother's voice booms over the din of noise. No one gives a crap, though.

Or almost no one. The table of Strikes are fully turned to me. Tinker Bell's the only one seeing how my fists ball up.

"Whatever. Where's Mom?"

My brother waves his hands in annoyance. "I'll get her. You know she doesn't like anyone with outside clothes in the kitchen."

"Yeah, Maxi Pad. You should know that." Leo shakes his head in an exaggerated way. "Why don't you sit here with me while you wait?"

I'd rather eat my foot.

But I don't want to make a whole scene of this with the Strikes watching my every move. I sit across from Leo, which puts me diagonal to Tinker Bell. Prime position to give her a let's-get-the-hell-out-of-here look when necessary.

"Look, your friends came too." Leo jerks a thumb at the Strikes' table.

I tip my head at them, because while far from my friends, I have no particular beef with any of them.

"Where are the rest of your friends, Maxi?" Leo puckers his lip out. "Or are all your friends girls? Is there something you want to share with the family?"

I expel all the air in my lungs. "Aren't you tired of acting like a middle schooler?"

"I just adapt to the level of whoever I'm talking with." He shrugs.

I can't help but glance at the girl I'm supposed to be on a date with. I don't find the patience I'm looking for in her expression. Instead, it's full of anger.

Yeah, Leo tends to have that effect.

"Or…" He leans closer, elbows on the table. "Were you gonna have a fivesome for your birthday?"

I have to sit on my hands so they don't find themselves wrapped around his neck.

"You're absolutely disgusting, you know that?"

One half of his face smiles, but the other looks ready for murder. "Someone has to keep you in check, Maxi Pad."

"Maxi Pad?" one of Tinker Bell's friends asks.

Oh, great. Now all of St. Cloud's going to start calling me after a sanitary supply for women. Even worse, the girl I like is hearing all of this, and I'm sitting here like a puppet, taking every punch.

Without a word, I push the chair back and stand. I wish I could cut Leo out of my life forever, but everyone else in the family adores him. He's only an absolute ass to me, and no one's ever believed me when I tell them he's a bully.

"Where you going, birthday boy?"

I ignore his calls. Mom may get pissed at me for walking into the kitchen like this, but that's better than dealing with my nephew. Problem is, right before I push the side door to the kitchen open, someone yanks me by the shoulder.

"How can you disrespect your elders like this, huh?"

I do a double take before pushing his hand off me. My brain isn't computing Leo's attitude right now. "What the hell is your problem, man? I just walked into this place, and you're trying to get all up in my grill for no reason."

"I don't need a reason." Leo pushes me. Hard. Then he pretends to fix up my jacket. "It's just that I get a glimpse of your mug, and I get pissed."

"Funny, I feel the same about you." I roll my eyes in just the way I know keys him up and make for the door.

"Don't think I'm the only one who feels that way." His harsh laugh freezes me. "Wanna know why no one's wished you a happy damn birthday?"

No, I don't. I don't care anymore. And nothing he can say will surprise me. Every theory possible has crossed my mind since I was a kid and everyone forgot my birthday the first time. Or the second time, a few years later.

"Just leave me alone. We're both happier that way."

He mustn't have heard, or he still wants to talk. Because he grabs me by my jacket and gets real close. "It's because you almost killed Nonna."

My lungs stop working.

"That's right." Leo grins, but there's no humor behind it. Only disgust. "A day like today, nineteen years ago, you almost killed your mother. You, who shouldn't even have been born."

If I was a volcano, I'd be erupting right about now.

I push him away with so much strength Leo can't catch himself in time and crashes to the floor. On his ass.

"Don't you ever mess with me again, shitface."

Half of the restaurant turns to catch the action. We're in a nook leading to a hallway of doors. The kitchen's behind me, the bathrooms and Dad's office beyond. The place is quiet now, but it wasn't a few seconds ago. I just hope that Tinker Bell didn't hear any of this.

Leo's eyes are wide and unfocused. I should've known he'd do something unhinged next, but it still catches me off guard. He swings himself up to stand, and before my brain can process, he straight-up socks me in the face.

Someone shouts. I can't tell who, because my bell is rung.

"That's the least you deserve, Maxi Pad."

Something snaps in me.

As if I'm watching someone else, my body takes a couple of steps toward my nephew, and I slam my fist into his chin. He flies back and lands half on a chair, half on the floor. But he can't stay down long. Of freaking course he can't. The second he tries to get up, I sit on him and punch his face again.

And one more time for good measure. Blood splashes from his nose or mouth, I don't know.

I'm about to hit him again when something clenches my arms and chest in a vise. While I'm dragged away, the buzzing in my ears starts clearing, and I hear screaming. Men's voices. They're shouting words.

"—wrong with you?"

"Grab him!"

When he's free of me, Leo tries to take a swipe at me. Suddenly, a boot appears on his chest, pushing him down. I look up at the jean-clad leg, then higher still until I find it belongs to Tinker Bell.

What is she doing here?

"Don't you even dare," she threatens my nephew.

"Hey." A girl's voice grunts in my ear. "Chill, big man. You already won the fight."

"What is happening?" The question cuts through the fog in my brain. It's my mother, who now stands somewhere behind me. "Massimo Cassiano! What have you done?"

Of course everyone thinks *I* did this. Leo's feral grin tells me I walked right into his damn trap.

"*Explain yourself!*"

I shrink.

Oh, great. That's my dad. He's going to murder me now. That tone of voice is the same one that preceded lashes with his belt when I was a kid.

"Maybe the one who should explain himself is your *grandson*, sir," Tinker Bell shocks me by saying. Her eyes meet mine for a second before she directs them behind me again. "Since Max walked in, all your grandson has done is antagonize your son."

The emphasis on the word grandson isn't lost on me. So she figured that one out, huh?

But it's like she's speaking to a wall. Dad shouts. "I don't care how this started! How dare you make a scene in the restaurant, Massimo?"

Yeah. How dare I, huh?

I pat the hands of one the three Strikes holding me back. At this point, I probably look more tired than willing to commit murder, because they let me go.

Slowly, I get up and turn to face my parents. And two of my siblings, the rest of the kitchen staff, and a whole restaurant packed mostly with strangers. Mom gasps when she sees my face. On cue, my lip starts throbbing. I figure it's split. I wipe at it. The stab of pain confirms it, even before I see the crimson stain on my thumb.

I snort. My shoulders keep shaking in a silent chuckle. "Happy damn birthday to me, huh?"

This one will go down in history as one of the worst.

Before anyone reacts, I step over and around my nephew and keep going, one foot in front of the other until they take me out of the restaurant.

Only when I'm a block away am I able to take in a full breath. I rub my head, messing up my hair even though I styled it to perfection just an hour ago. I wanted to look good for the date that was never destined to happen.

And what's the point? Luz would've eventually seen that I'm a loser in my own family. It'd have weirded her out like it did to my ex.

"Cassiano! Max, wait!"

"Go back to your friends, Tinker Bell." My voice comes out like gravel. But I don't stop walking.

"No, they don't need me right now."

"Neither do I."

Mentally, I kick myself. That sounded a lot worse than I intended.

"The hell you don't." Her steps pound on the sidewalk faster and faster until she catches up to me. "You need someone in your corner right now. And also to wipe the blood from your face. Jeez, that meathead got you good."

I stop with a sigh. That's when I notice she's on the side closer to traffic, and in the early night, it's still fairly heavy. Holding her by the shoulders, I push her gently until our positions are switched.

"Look, I appreciate it. It was badass when you stepped on him." And pretty hot too. I shake my head hard. "But it's probably best I'm not around anyone for a while so… just go back. We'll talk later."

I can see her brow crease deeper the more I talk. Before she begins her retort, I resume the walk over to where I parked the pickup.

But this is Tinker Bell. She doesn't obey anything but her own freewill. So even though I glare, trying to freeze her on the spot, she keeps following me.

At least she says nothing while we walk down the blocks. Which is both good and bad. Good, because I'm not ready to hear anything anyone has to say about that little spectacle. Bad, because my head is coming up with its own theories on what she might be thinking about.

I'm a brute. The kind who scares my roommate. With just a few words, I snapped and reacted violently. No doubt this will get to Coach Green's ears, if not higher up. I may be suspended from the team. Or kicked out altogether.

"Shit," I mutter. And again for good measure. "Shit. Shit."

I jam the key in the keyhole and swing the door open with more strength than necessary. The pickup creaks and groans as I climb into the driver's seat and slam the door closed. For one second, I rest my forehead on the steering wheel.

Then the passenger door opens.

# CHAPTER 24
## LUZ

His truck smells like Max. Sandalwood and soap, plus an essence that is only his. It envelops me as I climb into the passenger seat and close the door. The silence hurts my ears, but it only lasts a moment. Max breaks it with a jagged breath.

I want to comfort him, to make him forget what happened in there, if only for a minute. When I was a kid, before The Big Hurt, my mom would caress my back in circles when I scraped my knee. Maybe that would help him?

My hand wavers for a second, but I go for it and place my palm on his back. Even through the bomber jacket he wears, I can feel the ridges of muscles as I rub one circle, then another. His shoulders start to sag just a bit.

"Families are hard." I speak softly, as someone would to a frightened animal. "Wanna hear about mine?"

He mumbles. "Can't be worse than what you just saw."

"Hmm, you'd be surprised." I pause but don't stop rubbing his back. "I haven't talked to my parents in like four months. Because they really don't want me to play hockey."

"What? Why?"

Max turns his face slightly to see me, and I take advantage of it. Reaching over with both hands, I slowly push him back against the seat. I want to get closer to him, so I twist until one of my legs is bent under me, and I face him.

It's too bad his lip is hurt. I really wanted to kiss him again tonight. I should focus on the topic, though.

"Well, it's been an ongoing issue since I almost broke my back when I was twelve. They were at the game, saw me take the bad hit, slam against the boards at a weird angle, and then not be able to move. It was scary."

His eyes go wide as saucers in the dark. "Uh, scary's not how I'd put it."

"Terrifying?" I smile a bit. "Heart-stopping? A nightmare? Yeah, it was all those things."

It's annoying how my voice chokes up, even though I'm trying to be cool about all of this.

Suddenly, Max's hand reaches out and touches my cheek. Just soft enough that I barely feel it. Almost as if he needed to check that I really am here. Alive.

I grab his hand and hold it on my lap, eyes focused on it. "I know, I know. You think I'm off my rocker too."

"I don't," Max whispers. "I think you're strong. And amazing. And way, way out of my league."

The snort that comes out of me makes him startle. I push my hair away from my face and look back up at him. I wonder if he lost his screws when his nephew hit him earlier.

"I'm out of your league, Mr. I-look-even-hotter-a-little-beat-up?"

"See, now I think you're really off your rocker." He runs his free hand through his hair. "That back there... I never wanted you to see that side of me."

I tilt my head. "Why not?"

"Are you kidding me? My family hates me. I went absolutely berserk for no reason—"

"No reason? That guy's the poster boy for he-had-it-freak-ing-coming. If not from you, then from me. The girls had to hold me back a moment before you smacked him down." I screech out a weird laugh. "That jerk who turns out to be your nephew refers to you as a period pad. Then he attempted to mock your sexuality, and even said you almost killed your mother. A few blows are the least he deserves."

"Crap, you heard all that?" He pulls his hand from mine, his big body shrinking as if he wants to disappear. The expression on his face is absolutely stricken.

That's when I realize this boy is so hurt. The urge to hug him and kiss him and hold him tight almost overwhelms me. Somehow, I manage to keep it in check, but I still lean forward to him. I balance myself on my knees, one hand braced on the steering wheel, and the other one against his headrest. We're so close that our noses brush.

Max blinks fast. "Uh…"

"Yeah, I heard all that." I bring the hand that had been grabbing the headrest forward toward his face in a touch like his earlier one. "Your nephew is toxically jealous of you. And I also heard not a single person wish you a happy birthday. You don't deserve any of that, Max."

He chokes on his own saliva and clamps his jaw tight. My eyes travel the sharp length of it. I caress it slowly, at first wanting to comfort him. But then his eyes shift, as if this touch is even more important than the sadness plaguing him. How will it feel against my lips? Hard like the shell of perfection he wears around himself, I bet.

A little lightbulb comes on in my mind. "Oh, I finally found the perfect nickname for you."

"What?" The poor guy sounds confused by the topic change.

"You're a S'more. Singular." My finger brushes softly over his top lip, enough to put him on edge but not to hurt. "Slightly hard on the outside, but once you get through that little shell, you're all gooey on the inside."

"Hardy har har."

The sardonic quality of his voice makes my heart sing. He's so good at driving me up the wall with his teasing. It makes me appreciate the ability to return the feeling that much more. I want to tease him more. But right now, I don't want to tease him with words.

I swoop down and place a small kiss on his left cheek.

"Tinker Bell—"

"Shush, S'more. Let me give you your birthday gift."

He looks confused. But then I kiss his other cheek with as much care as the first. It's very important that I press my lips against his skin just so. Tender, so he knows someone cares about him. A little bit hot, so he knows how *I* feel about him.

Max keeps blinking up at me as I repeat the process on his forehead. "Uh, Luz…"

I pull back slightly. "It's too bad your lip's busted. I was looking forward to kissing you tonight."

A strange choking sound comes from his throat. I know exactly what's going through his mind, and I'm basking in the fact that I put the thought there.

Max holds my shoulders to push me away, but I resist.

"Let me kiss you, Max."

"Uh—This isn't a vampire movie. I don't want you to get smeared with blood."

"Not there." I touch the tip of his nose, smiling down at him. "Here."

"Did you just boop me?"

I can see the sparks in his eyes thanks to the lights streaming in from the street and from the passing cars. Good, that's what I wanted. He deserves a little fun on a day that should've been special.

"Also here." I run the tip of my finger across his delectable jaw. "And here." My finger travels lower, along the length of his thick neck, then around to the base of his throat.

His Adam's apple bobs as he swallows hard. I touch that too.

Max's breath comes out far shakier than normal. "Uh, maybe this is a bad idea."

I bite my lip. If he says no… he can, of course. But I'll just have to slink away, all the way to a cave and never be seen again. Or stand under a cold spray of water for an hour. Maybe put on a really long documentary about nature. Anything that can tear my mind, my heart, my soul, away from the fact that I want this boy. I crave him. And not just because I'm thirsty for him.

I want to be with Max Cassiano. For a long while.

His eyes are so intense they almost burn me. Slowly, he cradles the side of my neck in his hand and pulls me closer to him. I take it as a yes.

I lean down and kiss the spot where his jaw meets his neck, under his earlobe. My lips close over it in a soft, hot pull. His skin is warm, almost feverish. I climb over the center console and squeeze myself between his chest and the steering wheel. His arms easily fall around me. Then I trail my lips lower, leaving a hot patch that makes him groan. The sound makes my chest swell with pride. I'm making the great Max Cassiano lose his composure. Who cares if I'm losing mine too?

"Happy birthday, Max," I say with a breathless laugh.

"This is torture." He grabs my waist. "We need to stop before I embarrass myself even more."

My dangerously accelerated heart tells me he might have a point.

"Fine. Let's not get arrested." I place a butterfly-soft kiss on his nose, the innocent little gesture I should've stuck to for his birthday gift. "Let's go to the pharmacy to get you patched up."

He winces. "Sure, once my brain starts working again."

I can't help smiling the smug smile of a girl who knows exactly how to push her guy's buttons and is proud.

Except, well, Max is not mine.

Obviously, he's his own person. But I mean, he's not my *anything*. We say we're friends, but friends don't want to devour each other like this. We're definitely not strangers either. Or just classmates.

None of those things are what I want to be.

I bring his palm up against my cheek once more, inhaling the clean scent of his skin. I wish I could tell him. But I don't want to make him run. Guys tend to do that when girls throw big words of affection too early.

But then he stuns me.

"I like you, Luz Rodriguez."

I babble incoherent sounds for a moment. "You do?"

"Oh, yeah. A lot. And not only because you just kissed the lights out of me."

Max pulls his hand away, leaving a warm spot on my face that mourns its absence. It's not so bad, though, because he shifts the touch to one of my hands. His hand is so much bigger, rougher, with the same calluses on the palm that I have. Familiar and not at the same time.

"I like you a lot," he whispers in the dark. "Since I first saw you."

"Is that why you were a bit of an ass?"

A little laugh makes his shoulders shake, something I wouldn't have thought possible fifteen minutes ago. "Yeah, I was nervous."

I suck in air while lacing my fingers with his. "Well, look at that. Turns out I like you a lot too."

"Since you first saw me?"

"No, it took me at least one more try." I scrunch up my

nose in fake outrage. Guess I should ask him what I really want to know, though. "Max?"

"Yeah?"

I fix my eyes on his, unwavering. "Are we a thing now?"

"If you want." His response sounds careful.

Nervous as hell, I ask, "Do *you* want to be? After all, you said you're married to hockey." I give out an awkward laugh.

The last time we had the opportunity to be something more, we both said we should focus on school. But I can't stop thinking about him. About what he's doing. How he's feeling. If he misses me. If he wants to kiss me again like I want to kiss him. It's like he's worming his way into my heart. He's become a part of my daily life. I don't know what convincing excuse I'll give to my friends for taking off after Max, but right now, all that matters is what he's going to say next.

Finally, Max leans his head on my shoulder. "I want you, if you'll have me."

If I'll have him?

Ugh, this boy has no idea my whole heart is his already, does he?

I wrap my arms around his shoulders and hold him tight. "Then let's be a thing, Max."

# CHAPTER 25
## MAX

A few days later, Tinker Bell and I are on a study date. A date where we're actually supposed to work on our project for Intro to Entrepreneurship. The problem is that I keep staring at her like a buffoon who struggles to keep himself from salivating.

We're at the Thundercloud, the aptly named café on campus. It's as busy as the library during the week before Thanksgiving, with finals around the corner. But the café has three advantages. First, the drinks. Obviously. Second, we can be as loud as we want. Which means we can hide our words under the loud chatter around us. And third, seating is a smidge more comfortable for a big guy like me.

Although my knees are up to my ears with how low this couch is, my ass sure is happy with the plush seating. Much better than the hard chairs of the library. And, in theory, better for cozying up to my project partner.

Except that since we arrived, she's been trying to put as much distance between us as possible. Almost as if she regrets having left hickeys on my neck.

The second the barista called our names, Tinker Bell

jumped to go get them before I could even *think* of reacting. Her reward is that she now has to walk very carefully to not spill my tiny espresso, while in her other hand she carries her ginormous pumpkin spice latte.

Funny how she's basically wearing the same oversized St. Cloud hoodie as me—hers the navy version and mine the gray —but it looks amazing on her. Her long brown hair is loose over her shoulders, not in the tight braid she usually keeps it in for training or games. My eyes drift lower, to the leggings that don't hide her powerful thighs and calves.

I can't be faulted for staring. Fortunately, she's so intent on not spilling a drop of the drinks that she doesn't notice me.

"This is a fresh reminder that you're such an Italian guy."

"Huh?" I blink up at her as she carefully, slowly, sets the two cups on the coffee table.

Tinker Bell puts her hands on her hips, shrinking the span of her hoodie drastically. "Really? One espresso shot?"

"It's enough. And I'm not thirsty." Not for coffee, at least. "But that's because, in comparison, your drink looks like a whole vat of coffee."

"As it should."

The couch isn't big, but she still manages to squeeze herself so far into the corner she practically becomes one with the armrest. I cock an eyebrow at her.

"Tinker Bell, what are you doing?"

"What do you mean?" She reaches forward for her drink, but all she does with it is smell it. And not look at me.

"I'm this close to smelling my armpits in public to see if that's why you're avoiding me."

"Oh, trust me. You don't smell bad."

That makes me oddly proud of the basic skill of showering.

"Okay, so what's the deal?" I follow her example and grab my cup of espresso. It's not as high quality as the one we serve at Romano's, but it'll do.

Suddenly, Tinker Bell starts laughing. She pauses once to blink at me, then carries on with the full belly laughter. Even though I suspect it's at my expense, just seeing the joy on her face quirks my lips. The lower one stings a little at the stretch, but it's worth it.

"What now, woman?"

She wipes the corner of her eye. "I can't believe you grab your cup like that."

I look down. "Like what?"

"So dainty. Pinky pointing up and all."

Heat travels to my face, but I refuse to acknowledge it. "My hand is too freaking big for espresso cups, okay? My pinky's too far away to even cradle the cup. It feels lonely and wants attention."

"Sounds a little bit like you." Her cheeks are pink as she smiles up at me.

"Well, you're right. It is me." I grin down at her, and for a second, I forget where we are. The noise fades away, and I get tunnel vision. All I see is her, Luz Rodriguez, my... thing. That's what we said we are.

"Anyway." She snaps out of it first, setting the mug with her drink down and picking up her laptop. "We should probably get to work."

"I see you're avoiding my question." I sip my drink.

She clears her throat. "It's just... We can't be seen to be all chummy-chummy."

"Why not?"

"Are you kidding me?" After a sweeping a glance around and confirming everyone's minding their business, she still lowers her voice. "Our teams hate each other, and last I checked, we're the captains."

I shrug. "So what? It doesn't mean we're supposed to hate each other, right?"

"I wish I were that naive."

"Besides," I say, pretending not to have heard her. "I didn't bring my laptop. And yours is so small. It's hard to see the words from this far." And by far, I mean the span of my open hand. That's already too far in my books.

"Sure, Mr. I-have-one-of-the-best-dynamic-visions-in-the-region."

"Did you read that in a news article when you were stalking me?" The way her skin heats up makes me smirk.

"See, this is the real reason I can't get close to you. I just feel this really strong urge to punch you."

In a swift motion, I down the rest of my espresso and set the cup down. Then I scoot so close I'm essentially glued to her. She tries to lean away, but the armrest keeps her locked in place. A small squeak escapes her lips as I sneak my arm around her back, splaying my hand on her opposite hip. It's wedged against the sofa so no one can see it. And for good measure, I sneak it under the hem of her hoodie.

"Max—" She chokes on air and takes a few breaths before she can speak again. "You can't just touch me like that and—"

I freeze. "Oh. You're right. I should've asked first—"

Tinker Bell presses harder against my arm as I start to pull it away, halting the motion.

"That's not what I mean *right now*," she whispers, almost in a hiss. "And I do like your hand there—although yes, consent is sexy. But what I mean is that if someone *sees* us—"

"Laptop. Small." I point at the device balanced on her knees. "And you can always tell everyone how annoying it is that I'm all over you."

"It's not annoying, though," she murmurs as she fires up the Word document our project is saved on. "I'm just trying really, really hard not to lean into you."

That would be nice. I didn't know that was exactly what I wanted until she mentioned it.

Sighing beside her, I say, "We need an off-campus date."

A whining sound vibrates out of her throat. "Yes, please."

"How about this weekend?"

Her eyes travel down to my lips for a second. "Do you think your lip will be healed by then?"

"Do you like kissing me that much?" A chuckle rumbles in my chest, but she doesn't even get flustered.

"Um, have you never kissed yourself? It's almost enough to make a girl…"

The end of the sentence remains suspended in the air. And it's charged with electricity. Thundercloud Café, indeed.

"To make a girl what?"

She turns her attention squarely on her laptop. "Anyway. I'm kinda glad we worked backward and compiled all the references already—"

I lean down, nuzzling her hair until I find the shell of her ear. I give it a tiny nibble that produces a yelp. The whole café could be watching right now, but I couldn't give two flying turds.

"Finish the sentence, Luz."

A shiver travels down her spine. Since she doesn't say anything, I push her hair out of the way until a sliver of skin is visible. And I kiss it. Slow, with my mouth open. As if kissing her lips.

She makes an involuntary sound. Only I can hear it in the din, but she still covers her face with both hands. And jams her elbow into my stomach hard enough that I have no choice but to retreat.

"Are you out of your mind?"

"Yeah." I grin. "Because of you."

Through gritted teeth, she says, "Would you please just focus on our assignment? We have to deliver it after Thanksgiving, and at this rate, we'll be done next year."

"Okay, okay." I run a hand through my hair, for once doing my best to dispel the desire for her running rampant in my body, engorging my veins and heating up my skin. At a café, for goodness' sake. "What's the next step?"

"The motivation part." Her voice comes out shaky, and while I don't remark on it, I do bask in it.

"So, why are we opening a PT center again?"

Tinker Bell turns to me. Gone are the traces of the flirtation we had going on. In its place is abject shock.

"Wait, you just accepted my proposal of doing a PT center just like that?"

"Uh, yeah?" I ask, uncertain where this is going. "I didn't have a firm business idea in mind, and you seemed so passionate."

"Wow, I don't know whether to smack you or kiss you right now."

"My cheeks are always available." I point at one of them.

Her lips press into a tight line, but I can see she contemplates it for a second before focusing back on the subject. "I want to open a PT center after I'm done with hockey so I can treat people like me."

"Crap, I want to punch myself right now."

"It's okay." Impulsively, she places her hand on my knee but removes it before I can enjoy the touch. In response, I hold her hip just a little tighter.

"How personal do you want to go with the motivation?" I ask, because she has the sole decision power.

"It's going to be more impactful if I speak from experience." Tinker Bell lifts her shoulders like we're talking about the weather. "Besides, there are a ton of articles about me and my case online already. It's like free references."

"What?"

She pretends to be shocked. "You mean we became *a thing*, and you didn't even Google me?"

There's a little wrinkle between her eyebrows that tells me she's joking to try to cover for something else.

"Do you want me to?" I ask in all seriousness.

After a brief moment, she takes a shaky breath. "Yes, I think I want you to."

"Then show me the way."

She clicks over to the search engine and inputs just a few keywords. Many results come up with words like experimental treatment and spinal cords. She places the device on my lap.

"There it is." She clasps her hands together. "The naked truth."

Nervousness oozes from her pores, but why would she feel that way?

The first thing that catches my eye as I start reading the article is her name. Luz Maria Rodriguez. Twelve years old at the time of the accident. Just a child when she took an illegal hit during a game that caused a nonpenetrating spinal cord injury. I'm not entirely sure what that means until farther down in the article. The swelling meant she'd lost her ability to move and even control of her bowel and bladder.

An experimental treatment developed by our very own St. Cloud scientists, involving the injection of her own stem cells into the damaged area, was only partially responsible for her recovery. The biggest miracle, as explicitly mentioned in the article, came from her own willpower and the grueling physical therapy sessions she endured for more than two years.

And look at her now. Captain of the very first class of the women's hockey team at St. Cloud. There should be more articles about this. Heck, there should be a whole book and a movie.

I turn my attention back to her. Luz hides the lower half of her face behind the sleeves of her hoodie. "Yeah, real sexy, huh? Couldn't even hold my pee in."

"Luz." Her name comes out sharper than I'd like, but it does clamp her jaw shut. "Do you even understand how incredible you are?"

"I—what?"

I regret having pulled my hand to hold her laptop and scroll through the article at the same time. Instead, I wish I were hugging her.

"You're amazing. What you've overcome is… wow. I have no words." I huff, angry that I don't have a better capacity to communicate what I feel right now. Awe. Admiration. My chest swells, as if her victory over terrible adversity was mine. But that's ridiculous. She went through this six years ago. She probably still suffers the consequences. And yet she still fights.

"You're not grossed out? Or pity me?"

My eyes bulge. "Why the hell would I?"

"That's usually how guys react. Especially when my chronic pain flares up, and suddenly, I'm not so fun anymore." She bites her lip.

My whole face scrunches up. "You just tell me where those dipshits are, and I'll bash their noses in. No. You wanna know how I really feel right now?"

"How?"

The fact that her voice comes out in a little thread makes me angrier at whomever caused her to feel insecure about this. Is it because of the level of detail the articles go into about her ordeal? Or because they don't wanna accommodate her? Because anyone who meets her should only ever feel—

"I'm proud. Of you. Of how you pulled through something so terrifying I can't even comprehend it. I'm blown away that someone as amazing as you would give me the time of the day."

For the first time since the topic came up, her lips curve into the tiniest smile. "Well, I didn't do it all on my own. My medical team was amazing—professionals from all over the world. And because the treatment was experimental, the hospital bankrolled it all. Obviously, my family supported me too. They were there every step of the way. But it was my PT who really made a difference. She never gave up, even when I felt like quitting."

"Ah, so that's why."

"Yes." Light has returned to her eyes. I love to see it there. "Because of this, the injury and the chronic pain, my hockey career will be over sooner rather than later. So after that, I want to help people like she helped me. The unique selling point of my PT center will be that I also want to help the patients' families. I want to train them so they can continue helping their injured loved ones even after they can no longer afford my services."

"So that's why you want it to be a non-profit organization in a marginalized community."

"Exactly!"

If I were rich, I'd pour all my money into it just to see her smile like this forever.

"Did I already say you're amazing?"

Tinker Bell takes her laptop back. "Stop. You're gonna make me blush."

"You've been blushing all afternoon, for the record."

"What's this?"

We both jump as a new voice joins us.

Somehow, without either of us noticing, Nate and Conor have approached. Their eyes bounce from Tinker Bell to me, back and forth.

I put on my poker face, even though my heart's working as fast as a rabbit's.

"Hey, guys. What's up?"

"My question exactly." Nate narrows his eyes as he sips an iced tea. Even though it's chilly as can be outside.

"Uh, working on my class project with Rodriguez," I say, hoping they scram already.

"Really?" Nate's gossipy old woman expression would normally make me laugh. But not today.

Conor smirks. "Very cozy for a class project."

"Oh, trust me. I wanted to maintain a minimum distance of ten feet, but as you can see," Tinker Bell says while motioning around, "the place is packed."

"*Right.*" Nate takes a very loud sip of his drink.

"Anyway, carry on." Conor grabs our buddy by the shoulder and pushes him away from us. "See you at practice, Captain."

"Uh huh."

I wait until they're well away from the café to rest back on the couch.

"We were *this* close to being caught. What if they'd arrived a few minutes earlier when you..." She trails off, staring at me with her open mouth.

"But they didn't."

"For now." She frowns. "No more displays of affection on campus. Ever."

All the air in my lungs comes out. "Fine. But off campus, yes?"

"Oh, yes. Absolutely."

Grinning, I sneak my arm around her again. "Can't wait."

# CHAPTER 26
## LUZ

'm pretty sure Max can tell I'm three shaky rabbits in a trench coat. Not only did I convince him the date should be in the next town over, to *really* make sure no one from our teams catches us, but I'm also freaking out about the fact that I'm officially on a date with Max Cassiano. Only the hottest guy I've ever met. Who opens the door for me even though I can do it myself, but in a way that is so sweet it shows he's just trying to help.

"You okay?" He squeezes my hand in his, snapping me back to the present.

"Uh, yeah. Totally fine."

Totally burning up inside because of him is more like it.

Max put some product on his hair that keeps it in place, a perfect little wave that begs to be messed with. His outfit is simple, a crisp white button-down shirt under a black bomber jacket for winter, black jeans, and boots to match.

When we enter the place, an employee shows us to a room with lockers where people can leave their stuff. I hang back for a moment, admiring his frame as he removes his jacket and hangs it. The shirt has to be tailored, because there's no way they make it for shoulders that broad and a waist that narrow.

"Allow me?" He smiles at me, polite like I've never known him.

I turn around so he can remove my trench coat, about to tease him for the pleasantries, when he gasps.

"What?"

"Tinker Bell, you didn't have to attack me this hard."

I have to press my lips together not to bark a laugh because we're not the only ones in the room. When I face him, he's holding my trench coat as if it's a pillow. Those eyes I can't get enough of roam up and down my body, leaving a trail of fire in their wake.

"Like what you see, pretty boy?"

He shakes his head hard. "Like doesn't cover it." It takes him another moment to tear his attention from me and back to the task of hanging my coat.

I won't tell him it took me three hours to put together the outfit or that I still wasn't quite convinced about it when I left the dorm. But now I feel like I'm wearing a million bucks. In reality, it's just a black body suit that shows off what my momma gave me, blue skinny jeans, and combat boots I borrowed from Lynn.

"Ready?" I ask when he pockets our locker key.

"Absolutely not. Let's go." Something's off with his voice. It's too deep and a little choked. I take it as a good sign.

Our hands find each other like there's a magnetic force pulling them together. Earlier in the week during class, we spent the whole period holding hands under our desks. Once during training, we bumped into each other in front of the water coolers, and while no one was watching, we linked our pinkies together.

Tonight is about being all over each other without the fear of someone watching. That's why I proposed this place for our official first date. It's a former high school that has been turned into an entertainment center. Every room has different games, from dartboards to billiard tables to bowling to escape rooms, an arcade, and even axe throwing. With the fee we paid at the entrance, we can play in as many rooms as we want. There's also a restaurant and a bar, and while we can't buy alcohol, I don't think we'll need it to have fun.

"Wow, how did you find this place?" His eyes twinkle as he takes a look around. We're only in the lobby. There are game rooms to the left, and a bar and restaurant to the right. Every area is teeming with people, and the music is some alternative stuff that gives a chill atmosphere.

I shrug in a show of exaggerated modesty. "You'd be surprised what you can find on Google."

"I'll have to step it up for our next date, huh?" Ugh, I love his smile. How can an expression be so cute and sexy at the same time? "So, where do we start?"

"Bathroom for me first," I blurt out. Before he's able to respond, I say, "Be right back!"

I all but dash into the women's restroom located between the bar and the restaurant. After taking care of my nervous need to relieve myself, I'm washing my hands when two girls walk in.

"—will give him my number," one of them says.

The other one moans, and her body droops a notch. "Ugh, like, I cannot believe how hot he is. Too bad I just got a new boyfriend!"

They take the sinks on either side of mine. Both are absolute knockouts, and the first one is the kind of girl most guys go for. Tall, skinny, big curves in all the right places, and leggy. She tosses her blond hair over her shoulder and adjusts her boobs so her cleavage is on display.

"Lucky me," she says. "I bet tall, dark, and handsome at the bar won't be able to resist me."

"Get it, girl." Her friend laughs. She has a very similar appearance. Pretty girls flock together.

I finish washing my hands and sidestep the second girl to grab paper towels. From the corner of my eye, I see them redo their lipstick and primp themselves some more. Then I check myself in the mirror.

Yeah, so I'm shorter than either of them. My skin's several shades darker. And my hair is the opposite of golden. But I have plenty of curves, and my outfit tonight is absolute fire. There's no reason I should feel jealous of some random girls who may or may not be talking about my guy. Right?

I wink at my reflection and leave the restroom. If anything, the pit stop ignited my competitive spirit. The more time I spend holed up here, the less time I'll have to seduce Max.

I spot him at the bar, which raises my suspicions that the bathroom girls were talking about him. Two glass bottles sit at the bar in front of him, capped, as if he's waiting for me to return to open them. He often does little things like that to make me feel safe. It's why he's a S'more.

Like some fangirl who doesn't dare to approach him, I stand and stare at him for a while. The girls walk out of the restroom and straight to Max. I have to do a double take to confirm that, sure enough, the pretty girl is trying to chat him up.

Max's body language screams uncomfortable. He shakes his head and puts his hands up like a barrier, and still the girl tries to touch his shoulder. I want to save him, but will it look bad if I jump in? I'm pretty sure my dad said jealous women are called cuaimas in Venezuela.

To cuaima, or not to cuaima?

But then his eyes find mine, and the plea is unmistakable. To cuaima.

"Here we go." I put on my best strut. The two girls turn around, and it takes them a while to really see me. I don't even have to think too hard about what to do when I reach him. Max slides me up against his side, his arm around me and a hand on my hip just the way he likes.

"I do have a girlfriend," he says in a way that makes me think he tried to explain it already. He glances down at me. "Isn't that right?"

And then it clicks. If this is his way of asking me to be his girlfriend, I'm all aboard the Massimo Express.

I wrap my arms around his waist. "That's right, boyfriend."

"Ugh." The girl taps her friend and says, "Let's just go."

They look embarrassed, but there's really no reason. It takes some big ovaries to shoot your shot with a guy. Something I never really tried to do until Max came along.

I look back up at him. Thank heaven I realized he was too precious to pass up before someone else snapped him up.

"Girlfriend, huh?"

He doesn't even try to hide how his face flames. Clearing his throat, he says, "If that's okay."

"Oh, yeah. More than okay." I reach up to brush the wave of his hair, letting my hand travel down to hold his cheek. His lip's been healing pretty well. I'll be able to kiss him tonight. "I just have a simple question."

"What's that?"

"Why do you still have all your teeth?" I almost laugh at his bulging eyes. "Or, like, could we bust up your nose a little?"

Poor guy mustn't know whether to laugh or run away. "The what?"

"It's just—" I sigh dramatically. "Even with a busted lip, you look too perfect. I'm afraid I'll have to carry my stick with me at all times to beat women off you."

Max throws his head back and laughs.

"Are you jealous, Tinker Bell?"

Am I?

Yes, a little.

I shrug. "If the roles were reversed, wouldn't you be jealous?"

"Oh, I'd be pissed." That sobers him up. He brings me around until we're face to face, both leaning against the bar. While he keeps his hand on my hip, the other one sneaks up my back and through my hair, only stopping when he finds bare skin. "I've been doing everything I can not to go full caveman on a guy who's staring at you."

"Hmm." I circle my arms around his neck, which makes him bend down a little. "He's not worth it. Let's just keep our attention solely on each other tonight."

"Sounds like a great plan." The smile is back on his face, sending butterflies down my stomach. "I got us a couple of root beers."

"You're a genius." I stand on my tiptoes and place a soft, quick kiss on his lips. "And to answer your previous question, I want to start with axe throwing."

"After another kiss?"

And he pouts. Pouts!

"No." With all my willpower, I pull away from him and grab my drink instead. "If I kiss you now, I won't be able to stop. Can't you see my struggle, man?"

He also grabs his bottle and falls into step beside me. "But what if I don't want you to stop?"

"Stop giving me that cheeky look, Massimo. We came all the way here to enjoy the place. There'll be time to enjoy each other later."

Max chokes on his first sip of root beer, which must be painful. I leave him behind to get in line for the axe throwing room. When I glance back, he's wiping his chin with the back of his hand, eyes trained on me as if I'm the reason he drooled. It's sort of true, anyway.

I give him the same kind of smirk he gives me all the time.

The kind that tests my patience. I know it's having the same effect on him.

A good fifteen minutes later, one of the stalls clears up, and it's our turn. An employee gives us a safety briefing that mostly consists of *first, throw the axe forward and not back* and *second, don't drop it on your foot.*

Max whispers, "Almost feel like telling him we play with knives on our feet every day, and here we are."

I throw the first axe, and it's off center, but it wedged itself pretty nicely in the wood. After exchanging high fives, Max pushes his sleeves up his arms and grabs an axe. I enjoy the way his muscles flex. But I enjoy when his axe bounces off the wall and crashes to the floor even more.

"Looks like I'm gonna win this game, huh?"

"Tell me the truth. You've done this before, haven't you?" His entire face scrunches up.

"Once. I didn't suck that bad on my first try, though." I blow a kiss at him. With my hip, I push him out of the way to throw my second axe. "Ohh, closer to the center."

Max grunts. "Why's my beginners luck not working?"

I turn slowly, striking a pose. "Maybe I'm distracting you too much?"

"You are." Oh, he's serious. He runs a hand through his hair, messing it just enough to make me skip a beat.

"Come here."

Never has he been more obedient. In a second, Max stands before me, leaning down as if to kiss me. But I put a hand on his chest to stop him.

"Now," I say, smiling as he grows even grumpier. "Face the wall."

"Why?" But he does turn to it, which puts him in profile in front of me.

I run my hand down his arm, stopping to explain. "You put all the power here."

His eyes stray toward me as I step in front of him. With my boot, I push his feet apart at hip length. Then hook my leg around one of his to bring it forward. Max holds my back the second he sees me tip back. I wasn't planning to fall, but this is much better.

"Then," I say, grabbing his hips, "you pivot just a little on your back leg, bringing the power with your hips."

"Oh yeah?" He pushes me all the way up against him, arching forward to leave no space between us.

I can't help but kiss him now that we're this close. His arms embrace me, and I bring my leg higher, the friction revving me up. If his lip hurts, he must not mind it, because he kisses me hard, pushing my mouth open as if he's been drowning and only tasting me can save him.

The thwack of an axe hitting its target in the next stall over reminds me that we're not really alone here.

"Max, focus please. We don't want to get kicked out for public indecency."

He groans. "Okay, okay. I'll try."

Props to him for throwing his axe well this time, even though my aim is way off after that kiss.

It takes us a whole tour of the arcade to bring the heat down a notch. We decide to avoid the pool tables and head to the restaurant. A waiter sits us at a cozy round booth, and with Max's size, it's impossible to keep my distance. Somehow, we manage to order a couple of burgers, side salads, and a basket of fries before we're on each other again.

I snuggle up against him, one arm around him and the other hand on his thigh. Despite being a wall of muscle, when his arm's around me, it feels soft.

"S'more."

He sighs. "You're really gonna keep calling me that?"

"It's a compliment." I blink up at him, all innocence. "Soft on the inside, hard on the outside—” I pause to squeeze his thigh. “And very tasty.”

Slowly, Max starts shaking his head. “You do know you’re killing me, right?”

“Yup.”

“And that I’ll take my revenge tonight?”

“Yes, please.

He laughs. “You’re perfect. It’s too bad I can’t show you off on campus.”

I freeze a little. Max definitely notices.

“It’s just…” I bite my lip. “I almost let people’s expectations keep me away from you. It was going to be the easier path, you know?”

“Is that why you said it wasn’t a big deal? That time at the library.”

It takes me a moment to remember what he’s talking about. The memory of him standing before me while handing me a book comes to mind. Almost as if maybe, just maybe, that book was his heart. I took the book, but at the time, I was too afraid to accept the feelings brewing between us.

I rest my head on his shoulder. “Yeah. I was being a coward. Like now, I guess.”

“It’s okay. We can take it as slow as you want.” I feel him place a kiss at the top of my head. In retribution, I caress his thigh, and it makes his breath hitch. “Or not? I’m fine with that too.”

My laughter comes out husky. We’re probably moving a bit too fast, but it feels right. Max is right for me.

# CHAPTER 27
## MAX

wish the date could've lasted all night. Things were getting good after dinner, while Tinker Bell and I played table games in which I kept winning and she grew more and more irritated. The payback for her turning me on more than a fireplace was interrupted by a frantic call from Conor.

"Uh, dude, I don't know what you're doing right now, but you need to drop it and come here."

"What the hell for?" I didn't even bother hiding my irritation.

"The guys are drunk out of their minds, and Boucher's making a scene again."

I considered telling him to deal with it, but then Tinker Bell got a text from a teammate saying they were getting into a situation with the Bolts. I put two and two together and figured the scene Boucher was causing involved the Strikes. That effectively ended the date earlier than I wanted.

Now, a day later, the hangover has most of the Bolts skating like snails during this game. I'm this close to batting each of their helmets off with my stick in the hopes that it'll snap them out of the trance. Coach Green has already screamed himself raw and no longer has any juice. He stands with his arms crossed so tight there's probably no circulation left in his fingertips.

It's the third period, and no one's scored a single damn goal. The other team is one of the bottom feeders of the conference, so this should be a pretty smooth win. But every time I try a play, everyone else is too slow for the passes to connect.

"Cassiano." Coach barks my last name as if all of this is my fault. And maybe it is, by default. He grabs the loose straps of my helmet to pull me down to his eye level. "You're the only one even trying. Just one goal. That's all we need. I don't care how you make it, but get it done."

I clench my teeth so hard I'm surprised they don't break. "Yes, sir."

After strapping my helmet back in place, I wait until Coach calls the first line out to play. I swing over the board and land on the ice like a beast looking for a victim. If I have to play forward and defense at the same time, I freaking will. We'll skate away with a victory tonight, even if it's a lousy one.

Boucher passes the puck to me, and I have to remind myself that he's a Bolt. Otherwise, I might just ram my shoulder into his solar plexus. I channel all my frustration into this play. An opponent tries to block me, and I slide the biscuit between his legs as if he's a child. Another one tries to get in the way. I feint left and twirl around him on the right just like I've seen my girlfriend do. Not a single Bolt is in sight to help me out. It's all on me.

A big D-man from the other team rushes over with the clear intention of turning me into a pancake. He's the last man between his goalie and me. I grin in the face of danger. Just before the dude connects, I bend down all the way and ram my shoulder against his legs. I feel him fly over me and keep going. The place isn't packed, but the thin crowd is screaming now.

It's a breakaway, suckers.

I skate like the wind. The goalie shifts left and right, trying to anticipate my movements. I lock eyes with the dude. The panic I see in them tells me I've already scored. I swing my stick wide. The goalie leaves a big hole on the top shelf. Faster than he can blink, I swing again and snipe a slapshot that makes the net slide back.

The buzzing sound makes this sham of a game worth it.

"Nothing but respect for my captain!" Nate comes in for a high five, and I give him a face wash instead.

"Get your head in the game." The way I snap makes me sound a lot like Coach. "If you have to leave your guts all over the ice to win this game, do it."

"Aye, aye."

I end up scoring a hat trick in the last five minutes of the game. Which, on the one hand, will look great on my stats, but on the other is embarrassing.

"That was the worst game I've seen in my life." Coach Green makes sure to tell us how he feels, huh? "Everyone was slow and unfocused. We only made it through because Cassiano wasn't suffering from a hangover like the rest of you zombies."

"But we can't be a team that revolves around a single player." Spittle flies out of Coach's mouth as he attempts to scream. We can tell he's an erupting volcano, what with the protruding neck veins and the red face, but his voice comes out as a whisper. "Especially not when we face the Bulldogs after Thanksgiving."

If I didn't already feel like garbage, that reminder sends me into a pit. The silver lining is that I'll have another chance to get back at my nephew. And I'll probably need it, after seeing his face again during Thanksgiving.

"Do you think you'll all get your shit together by then?"

"Yes, Coach."

"You better. Otherwise, I'm making you do burpees around the entire campus perimeter."

Something in his face tells me he's not bluffing. We're all absolutely screwed if the next game is a mess like this.

The shameful silence in the locker room only lasts about two minutes before Nate opens his big mouth.

"So, O'Malley's tonight?"

My jaw slacks as everyone agrees right away. "You gotta be kidding me."

"We gotta celebrate your win, bro." My alternate captain slaps my back, grinning as if he played any part in the three goals. He didn't. Conor took one assist. The other two goals were unassisted.

"I fully intend to kill you."

He shrugs at my threat. "Sure."

But I have no option except walking out of the locker room, using the same path the rest of the team does. Only to come face to face with a small group of people—mostly girls—wielding quick and dirty posters in support of the Bolts. One is a cut-up cardboard box that reads *you guys are hot. Single?*

Someone hoots behind me.

"Are those…" Conor's voice trails off for a moment before he recovers. "Our first fans?"

"Puck bunnies!" The way Nate screams it is the same as someone who is wasted at a party, about to jump into a pool naked.

"It's him!" A girl squeals and points at—

Me?

Her group surrounds me. I wonder if they're magicians, because they crossed the distance in the blink of an eye. Now one girl hangs off my left arm, another one from the right, and a third tries to cozy up in the middle.

"I—" My friends snicker at the scene. "Help me out, jerks!"

"Wow, you're so strong." The girl on my left fondles my

bicep hard enough that her fingers dig into my layers of clothes. "Is the rest of you this hard?"

It takes more effort than I care to admit to extricate myself from them. I grab both of my friends by their shoulders to steer us away. To steer *myself* away.

"O'Malley's you said? Let's go." Anything has to be better than walking alone to my dorm room, only to be assaulted by some random girls.

"Aw, yeah!" Nate pumps a fist in the air. "Let's party all night."

I glare at him so hard he backpedals. A bit.

"Let's party some of the night. How about that?"

Conor laughs.

The whole team plus fans, or whatever the hell they are, cram into an already busy pub. I wish I'd had time to get changed into more comfortable clothes. I'm here in a whole suit and coat, nursing a Sprite like I'm a child at a grown-ups' party.

"Hey, good game."

That comes from the least expected person. I turn to find my roommate next to me, glass of apple juice in hand. He scratches his head like it hurts him to have spoken civil words to me.

My eyebrows go up. "Thanks, man. You watched it?"

"Yeah." He shrugs, like we're not making some sort of breakthrough here. "A few of my buddies wanted to see a game. See what all the hype is about."

"And?" I'm fishing, I know. He knows, especially considering how he cringes.

"It was pretty cool."

I chuckle. "Did it hurt to admit it?"

"A little." Brett clears his throat. "But after hanging out with you guys a couple of times… you're not so bad."

This conversation would probably be smoother and end

faster if I could keep my face neutral. But I can't. For the first time since last night, I grin wide.

"Told you." I nudge him with my elbow. "Wait, first there was my birthday. When was the second one?"

"Last night." He pauses to take a sip of his juice and makes a face. It either tastes like piss or he wishes it were a beer, like I wish I were drinking instead. "The party was at my friend's place."

"Hey, Brett!" Nate raises his hand, and to my surprise, my roommate high fives him. "Pretty wild last night, huh? Did you get that girl's phone number?"

"No," my roommate grouches.

My head's spinning with all this new information. Then again, theirs might spin right off their necks if they learn who I was with last night.

Stifling a sigh, I take out my cell phone and find her contact. I miss her. I want to pick up where we left off. We'd been playing a shooting arcade game, and Tinker Bell couldn't get her aim right. So like she did with me for the axe throwing, I tried to give her some instructions. The kind that made her break out into goose bumps and that let me sneak in a few rogue kisses down her neck.

ME

At O'Malley's. Wanna come so we can escape together in secret?

She doesn't respond right away, but I can feel someone trying to snoop. Except that as I tuck my phone back into my pocket and glance up, I don't find Nate watching like I expected. Rather, it's the girl who thought it was okay to take liberties earlier.

"Hey there." She probably thinks she looks hot licking her lips like that. They're red like a fire engine, and some of the tint sticks to her front teeth.

"Have you met my friend Brett?" I ask, pulling at my room-mate's shoulder.

The poor guy blinks like an owl. "Uh…"

But the huntress doesn't even give Brett a glance. She pushes Nate out of the way and slides up against me. As in, she wedges my arm right between her boobs. Resting her chin on my arm, she looks up with bedroom eyes and says, "No, sorry. All I can see is you."

And all I can see is the exit. Which is, of course, where I find Tinker Bell surrounded by Strikes, walking into the pub. And their captain's eyes are trained on me.

# CHAPTER 28
## LUZ

Our last game before the holiday break is tomorrow, and instead of nursing their nasty hangovers in bed, all my teammates want to do is hit O'Malley's.

I check my phone on the way. The school's website is open on my browser. I take a quick look at the results from the Bolts' game and scream on the inside. They won, thanks to a hat trick from my boyfriend. I wish I could've seen that from the stands. I would've screamed his name so loud it probably would've gotten me kicked out of the arena.

But I can't do that. The Strikes would pile on me if they knew I'm dating the leader of the enemy. Even though they collectively agree that Max Cassiano is the nicest one of the bunch. And they also think he's the hottest. Because he is.

His text message pings right then, as if he can read my mind. Like he knows I'm thirsting for him from wherever he is. Before I can read it, though, Chelsea snatches my phone from my hand.

"S'more? Who's that?"

"Give it back if you want to keep your nose intact." Maybe

she sees the threat is serious, because she places the device on my open palm.

Not without giving me a chill-inducing smirk. "Are you dating someone, Captain?"

"Me?" I laugh like it's the silliest prospect. Even though I very much am dating, and not just someone, but the sweetest, sexiest guy I've ever laid eyes on. And hands. Although I want to lay them for longer. "Uh, where do you get that idea from?"

"Who are you trying to escape with, Rodriguez?"

"Oh?" JT picks up on that thread. "Are you off to some secret tryst?"

That *was* the plan. Obviously, now that's impossible.

Huffing, I walk into the pub. There are more bodies here than in front of a goalie during play. But even then, I sweep my eyes across the place just once and find him right away. Max. My delicious, secret little S'more. With some unknown girl hanging off him.

I'm glad no one can see how I ball my fists, since they're stuck in the pockets of my winter coat. My feet are rooted to the spot, blocking the way for the rest of the Strikes.

"What's up?" JT gives me a weird look, which means I'm severely at risk of leaking the truth.

That I am jealous as can be, even though I have no right to be. It's not like I've staked a public claim on Max. I know he wouldn't take advantage of that to see other women on the side, but I still can't help fantasizing that I part the crowd in a smooth sweep, march up to them, and replace the girl. I want to be the only one pressing up to him, holding his hand, taking in his sandalwood scent.

Damn it. My eyes are prickling. I wasn't even this affected last night when this happened too.

"Nothing's wrong," I say through gritted teeth, allowing her to pull me the rest of the way in.

As we make a slow journey to the bar, Max's eyes don't

leave mine for a second. They want to tell me something I'm not getting. And thanks to Chelsea, who should probably be hired by the freaking FBI, I can't just sneak off with Max now.

I take several deep breaths. Waiting for a bartender to acknowledge our existence helps me bring my blood pressure down. Maybe I can still salvage the night. I could hang out with the girls for an hour or so before claiming a stomachache, and *then* text Max with a meeting place. Away from the puck bunnies he now seems to be attracting. Somewhere we can be all by ourselves.

Sounds like a plan.

While my friends are embroiled in a discussion about whether to dance or hit the dartboards first, the cranky bartender appears before me.

"What do you want?"

"A backbone?" I ask, sighing.

"We only sell sugar and regret here. Which will it be?"

"Sugar." I slap a five-dollar bill on the bar. "Of the soda variety."

"You got it." Was that a tiny twitch of his lips? The beginnings of a smile?

While I contemplate whether I just made a new friend, a sudden shiver trickles up my back. The jerky motion gives me a bit of pain, and I wonder what caused it. When I glance over my shoulder, I catch Max still looking at me. There's a crease between his eyebrows, as if he's upset. At me. Or about me. Even though that girl is still trying to chat him up.

"Uh, Luz?"

It takes me a moment to find where the voice is coming from. Amid apologies to my teammates, Brett emerges to stand beside me. His face blocks my view of Max.

"Hi." I'm careful that my tone of voice doesn't show that I'm one second away from cringing.

Maybe he can tell, because he laughs awkwardly and says,

"I know I'm probably the last guy you want to talk to, but I've been on a journey of sorts."

Oh, boy. What the heck does that have to do with me?

"And I've realized I've been a jerk to you, so… I'm sorry?"

My shoulders deflate. "Oh. I have to admit I wasn't expecting that."

He wrinkles his nose as if he catches a whiff of all my previous feelings about him. "Yeah, Max was pretty shocked too. It's just, I've had really bad experiences with jocks in the past, and I projected. But you guys are pretty decent."

I try to make eye contact with my boyfriend again, but the space is too packed with people trying to get a spot at the bar. My drink's still not here, but the five bucks is definitely gone, so I have to hang on.

"I appreciate it," I say in something close to a shout.

"So, friends?" Brett asks, offering his hand for a shake.

Eh, what the heck? I shake it. "Sure."

"Rodriguez."

The deep growl is unexpected but comes from the person I most wanted to see. Somehow, in a matter of seconds, Max managed to weave through the crowd and now stands beside me. In his suit and black coat, he looks like some rich guy in the middle of a crowd of peasants. My tongue grows thick, and it takes all my willpower not to open my mouth and drool. Why does he have to look so fine all the time?

Not only Brett gives him a funny look, but so do the Strikes all around us.

Max doesn't care, though. Loud enough for everyone who cares to hear does, he says, "We need to have a talk. Captain to captain."

I can't tell from his expression if he's truly mad. But it does seem like it.

"Are you out of your mind?" I try to whisper to him, but I'm not sure the words carry. Every eye in the area is stabbing me in the face. I can feel my blood rushing to it. "We can't be seen together—"

"About what happened at that party last night," Max says, enunciating every word with all his lungs. "And how it affected my team's play tonight. Let's go."

"What?" I glance back just as the bartender places my expensive Coke on the counter. But Max has my arm in his grip, and he's pulling me away. "Cassiano, would you stop?"

"No" is all I hear.

"Luz, you need help?" JT glares at the back of Max's hair.

"I'm okay. I'll just hear him out. See you in a bit!"

The last glimpse I get of the Strikes is Chelsea's face. She's wearing a frown, like she can't quite finish a puzzle that lives in her head rent free.

I think I know exactly what it is. She's been suspicious of Max and me since my drunken incident. A few sly comments after I walked out of Romano's behind Max also make me think she's right on the money. But Max is giving such a weird vibe right now. Maybe her theory's crumbling.

Frankly, I'm confused too.

An eternity later, we're out in the chilly November night. Our shoes click on the sidewalk as Max pulls me away from the bar. He still hasn't glanced back at me once, even though we've been alone for a whole block.

"Max?"

My voice finally snaps him back to reality. I almost crash into his back when he brakes abruptly. He releases his hold on me as if I'm scalding, and I hear him inhale a shaky breath before he turns.

"I'm sorry." He rubs his nape. His cheeks and nose are red, but I don't know whether it's from embarrassment or from the chill that makes his breath come out in white puffs.

I shake my head. "Yeah, you should be. What if they start connecting the dots?"

"Do we really have to do this? Sneak around as if we're criminals?"

"Well, you saw what happened yesterday." We timed it so we'd arrive at the party at different times, but the scene remained unchanged during that span. Strikes versus Bolts once more. A beer pong game gone wrong. Boucher spewing out insults that will never get him laid in this town. "They're so entrenched in this ridiculous feud that they'll never understand how we can possibly date."

"So, we have to hide forever?" Max's blue eyes are almost black in the night. I finally realize he's mad. For real. "I have to stay a million miles away watching other guys try to pick you up at a bar without being able to do anything?"

"Excuse me? That's rich." I throw my head back and laugh. "Says the one who had a puck bunny stuck to him like Velcro."

"And you were jealous."

I huddle into my coat, glaring up at him from over the thick collar. "So were you, in case you forgot. And oh, by the way, you had no reason to be. Your roommate was just apologizing for being a jerk, which you're acting like right now."

"Yeah, I'm jealous." His voice isn't loud, but it still hits like the crack of a whip. "And I don't want anyone beside me but you. Except that can't happen, huh? The teams are more important."

Understanding zaps through me like thunder striking me down.

Max is not jealous that his roommate was having a little chat with me. He obviously doesn't care about the puck bunny either. What he's jealous of is that I'm choosing the delicate balance between our teams over being with him openly.

I open and close my mouth. The anger in his expression cracks. Probably because there are tears forming in my eyes and my nose is starting to run already. I stomp my foot on the concrete, trying to force every chip of my breaking heart to go back to its rightful place.

"What do you want me to do?" My voice comes out in a whisper. It makes him flinch.

"I don't know. I guess I want to have my cake and eat it too."

"So do I but… I don't know how."

When the irritation fades away, all that is left is a throb in my chest. I want Max so, so much. Thinking about not being with him would be the same as drowning, even though my lungs will continue to work just fine. But we're the captains. We can't just throw our teams into a disarray.

"Where do we go from here?" Max asks.

He hunches forward, trying to meet my eyes. But I can't. If I look into his eyes, I'm afraid I'll say something I'll regret. Like how I think I love him, but that maybe this isn't meant to be if it's so damn hard to find a quiet moment to be together.

I shake my head. "I don't know."

Neither of us says anything else. In the next few days, we don't even exchange a single text. That's how we leave campus for Thanksgiving. I wonder if he has a pit in his stomach the same way I do.

# CHAPTER 29
## MAX

I f not for my mom's demand that I join the family for Thanksgiving—as if I wasn't there every single year—I would've stayed at the dorm. Look at me, getting the point.

Still, out of the many things that have changed this year, chief is the time she insists I arrive: noon and not a second before. In my family, we have our big meal at lunch, but preparing for it is an affair that starts the night before. And because Alessandra Cassiano runs a tight ship, absolutely everyone contributes. Yes, including the men. At the end of the day, everyone but Leo and me works at a restaurant, so no Cassiano man has the excuse of never having visited a kitchen.

Which means she doesn't want me to contribute. And I suspect that the late arrival time is to shorten the number of hours I'll spend with the whole family. It's a very nice and subtle way of saying they don't want me there. I'm not shocked. They've basically spent my entire life drilling home that point.

In addition, this time, they're probably concerned that Leo and I will get into another tussle. A likely prospect, considering how high-strung I feel.

Since I made it with about fifteen minutes to spare, I've been sitting in my truck on my own. I parked on the parallel street so no one can see me. After running my hand through my hair several times, I look like I was electrocuted. The ache in my chest could very well be because of that, or because no one in my life cares about me enough. And I don't even have anyone to vent to because, what kind of guy does that?

One who actually has people who care, I guess.

I rest my head on the ice-cold windowpane. Between my weird family, the prospect of seeing them again, and that awkward fight with Tinker Bell, I'm unmoored. Like the gentlest autumn breeze might sweep all two hundred and ten pounds of me away.

The oppressive feeling in the center of my chest doesn't let me breathe properly, and I know it's all because I miss her. Because I want to tell her how I really feel—about her, my family, myself—and see if she cares. But after that talk, I'm afraid the most important thing to her will be to continue with the status quo. And I get it. I don't want to deal with the fallout either. But she's worth it.

Is it that maybe I'm not worth it? To anyone?

"Ah, shit." I run my hands around the steering wheel, trying to stay busy enough so I don't start wailing like a baby.

My phone buzzes with an incoming call. Mom.

I press the green button, and immediately, she says, "Massimo Cassiano, where are you? We are hungry."

"On my way."

"You better be here in five minutes, or else." She hangs up before formulating the rest of the threat, but the shouts in the background told me everything I need to know.

"Let's just get this done and go back to the dorm," I say into the silence, sighing. Every cell in my body wants to be elsewhere. Preferably where Luz Rodriguez is.

Too soon, I'm parked in front of the house. I'm surprised

there was even a spot left for me. The small Georgian house I grew up in looms in front of me. It was my whole world until recently, until I thought I had finally escaped it. I don't know what I was thinking by attending a college in town—that I wouldn't have to come back here again?

The door flies open, and out comes my second brother, Alessandro. None of the Cassiano men were cursed with a balding head, and his full hair bounces as he takes the steps down toward me. He's the hardest to read, the one I've always had less of any relationship with, and I'm confused as to why he's the welcome parade.

"I have to warn you," he says in greeting. "Don't go in there and be an ass."

Obviously, it makes me want to be an ass. Instead, I say, "Okay?"

"Cossimo Jr. already gave the same speech to Leo. We're all on a tightrope with Mom and Dad right now."

My brow furrows. So this is a legit warning, huh?

"Thanks."

"Let's go. My stomach's starting to eat itself."

What little amusement I can conjure up comes out as a snort.

I follow behind him, taking off my thick jacket even before I make it to the threshold. No one else so much as glances my way as I dump it on the pile by the door. It'll stay on top, which means I can grab it quickly and make a dash out before anyone else.

That gloomy thought poofs like a cloud when I hear the voice of the best Cassiano.

"Max! My favorite brother!"

I whirl around, searching among the faces until I find Alessio coming out of the kitchen. His arms are spread wide, and before I can react, he squeezes me into a bear hug. He can no longer lift me up like he used to when I was a kid. In return, I squeeze him right back.

"Alessio?" I pull away and grab his face, turning it this way and that. "It's really you?"

His grin is infectious.

"That's right." He lowers his voice to a whisper. "Listen, if they didn't disinherit me for leaving and not contributing to the family business, you're in the clear."

A few paces behind him, Leo sees the whole thing with a deadpan look on his face I'd love to sweep the floor with. The second he opens his mouth to say any shit about Alessio, I will.

Maybe he can smell the hostility radiating off me, because he turns around and goes back into the kitchen.

"Missed you, piccolo." Alessio pats my shoulder and uses the motion to steer me toward the dining area. "I've heard things around here have been tough for you."

I jam my hands into the pockets of my jeans. "The fact that you even heard about me is a shocker."

"Well, you did break Leo's nose. That kind of news travels fast."

"Just don't let me sit anywhere close to him," I mutter.

I end up sandwiched between Alessio and Lily, Alessandro's wife. Leo sits farther down with the rest of my nephews and nieces at a second table that I know is normally in Dad's studio. The kids are the nicest of the Cassiano bunch, but they're far more interested in their phones and tablets than in any of the adults. But hopefully they keep the eldest grandson of the family away from my face.

Mom and Dad finally appear from the kitchen. Somehow, their eyes are trained on me. My alarms go off, but for what? I have no idea.

Dad places a mutant-sized turkey on the table, close to his seat, where he can carve it comfortably. That's the only American part of our Thanksgiving meal. Maria, Cossimo Jr.'s wife, pushes a gigantic Pyrex with lasagna out of the way so Mom can place her tray and—

It's tiramisu. Normally, the dessert comes last, especially for something like this that is best served cold. So I'm confused about why it's out this early.

Mom clears her throat. The raspy sound is enough to halt all activity, which is another abnormal thing. Too many eyes turn to me instead of to her. When even my youngest niece looks at me, I confirm something's up.

I glance at Dad. He stands beside Mom with his hands on his hips, lips pursed in a way that usually signals that he's about to go on a deafening tirade.

Well, I did basically run away after hitting Leo. And after that, I went no contact. I suppose this is when I get what's coming to me. I clasp my clammy hands below the table and wait.

"What happened on your birthday was a disaster," Mom says, already making me flinch.

Dad picks it right up. "It can never happen again."

"Family is family." After forty-five years of marriage, it makes sense that they complete each other's sentences. Especially to tell me off. "And family doesn't hit each other. Or tell one another that they almost killed their mother."

"Is that clear?" Dad first gives me a pointed look, then Leo.

"Yes." I tuck my chin down.

"Fine," Leo mumbles from his spot.

"Good." Mom's expression changes just a tad. Gone is the stern facade, but I have no idea what's in its place. She wrings her hands with the apron tied around her waist. Is she nervous? Mom? My unflappable mother made of steel? "And now, we do a do over."

Cossimo Jr. leans back, putting his arm on the back of Maria's chair. "We *get* a do over."

Mom waves a hand. "That. Massimo, we will pretend today is your birthday."

I blink. Fast.

When I see no one's laughing and saying *gotcha*, I realize they're all serious. Expectant. Of my reaction. That's why everyone's been looking at *me*.

They planned this. This is why Mom told me to be late.

I rub my chest. Something in there feels like an elastic band that was stretched too thin and has snapped. Now it's a loose noodle, and it's making my eyes prick again.

"Uh… thanks."

"Is that it?" Alessio tilts his head forward to get a really good look at my face. Which I'm trying to hide. "Oh. He's crying."

Damn it. I punch him in the side, but there's no hiding the sniffle.

"Oh, baby." It's Lily who pulls me into a hug. "Happy birthday, Massimo."

One by one, they all wish me a happy birthday. No one makes fun of me, even though none of them have ever seen me cry. But once I start, I can't seem to stop.

# CHAPTER 30
## LUZ

Growing up, I always wished we did things differently at my house. That we did them the same as all my American friends. They got a big stuffed turkey, mashed potatoes with dollops of gravy, cranberry sauce, green bean casserole, and so many pies.

Instead, my parents made pabellón criollo. Every. Single. Year.

That's exactly what's on the table, which, by the way, is round. It was always a big joke, since my dad's name is Arturo. He said it was so he could look at all of us easily, so that everyone could speak freely to one another. Except no one is speaking right now, and there's a lot of staring in my direction.

I love the pabellón criollo now. It took a hot minute to recognize that I've always been different from my friends, and it's not necessarily a bad thing. The struggle has continued inside the house, though. It's one thing to reconcile my identity with my peers, but it's completely different to do the same with who my parents always expected me to be.

That's why they don't talk. They keep stuffing their faces

with tajadas and black beans and pulled beef and rice and arepas, to keep the words they want to say inside.

*Why do you keep playing hockey? It almost killed you. You got a new lease on life, and you're risking it all for that violent sport. So many people who went through accidents like yours didn't get the miracle you did. What are you thinking? Are you* even *thinking?*

Those were some of the things Mom and Dad volleyed at me the last time I sat at this table. It was a couple of days before I left home to start the summer bootcamp. We haven't exchanged a word since.

Maybe I should be glad to still have a seat at the round table, huh?

To my right, Mom keeps sneaking glances at Dad. Estela de Rodriguez never does anything her husband doesn't want, which sounds worse than it is. They're just shockingly in sync at all times. But right now, I have a feeling even Mom can't read him. I certainly can't, even though I was Dad's little girl until I started playing hockey again some three years ago.

To my left, my brother, Aran, gobbles up food like it's oxygen and he's drowning. Sixteen-year-old boys can be like that, but he's worse. He's already as big as Max, and if he keeps eating like this, he'll more than pass him. With how he attacks his food, it would be impossible for him to talk, even if prompted.

Almost across from me is my baby sister, thirteen-year-old Olivia. She *wants* to be called Liv, but everyone in the family calls her Aceituna, since her name is one letter apart from *oliva*. Maybe that's why she's always cranky. Today is no exception. There is no way she'll be the one to break the ice we're all treading on.

It will be up to me. The question is whether to break the ice with something akin to weather talk or by pointing at the big elephant in the room.

"Are we going to talk, or is this going to be the most silent meal in Rodriguez history?"

My sister's eyes go wide in that very obvious do-you-have-a-death-wish way.

"We can talk when you're ready to hear what we have to say." Dad's voice is gruff. He washes away the unpleasantness with a swig of papelón.

I spear a mound of meat with my fork. "Conversations go both ways." Then I eat, watching as his face goes from normal to streetlight red in a second.

Here we go.

"I don't understand you, Luz Maria!" His utensils clang against the plate. "How can you not be afraid of getting injured again?"

Mom crosses herself. "I pray every night, mijita. I pray for the Lord to keep you safe."

"So do I," I say, not even lying. "But people can get injured really bad from a simple fall. You're not saying I should stop walking just because I might trip, right?"

"That's not the point." Dad takes deep breaths before pushing himself off the table. He stands up for the higher vantage over me. "Walking is okay. Walking is what we hoped for after the accident. What you're doing is reckless."

"No, that's what *you* hoped for." I toss my napkin onto the table and stand up too. My voice rises to match. "Do you know what *I* hoped for, during all those years of PT? To play hockey again! It's why I fought so hard even though every exercise hurt like the hit itself, over and over."

My eyes are welling up. I wipe the first tears away with the hem of my fuzzy sweater. Mom's hands move, as if to reach for me, but she stops herself.

"Why do you treat me like I'm a fool for wanting what I had before the accident?" I hate that my voice, my entire body, quakes. But I don't regret it. I don't want to go back to the tense, artificial silence of five minutes ago. Taking a deep breath, I say, "I already know I won't be able to play hockey all my life, like I dreamed of as a child. But it's what makes me happy. It's what makes me *me*."

"But, mija." Mom looks like she's on the verge of tears, but she's holding out much better than I am. Slowly, she gets up and engulfs me in the first hug she's given me in months. "Isn't it better to give it up now, before something bad happens?"

I sigh into her shoulder. "Why are you so sure something bad will happen?"

"Because…"

"Because we're afraid," Dad says to finish Mom's sentence. I look up and catch him run a hand down his face. Like magic, in that sweep, he looks ten years older. "We're not rich. If anything happens to you again, and we're not able to help—"

"I know that. And it's another reason I'm playing." I pull away from Mom and glance from her to Dad. "Full ride, remember?"

"You could study somewhere else," Mom mutters. "Somewhere cheaper."

"No, I really can't." I shake my head. "Please, I don't… I don't want to live full of regret."

Silence settles like a heavy blanket over us. Our shoulders sag, and one by one, we return to our seats at the table. The food's gone cold, but I don't really have the energy to get up and heat it in the microwave.

"Are you gonna eat that?"

My eyes snap up to Aran. He points at my plate. Bless this fool.

I push the plate to him and watch, equal parts marveled and horrified, as he polishes it off in two minutes flat. My mind goes blank as I watch him, which I guess is why people watch reality shows.

A snort echoes around our small kitchen. It becomes a laugh. Aceituna shakes as amusement comes off her in waves.

"You guys are so weird." She points at Aran and me, as if she also isn't completely off tune.

Dad puts an elbow on the table to rest his face on his hand. "Luz Maria."

"Arturo," I say in return. It makes his lips twitch.

"This is serious. Are you going to keep playing hockey?"

"Yes."

He inhales deep through his nose. "And if you get injured again?"

"And if I don't?"

"Even if you don't, you still have chronic pain for life, mija." Mom finally reaches for my hand. I stare at our linked fingers for a moment.

"So do millions of Americans, Mom. And thousands of elite athletes too."

"You can't tell," Aran says all of a sudden. He's done eating and now leans back, rubbing his stomach. "You should come watch Luz play."

"It's true." Aceituna shrugs. "Even I can tell she's good. Better than the girls who probably don't have chronic pain."

Because I want it more. None of my teammates know what losing hockey is like. Not yet. Most of them will probably not go pro, but they're all working toward that chance of making a career out of the sport. The risk of injury is the same for everyone, but the sense of loss is still something they know they'll deal with down the road.

That visceral hunger I feel for every second I get to play is what I displayed during bootcamp. I was on medication twenty-four-seven, but damn it, I busted my ass. I connected the plays. I never quit the drills. I puked just a little less than everyone else. And I became the captain of the team because of it.

Taking encouragement from my siblings, I say, "I'm the captain of the team." Both my parents turn to me, eyes wide. "Not to brag but, yeah, I'm pretty good."

"Are you?" This is what makes Mom's bottom lip start trembling.

"Sometimes." Aran's face is serene, as usual. Most people think he's a sarcastic little shit, but I know better. Nothing that goes through his mouth is ever a lie.

I narrow my eyes at him. "I thought you were on my side."

"I am." He shrugs. "Sometimes you're spectacular. Other times, you give me secondhand embarrassment."

Olivia chimes in, "If it helps, you *always* give me second-hand embarrassment."

"It definitely does not help."

Abruptly, I'm pulled into a hug so fierce it twists my body in a way that will make me hit the foam roller up in my room. Mom sniffs against my shoulder, where she's buried her face. Her words come out muffled when she speaks.

"I'm so proud of you."

The scrape of Dad's chair against the linoleum alerts me to his movements. While rigid in Mom's embrace, I feel Dad's hand caress my head.

"We just worry, mijita. We don't want anything bad to happen to you—to any of you."

"I know." I sound like I did when I was five and being reprimanded for something I definitely did do. "But you also have to let us live."

"Agree," Aran says.

Olivia starts snapping her fingers.

"You two still live under this roof," Dad says, his gruff voice back. "My roof, my rules."

My siblings groan and shake their shoulders like the children they are. My silly, adorable, annoying siblings.

Before the accident, we were like any other kids, fighting

over everything. Aran has always loved hockey as much as I do, and he used to try to one-up me while we played in our backyard. Except he was a ten-year-old runt back then, and I was a whole head taller. Never winning a faceoff against me, always being fooled by my dangles—me, a *girl*—made him absolutely hate my guts.

Meanwhile, seven-year-old Olivia couldn't possibly care less about hockey. Or us. She's always been a bookish girl, and the ruckus Aran and I made grated on her nerves. Often, she'd tuck herself inside the laundry closet just to have a quiet moment to read. Until we found her and forced her to play with us. Aran and I were the easy ones to handle for our parents, because Olivia has always had severe food allergies. Maybe that's part of why she felt so different from us.

After the accident, everything changed. Aran and Olivia had to make room for my needs in our parents' lives and their own. They went through the whole five steps of grief at their own pace, but at the end, they somehow grew up more than I did. Or maybe I'm still trying to make up for my lost childhood, while they have resigned themselves to a wild older sister who doesn't fit the mold.

I extricate myself from my parents, then wrap one arm around my sister and the other one around part of my brother. He's too big for my grip, but I still squeeze him tight against Olivia and myself.

"What the—"

"Air! I need air!"

"Shush. Let me love you." I grip them even tighter and, because I know it will annoy them, I smack a loud kiss on each of their cheeks.

"You're so embarrassing." Aran grunts, but while he could easily overpower me, he stays put.

Olivia sniffs me. "I like your perfume. Can I have it?"

I let them go, but not before rubbing their heads and

messing up their hairdos. This will be my God-given right forever, as the eldest sister.

Mom and Dad stand together, hand in hand, watching the whole thing, as if they can't believe it's happening. It's not like they now want me to keep playing, but the fact that we're not screaming at each other is major progress. And not at all what I expected.

It's wonderful what can happen when people just… talk. We don't always have to agree. All we need is to understand one another.

I don't think that's a courtesy I've extended to Max these days, but I want to try. Just like my parents can't magically fix my back and my life, Max and I can't fix our teams. But it doesn't mean we should continue not speaking to each other just because it's easier than to deal with a messy conversation. All week, I've been afraid that another fight may break us up, but I've missed him. Just like I've missed my parents all these months.

The difference is that my parents are mine forever. But if I don't do something, I may lose Max. And that's a pain ibuprofen can't mitigate.

Once we're done clearing the table, I sneak off to the quietest area in the house, the laundry closet. I pull my phone from my back pocket and find my S'more.

ME

I miss you

I'm sorry

Can we please talk?

I hit Send. And wait.

# CHAPTER 31
## MAX

As I drive over to Luz's parents, I'm determined to grovel if I have to. I practice a speech in my head that will hopefully lead to the desired conclusion of staying together, no matter what.

My body vibrates with nervous energy because I'm not quite sure if that's what she wants. If she doesn't, I'll respect it. I'll always respect her above any of my wishes. But I will also be absolutely destroyed. We can't always get what we want, right? And the hardest part is dealing with the aftermath.

Of course, every stoplight on the way is red. My watch beeps a couple of times, marking a too-high heart rate. It happens every time I imagine Tinker Bell saying that she can't see us working out under these circumstances.

In one of those scenarios, she throws my old words back at me, and I picture her saying, "I'm married to hockey, you know? That's what I came to St. Cloud for."

I glance at the enormous Tupperware full of Mom's tiramisu. I'm not above using it for bribery. The problem is that Luz didn't get to try it before, so she doesn't really know what she'd be missing out on if she sends me packing.

When I finally park in front of the right address, I have to take several bracing breaths before getting out of the vehicle.

The little suburban house appears cozy and welcoming. My feet freeze on the asphalt as I stare up at it. Somewhere inside is the girl I like. Somewhere inside, we'll have a conversation that, not to be a melodramatic drama king, is going to change the game.

I run a hand through my hair. The longer I stand here, the longer I prolong my own torture. The air is so cold I can see my own breath as I walk around the car. On the way toward the front door, the perspective makes the little house loom over me.

I'm halfway up the front lawn when the door bursts open, and there she is. Luz stops on the porch for just a moment, as if to make sure it really is me. Without a word, she launches into a sprint. And nothing in her expression hints that she's considering stopping.

"Uhh… Luz?"

Just like the day we met, she jumps at me, except this time it's not to wrestle a foam roller from me. Air comes out of my lungs in a grunt as I catch her. My whole attention fixates on not letting her fall. I don't think too much about hand placement, but this time, she doesn't care. Luz wraps her limbs around me and kisses me.

Well, this is going better than I expected.

I close my eyes and leave her in charge. One of her hands holds the back of my head, fingers laced with my hair. The subtlety of this kiss is minus one hundred, because not a second after her lips touch mine, she coerces them open. Feeling the urgency behind the kiss tears a moan from my chest. Luz's thighs cinch tighter around my waist as she braces to shift her angle.

Luz makes a sound like she can't get enough. Every cell in my body feels like it's been dipped in lava, even though the day is cold as ice. I grab her tighter, trying to pull her closer. But there are too many layers of clothing between us, and that's probably a good thing—we're in front of her house, after all.

Wait, are my hands on her butt?

It takes superhuman effort to pull away from her lips. Stars dance in my vision with the effort to keep myself in check.

"Luz." My voice comes out like gravel. "Uh, we're in public."

Her eyes are half-mast as she stares down at me. She runs a hand through my hair, the other one down the side of my face, observing my features as if making sure this is real life and not a fantasy.

"Shame," she mutters. Leaning down, she places a small peck on my lips again.

My grip falters. Tinker Bell starts laughing. She slides her legs down one at a time until she's on her feet. Looking up at me with sparks in her eyes, she wraps her arms around my waist under my coat. And of course, this is when I notice her entire family is on the porch, staring wide-eyed at us.

"You're killing me," I say in a tiny, squeaky voice.

She rests her chin on my chest. "They're all watching, aren't they?"

"Yeah. Does your dad own a gun? He looks like he wants one to appear in his hand right now."

She bites her lips, but her shoulders shake with obvious amusement. Without looking away from me, she tells them something in Spanish that reluctantly gets all four of them filing back into the house. I only catch the tail words—por favor, which is as far as my Spanish skills go.

I lower my forehead to hers. "Not quite the way I wanted to introduce myself to your family."

"I couldn't help it. I just saw you and—I don't know. I just missed you so much." She shrugs, which makes me notice she's only wearing a sweater. I wrap the flaps of my open coat around her.

"So I take it you don't want to break up with me?"

Luz does a double take. "What? Where did you get that idea from?"

"Uh." If my face isn't red like a tomato from making out with her in the cold, it has to be flaming right about now. "I don't know. Pessimism?"

"You absolute fool." Her words are barely above a whisper. "Can't you see how you make me lose my mind?"

A slow grin stretches my lips. Somehow hearing her say that sends my pulse to new levels. "Okay, that's good. Because I came prepared to beg. I even brought tiramisu to sweeten the pot."

"Oh?" She shifts her weight from one foot to the other. "Wait, that's not the point."

"What's the point? Because I'm having trouble thinking straight here."

Luz snorts, but she does nothing to reduce my suffering. The glint in her eye tells me she's actually enjoying it. "The point is," she says very slowly, as if maybe she's having trouble focusing too, "that I'm sorry I even made you think you had to beg. I don't want to break up with you. Not for a second."

I turn her words over in my hormone-addled brain. I like the sound of them, but the fundamental issue remains. Or rather, I need to make her see it's not an issue anymore.

"Good, because I'm sorry I acted like a Neanderthal. If we have to date in secret until we graduate, then that's fine by me."

"But that's not fair to you." Her dark eyes bore into mine, so intense I couldn't look away even if a meteor crashed down next door. "You don't deserve to be kept a secret."

"Neither do you."

Her swollen lips draw into a little arch, a tiny smile that

seems almost shy. I capture them with mine for a second, enough to sear the feel of that smile in my mind forever.

"Max." She says my name like a sigh. "Let's just tell everyone."

I'm quiet. On the one hand, yeah, that's exactly what I want. I want to scream to the four winds that *Luz Rodriguez is my girlfriend.* I want to hold her hand in class, sneak kisses between practices, go on dates, put my arm around her at O'Malley's, act a proper fool every time she's around.

But I can see the teams losing their collective marbles, toppling what little respect they may have developed for us as captains these past few months. If they live up to their pot-stirring potential, it may even throw our seasons altogether. That's also not what this relationship deserves.

I summarize all that by saying, "Are you sure? Shit could hit the fan."

"I know." Her nose wrinkles, as if she's smelling the sharticles already. "And I definitely think we should find the right moment to break the news. But I don't want this double life forever."

"What if we tell them after the season's done?"

She tilts her head. "What if we make it all the way to the playoffs?"

I narrow my eyes. "What if we tell them *after* we win the playoffs?"

"Atta boy." Her chuckles vibrate through me too. "Or we could just get them drunk off their minds and break the news then."

"That might be quicker." Movement from the corner of my eye catches my attention. A curtain swooshes shut as a spy tries to hide from view. "By the way, we've had an audience this whole time."

"I bet." She snorts through her nose. It's as red as a stop sign. "What do you want to do now?"

"What do you mean?"

"The way I see it, you have two options. One, get in your truck and drive away as fast as you can. Maybe with me in it, once I get a coat."

I nod seriously. "That's an option. What's the other one?"

"Go inside and face the inquisition." She makes a point of looking down at my pants.

"Okay, uh…" I clear my throat. "I might need a moment first."

Luz bites her lip, her cheeks darkening in realization. "I'll wait for you inside, okay?"

"Yeah, sure." My hand shakes as I push my hair away from my forehead. "If anyone asks, just say it took me a whole ten minutes to grab the tiramisu from my truck."

That's about how long it will take me to will away the desire coursing through my veins. The two options are really only one, because if I drive away without facing her parents, they will never, ever forgive me. And I want to stay in Luz's life. Knowing I have to face them after that little, uh, spectacle, sends my nerves into overdrive. That alone is enough to sober me.

I grab the Tupperware and realize its purpose hasn't changed. Instead of bribing Tinker Bell, I now have to use its powers on her family. Who all probably think I'm some sleazy horndog.

I still knock on the door, as if nothing's amiss. The spy from earlier must've been Tinker Bell's little sister, because she's the one who opens the door. Her eyes are wide as saucers as she looks up at me.

A hand falls on her shoulder, and I trace it up to a very angry man. The dad. To be honest, if looks could kill, I would've died the second his eldest daughter kissed me.

"Um, hi. My name is Max Cassiano and I'm—"

"Just let him in. He's freezing!" The scream comes from Luz, who's somewhere inside the house.

Wordlessly, her dad steps aside to let me in. I keep as wide a berth as I can, even though I'm a whole head taller than the man and significantly bulkier.

"Sit." He points at the couch.

I do, placing the container with cake on my lap. In an armchair across the coffee table sits Luz's mom. Her expression is blank, as is her son's. Luz mentioned he's the middle kid, but he's as big as I am. If I didn't know better, I'd have thought him to be our age or even older. The kid cocks an eyebrow, as if defiant.

The couch sinks beside me. Luz sits perhaps a bit closer to me than she should. I take the steaming mug she offers me, so relieved by the warmth I don't even care that she swipes the Tupperware from my grasp. She lifts the lid and stabs the cake with a spoon.

I watch her take a big bite. Her eyes widen as my mother's culinary talents hit her.

"Oh my."

"That was supposed to be for your family, you know?"

She shakes her head. "No way. All mine."

Her dad sits on the other armchair, diagonal from me. The glare hasn't dimmed even a notch. "What are your intentions with my daughter?"

If I'd been drinking the tea, I'd have choked.

"Ugh, Dad." Luz groans but doesn't stop chewing. "That is so old school."

"He needs to answer the question, Luz Maria. Especially after that—after that—"

"For your information, I was the one who kissed him."

"But he grabbed your..." He can't even say it. His whole body shakes. "In public!"

She has the nerve to shrug. *Shrug*. Even though I feel like death is creeping over me.

I smack her thigh softly with the back of my hand and hiss. "Luz, you're really not helping."

Is that amusement in her mom's face?

Behind us, I hear the younger girl say, "I told Brooke that Max Cassiano is here, and he's on his way."

Who? What?

I do a double take and glance back. "Do you know me?"

It's her brother who answers. "Everyone who follows hockey in this town knows you."

"You can't date celebrities, Luz. Fame corrupts those people," her dad says.

"Are you hungry, Max?" the older woman asks, completely ignoring her husband. She has the same light brown skin as her daughter, the same head of hair. But Luz's eyes are more like her dad's. The man who is still staring daggers at me.

I'm not completely clueless. Even though I ate a full meal at home, I'm not about to decline an offer of hospitality. "Um. Yes, ma'am."

"You have not answered my question, young man." If anything, this ruckus seems to have made Luz's dad angrier.

I rack my brain, trying to remember what he's talking about. Without thinking too hard, I blurt out, "Honorable ones, I swear."

"That's not what it looked like to me!"

"Dad, please."

Her mom stands up and brushes the wrinkles out of her cardigan. "Do you like arepas? I can make you one right now."

"You don't have to bother—"

"Oh, it's not a bother."

A scream outside the door makes me jump out of my skin. No one else bats an eyelash, though.

"That'll be Brooke," Luz's sister says. A moment later, the door opens, and I hear frantic steps.

"Where is he?" A boy the same age as Luz's sister appears before me, puffing air as if he ran all the way here. His messy, dirty blond hair confirms he probably did. "Whoa, it really is him. Can I have your autograph?"

I blink really fast.

My supposed anchor to reality offers me a spoonful of tiramisu. "Say ah."

All the emotions of the day rush up my throat in a guffaw. My chest was full of them, the sadness, the anger, the fear. But a single emotion dominates over them now. Happiness.

Tinker Bell's lips twitch, and soon, she's joining in too. Hearing our intertwined laughter echoing in her living room makes this the best Thanksgiving of my life.

# CHAPTER 32
## LUZ

The Sunday night before our big business plan presentation, Max and I are holed up in a secluded corner of the library. There has not been a single table available all day, so we had no choice but to camp out on the floor behind the bulky shelves in the history section. The old Tiffany lamps overhead that pepper the entire building are dimmer in a few areas, and this is one of them. If I were on my own, I'd feel like I was in a horror movie.

The true horror here, though, is that despite having worked so hard all semester, there was still so much crap left for the last minute. Even worse, every time Max takes a break from working, his hands find me and threaten to topple my concentration too.

"Max." I hiss his name like a warning when I feel him sneaking behind me. His arm circles my waist, and I feel his chin rest on my shoulder. "Someone might see."

"And what are they going to see, exactly?" His breath is hot against my ear. I'm glad it's cold enough that I'm wearing thick leggings and an oversized hoodie. This way, he can't see how he's given me goose bumps everywhere. "We probably look like two cave trolls in this corner. No one will know it's us."

"Even then, I'm pretty sure PDA isn't acceptable here."

"Isn't it?"

Max obviously takes this as a challenge.

His teeth close around my earlobe ever so softly before he trails his lips down my neck. He places hot little kisses, suckling strategic areas that won't be too visible if they leave a mark. My spine melts, and with his arm, he pulls me back up against him.

I abandon the keyboard of my laptop and trail my hands up and down his legs where they frame mine. I feel him pull my hoodie over my shoulder, and with it, the T-shirt underneath, so he can bite my shoulder just enough to make me shudder.

Oh, this is getting too dangerous.

It takes a lot of effort to unstick my tongue from the roof of my mouth to say, "If you keep this up, we won't be able to finish the presentation and get any sleep before practice."

"Worth it," he murmurs against my skin. "Can I touch your stomach?"

I gasp a little. The fact that he's asking is even sexier than if he already was.

The problem is that I know I should say no. Not because I don't want to, but because this is too risky. And we really need to work. Plus, I feel gross after sitting on this ancient carpet all day. And I'm wearing some comfortable granny panties that don't show any lines with my leggings. Obviously, there are more cons than pros.

Which is why I sigh a "yes."

Even though it makes him chuckle, he wastes no time sneaking his hand under the layers of clothes to find the skin he seeks. His hand is so big that, even without splaying it, it spans most of my stomach. He explores no further, which is both disappointing and relieving. It's almost like he craves intimacy, but little by little. I'm fine with that. I plan to keep him around for a long, long time. There's no hurry.

As his thumb strokes my skin, he says, "I've heard people say that consent is sexy."

"Hmm, sure is."

"So I wanted to tell you that you have my consent."

As the pause grows longer, I twist a little until I can look up into his eyes. "What for?"

"Whatever you want. Whenever you want."

My mouth unhinges. His lips are curled into a little smile that has the power to raise goose bumps all over my skin once more. It's the smile that shows that one dimple. Meanwhile, his eyes are darkened with very obvious hunger. And not for food.

"Uh…"

"You can touch me where and whenever you want." He shrugs, like he's talking about our assignment. "Not in circumstances that will get us in jail or something, but you know what I mean. And, of course, I'll wait until you're ready too, because, again, consent is sexy."

The way he grins, so cheeky and with a touch of shyness, sends my heart into a faster pitter-patter than even his words do. If not for this damn assignment, I'd take him up on the offer.

I have to shake my head hard to rattle my brain back in place.

"How about—" I stop to clear the rasp away from my voice. "How about we save this for a later date? After finals, maybe?"

His eyebrows twitch. "I'm sure that can be arranged."

"Great." I turn all the way until I'm kneeling in front of him. He has the hood up over his head, wisps of black hair escaping their confines and framing his face. I clear them out of the way and place a soft kiss on his forehead. "Can we get back to working now?"

Max frowns. "My plan has been foiled."

"Stop being so adorable and get back to work."

It's quite amusing to see the hulking figure of my boyfriend tip tap away on his tiny laptop. Especially because he can't stop frowning down at the screen.

Two more coffees later, and we finally finish the presentation. The sleek and didactic slides are the brainchild of one Max Cassiano, who turns out to have a knack for this kind of thing. Additionally, the content is concise but robust. There is not a single weak area. The numbers are perfect, and the storyboard is compelling. I would give us an A freaking plus. I really want to see the lecturer say that we're still not at the right level after this.

It's two in the morning by the time we leave the library. Under the light of the streetlamp, I can see that Max's nose is red. I probably look like a mess, with my mop of hair in a messy bun atop my head and more layers of clothing than a single person should have. Even then, my S'more looks down at me like he can't get enough.

We stop at the entrance of my dorm building, and for a long time, it's impossible to let go of each other's hands. Little by little, we've tried. Now we're down to linked pinkies. A few days without him last week were enough to convince me that, nope, I don't want to be apart from this man for a whole second again. He has stolen my whole heart. I only *feel* again when I'm close to him. It's not like hockey's any less important, like I feared. I just have him to share it with now.

"I'll wear a business suit in St. Cloud blue tomorrow," I say. My breath fogs up the vision of him for a moment, and I resent the air. "You're absolutely going to fall in love with me when you see it."

He tilts his head. "What makes you think I haven't already?"

The night is absolutely quiet. All I hear is the drumming of my own heart in my ears. "Max."

Smiling, he leans down to press his lips to mine for just a second. Then his pinky lets go. "I'll wear a matching tie. See you in the morning, Tinker Bell."

I watch him walk away until the cold seeps into my bones.

It takes me far too long to find sleep after that, and what little I catch is restless. When I close my eyes, I can still see us sitting in the library. Just as the dreams are about to turn saucier than real life, they shift until I'm standing in front of the classroom, bombing the presentation so badly that Max decides to break up with me.

I'm a wreck during morning practice. This is probably my worst practice ever, but Coach Young doesn't seem to mind. It could be because everyone else is a mess too.

"I have a calculus exam in two hours," JT says, eyes like a deer caught in the headlights, when one of the trainers asks her why she can't nail down a drill.

"And I have two exams today," Chelsea volunteers with a cringe. "One is oral."

Coach Young puts her hands on her hips and glares up and down the line of Strikes. "You need to learn to perform under pressure, no matter what."

"Yes, ma'am."

But the second she blows the final whistle, everyone runs into the locker room to get ready for the academic side of this college gig we got going on. I take a record-breaking quick shower and spend most of my available time blow-drying my hair to perfection and applying makeup good enough for TV.

"Va-va-voom." Chelsea whistles behind me. "Are you sure you're okay with becoming a killer? Because people are going to die when they see you like this."

"You think?" I smack my lips as I finish applying the red lipstick. Aside from it, the rest of the makeup is simple and muted, just highlighting the contours of my face and eyes. I take a bracing breath once I'm done, and say, "Wish me luck for this presentation, ladies."

"You won't need it. They'll be too dead to even hear what you're saying." JT laughs, and I appreciate the sentiment.

I want to dazzle the class with the excellent work we've done. This is just the final battle armor I need to brook no doubt that I mean business.

Max waits for me in his truck. If anyone who sees us leave together wants to give us crap, we have excuses. First, it's freezing, and second, we're going to the same class. I hop in the passenger seat and stop.

He has slicked his hair back with wax and, along with his well-tailored coat, he looks one hundred percent like the rich guys that pullulate on campus.

"Ready?" Max asks.

"Yeah." It takes me a moment longer to realize he's talking about the presentation and not about taking this a step further. "Uh, I mean, absolutely. They won't know what hit them."

Neither do I. The moment we find our seats in the classroom and Max removes his scarf and coat, I realize I'm not ready for the strength of my emotions. He's in a suit and a St. Cloud blue tie. The quiet confidence with which he wears it is probably due to the fact that he wears these suits after every game. But even then, it fits him perfectly enough to not hide the power in his shoulders, arms, and thighs.

Max catches me, frozen in the act of removing my own coat. "Need help?"

"Yes."

But not the kind he gives me. While he removes my coat, I beg my lungs to work at normal capacity again. I cannot climb this man like a tree in the middle of this classroom.

A little hiss behind me gets my attention. "Luz, I did not bring my stick."

"What?"

"So I can beat other men off you."

As we take our seats, I lean closer to him. "Flattery won't get you further than you already are."

Max cocks an eyebrow at me. Somehow, he keeps it locked in place even as I place a hand on his knee. The only reaction comes from his muscles, which tighten into rock-solid form. He puts his hand on mine, and we stay like that until the lecturer comes.

By the time our turn comes, you wouldn't think we only slept for three hours, with the way we walk down to the podium. Or by the way we speak with equal levels of confidence, leveling our stares on the panel of investors that will be grading us.

While Max presents as though he's been doing business for years, I take a moment to glance at our classmates. Brett nods with a frown on his face, as if he can't quite believe he agrees with what his roommate is saying. Every girl is rapt, probably going through the same thought process as I did when I first saw him in this suit. One of the investors looks half in love with Max too. Meanwhile, the lecturer has a perfect poker face that doesn't fool me. He's surprised by how good we are.

The closing remarks are mine, so I step back up to the podium. Max's hand brushes against mine as we exchange places, and I draw strength from the little touch.

I look at him and take a deep breath.

"Business is not supposed to be about emotions." I fix my attention on the panel, even though I'd rather look into Max's eyes forever. "But this idea was born from the paraspinal scar on my back. I was once one of the patients we hope to serve with your support. And in a healthcare business like this, no one will care to make it flourish as much as someone who once lost everything she knew. With your help, we can make a difference in someone else's life too. That's why we're asking you to please invest in our proposal." I manage to deliver all that with an unwavering voice, up until the closer. "Th-Thank you very much."

My heart beats as fast as if I were in the middle of a breakaway, with the opportunity to either score or fail to put my team on the scoreboard.

The panel deliberates in hushed whispers. I stand beside Max and link my pinky with his. This assignment is pass or fail, a vote on investment or a rejection of the business plan. Only a third of the previous groups passed.

This is more than just a grade. It's a confirmation that my plans are good. Max might be sensing the turmoil in me, because he shifts until his whole hand engulfs mine.

And then the jury delivers the result. The words echo across the silent classroom as the woman says, "Approved. We would absolutely invest."

# CHAPTER 33
## MAX

can tell the bottled-up emotions inside her are about to explode. It's in the way her eyes glaze over, how her cheeks grow red as apples, and how she has to bite her lips.

"Next team," the lecturer calls in a bored tone of voice. I wait until he's jotted down our passing grade on his notepad before moving.

First, I offer my arm to Luz. She takes it, as though she hasn't just walked all over the place in her heels without issue. Second, I wait until we're right beside the lecturer to speak.

"So glad we got paired together, huh? That way we didn't hold anyone else back."

The lecturer's eyebrows crash. Maybe he thought we were such airheads we'd even forget his thinly veiled insults. But no, I'm a sensitive little prick, and I remember every stinking little slight ever done to me. And now, I will remember each one done unto my girlfriend too.

As we climb back up to our seats, twinkles dance in her eyes. "Oh, you're so petty. I love it."

It. Not me. But I'll take it.

I push my chair blatantly closer to hers when we're back in our spots. Our thighs are glued to each other, and so are our hands. I wish I could celebrate this victory by wrapping my arms around her and staying like that for a long time. Instead, another half hour of presentations passes, and I struggle not to doze off.

"Follow me," Luz whispers once class is done and we're shrugging on our coats.

At the rate things are going, I would follow her into a black hole if she asked. I tag along behind her in silence as we weave through clusters of students in the hallways. Our super fancy attires catch quite a lot of attention, but I don't care. All I see is the back of her head and the smooth dark hair that cascades down her back and swings with every one of her powerful steps.

She rounds a corner and opens a random door. Except it has a small sign plate that reads STORAGE, and I realize this isn't random at all. Luz waits until I cross the threshold to close and lock the door. I take only one moment to take in the dusty shelves stacked with papers and books in the too-small room lit only by the sunlight coming in through a tiny window. Because in the next second, she slams me against the door and pulls me down by my tie.

The last thing I see is her wide grin before she kisses me. I inhale her scent, something that is only hers. There's a crashing sound as I let my bag drop to the floor. Finally, I reward myself by wrapping my arms around her.

"You were incredible," I murmur against her lips. "Gave me a thing for CEO women now."

"Women?" She pulls back to frown.

"Hmm." I pretend to think about it. "No, only you're the CEO of my heart."

A little exhalation escapes her lips. "Max."

"Stop, I can see the engines in your head whirring." I reach up to smooth her brow with my thumb. "You don't have to say anything. I'll stop if it bothers you."

"Precious fool." The words surprise me, not gonna lie. Luz clasps her hands around my head, forcing me to lean down another notch. She traps my lower lip in a soft kiss before releasing it with a pop. "You have no idea how lovable you are, do you?"

"I have no idea what my name is right now." Especially not with my hands around her hips.

"Max." She sounds surprisingly serious. I stop staring at her smudged lips and focus back on her eyes. "There's something you need to know."

I cringe. "Oh, that sounds bad."

Luz bites her lower lip, giving me no indication as to whether this is good or bad other than the fact she hasn't stepped away.

"I am absolutely"—she draws in a breath—"irrevocably into you in a way that scares me."

"Oh?" I lift my eyebrows. "Why does it scare you?"

"Because you have my fragile little heart in that big paw of yours, and you could crush it so easily."

"You're wrong." I kiss the tip of her nose. "We exchanged hearts. That's all."

Luz groans, the sound coming out muffled as she buries her face in my chest. "Oh my word. This is next-level cheesy."

My laughter echoes a bit too eerily in this room. I peel her away from me, enjoying how her face and neck are flushed. "Should we get out of here? I'd like to continue our love declarations in a less musty place."

"No more love declarations." She glares. "Ever."

I grab my bag and am about to open the door when she presses the palms of her hands against my chest and stops me. "Wait, one more kiss."

"Happy to oblige." I spread my feet wide so I'm lower,

closer to her eye level. Luz's expression appears intrigued by the concept. I curl my finger at her. "C'mon."

All too easily, she presses her lips against mine. I sneak my hands under her coat to find her back and trail them down until they find her curves. Luz's lips pry my mouth open harder, and I squeeze her closer. My reward is a groan from her throat that will haunt me all day.

Not to be outdone, she runs her hands down my chest, stopping to really feel the muscles under my button-down shirt. When she gets to my belt, she pulls away from the kiss. Our stares find each other, unflinching even though we're both panting like dogs.

She doesn't remove her hands from my belt. I don't move mine from her butt.

"You move first," she says.

"I am physically incapable of moving right now."

Her lips twitch. Slowly, she takes one step away. And another. As if she's dealing with a feral raccoon that has just found a full trash can.

Clearing her throat, she says, "Anyway, you did amazing too. You sound like you care about this as much as I do."

"I do." My whole body shakes with pent-up desire, but I have to force my heart rate back to normal levels. "It's your dream."

Something different shines in her eyes now. "No more love professions, I said."

Chuckling, I point at her face. "By the way, your lipstick is smeared all over your face. I assume I look the same, right?"

"Yup. I also messed up your hair and your tie." By the way she grins, she's as proud of this as she is of acing the Intro to Entrepreneurship project.

After a few minutes of dabbing our faces with wipes from her bag, we're finally decent enough to rejoin civilization. We walk down the hallways with hooked pinkies until it's time to go our separate ways. I have to endure one more class and then an exam with the ghost of her kisses tingling on my skin.

Twice during the exam, I have to stop to stare at my hands. Never would've pegged myself for a butt man, but Luz's is spectacular. I have to drop my forehead to the cool surface of the desk to cut through those thoughts and focus back on the test. How I'm going to get through practice later today is a mystery. My body is primed for one thing only, and it is not for dryland training.

For the first time in my life, I stop by the dorm bathrooms to take a cold shower *before* training. Maybe after practice today, I'll start planning our next date, pour all my fantasies into that instead of walking around with a tent in my pants all the time.

With that plan, I head over to the training facility with a clearer mind and the plan to steer clear of my girlfriend for a few hours. Maybe this dating in secret thing isn't so bad after all. Otherwise, I might've gotten us in trouble publicly a few times already.

I even whistle when I step inside the front door. Only when I find the men's locker room to be completely deserted do I realize something's up.

"Anyone here?" My question echoes around the walls and back to me. I pull my phone from the pocket of my coat and check the time. But I'm not late, like I feared. In fact, I'm ten minutes early. This place should be teeming with guys getting ready to hit the gym.

After I shed all my winter layers, I make my way to the gym and find pandemonium.

Coaching staff from both teams struggle to keep the Strikes and the Bolts away from each other. I recognize Coach Green's hunched back over someone who's lying on the floor. I can't see who, but it's a Strike going by her clothes. One of her legs is bent at an unnatural angle.

The screaming and insults fade away. I stride forward,

fearing that the girl whose season is over is Luz. But I freeze when I find Luz kneeling opposite Coach Green.

The world resumes spinning as she looks up at me. Her face is pale, but she's not the one who's injured. The relief that hits me almost makes me crumple. But then I immediately feel like an ass. Someone else's season just went into the crapper.

"What happened?" No one will care that I sound choked up in these circumstances. I recognize the injured girl. I think her name is JT. One of Luz's friends.

Her jaw is clenched as she tries to hold back what has to be excruciating pain. But even then, she manages to say, "One of your guys did it."

"What?" I look around, trying to find who I need to murder. But I don't even have to go on a whole quest to uncover the culprit when he does it himself.

"It was an accident!" Boucher throws his hands up in the air as if he's talking about a spilled drink. "I just wanted to get her off the machine so I could use it and—"

"You broke her damn leg?" I shout. The edge of my voice is razor sharp, enough to cut through the chaos.

Frankie Boucher hunches over. "It really was an accident."

"You're an asshole," the other one of Luz's friends spits out, with tears in her eyes. "You couldn't just wait your turn like everyone else, huh?"

"Well, she was taking too long…"

"Shut up, Boucher," I bark, running a hand through my hair hard enough to hurt. "Just shut the hell up. Not a single word more."

"That's enough," Coach Young says. "If anyone else utters one more word, you'll be suspended. I don't care if you're a Strike or a Bolt."

"Captains, you're in charge until we come back." Coach Young glares at both of us. I notice that while we were being fools, he and a woman from the Strikes' staff patched up the injured girl enough to take her to the hospital.

"Yes, sir." I ball my fists, watching the procedure without being able to help, feeling like this is very much my fault for not keeping Boucher and his buddies in check.

# CHAPTER 34
## LUZ

After JT was taken to the emergency room by the coaches and the rest of the staff herded us into our respective locker rooms, it took a hot minute for everyone to go from keyed up and wanting to murder somebody to quietly seething. Once that transition was complete, Chelsea was able to tell me what happened.

JT and Boucher got into a verbal fight. It wasn't that Boucher was violent toward her, or at least not intentionally. But as they fought, he tried to pull her away from the leg extension machine, and her leg caught on the mechanism. While she tried to free herself, JT fell down on the other leg and broke it.

The second I walked into the facility, I heard screaming. I raced over to the gym with my heart hammering in my throat, fearing I'd find an axe murderer running rampant. Instead, I found my friend lying on the floor with tears streaming down her face thanks to the excruciating pain. And that jerk Boucher standing over her, a stricken look on his face as if he were innocent of any culpability.

Two hours later, hackles are still raised and feathers are ruffled. I pace up and down the women's locker like a caged lion. We take turns restraining each other every time the urge to go kill Boucher overpowers one of us. I feel it creeping up inside me again.

"Sit down, Captain. You're riling everyone up."

Brit's voice snaps me out of it. I glance around, and sure enough, the scowls around the room would normally be enough to make a grown man cry. Except Frankie Boucher is not a grown man. He's a man-child.

I drop down on my bench and clasp my hands together. One of my knees bounces so violently, it rattles the row of lockers behind me.

When my phone buzzes, I almost confuse it for the noise I'm making. I pick it up and find a text from Coach Young ordering us to go into the big conference room. Typically we use it to review games, discuss plays, and make big schedule changes, but I have a feeling we're headed toward the slaughterhouse this time.

With a bracing breath, I stand up. "Everyone, follow me."

"Where are we going?" Chelsea's voice is a mumble. That's all she's been capable of since earlier.

"Probably to go get our eardrums blown," I respond.

I march us over to the conference room, my steps growing heavier. They're not getting us all here to tell us even worse news, right? Like the injury's so grave JT might never get to play again or something like that, *right?*

It's perfectly warm in the corridor, yet I grow cold as an icicle. I fall back behind the group of Strikes entering the room. I just can't bring myself to go in yet. Rubbing my hands up and down my arms, I tell myself I'm probably overreacting. JT's leg looked bad, yeah, but I shouldn't really project what happened to me onto this incident. I need to cling to hope that she'll pull through without a hitch after a couple of months.

From around the bend, I catch sight of Max herding the Bolts over. His eyes widen, and he halts. One by one, the Bolts stop behind him in time to keep from toppling like dominos. I shut the door to the conference room and head over to him.

He glances back at his guys. "Stay back."

For once they obey, maybe collectively embarrassed by one Bolt's behavior. As they should be.

Max and I meet in the middle. His eyes roam up and down my frame, looking for injuries.

"Hey." His voice is feather-soft. "Are you okay?"

I hug myself and consider putting on a brave front. But there's no point. The concern scrunching up his eyebrows tells me he can see right through me.

"Not really. I'm a mess. Everyone is."

Max takes in a shaky breath. "For what it's worth, I'm sorry. I should've sat Boucher down for a talk a long time ago."

"It's not your fault." I shake my head, which brings into view how the entire Bolts team watches like hawks. "And you know, I shouldn't have fanned the flames so much every time I had a chance."

A corner of his lips rises in a mirthless smile. "You mean if we play with matches, we get burned?"

I know he's speaking in general, but shame consumes me from the inside. So many instances come to mind. Times when I was so damn sure I was doing the right thing, standing my ground, fighting the good fight. I was fanning the flames and got my friend burned—not even myself. There was probably a better way to go about each of those occasions, but hindsight is a jerk, because I still can't see how I could've done better. And in turn, that pisses me off.

Because I realize now that I've been helpless all along, despite all my carefully constructed bravado.

"Luz—"

Whatever Max is about to say gets drowned out by a murmur. I wipe the evidence of tears from my cheeks just before both team coaches appear beside us.

"Everybody in the room," Coach Young says.

When it's clear that this is supposed to be an entire assembly, both teams scoot to opposite sides of the room. No one wants to sit at the table.

Somehow, I'm the first one who finds her voice. "How's JT?"

"Back at her dorm room," Coach Young responds, nodding more to herself than to us. "Transverse fracture. She'll be out for about two months."

Someone shouts, "No!"

But I sag as all the adrenaline leaves my body. That doesn't sound career-ending or life-altering.

"Needless to say, this never should have happened," the Bolts' coach adds, sweeping an angry glance around the room. "It's about time we stop this nonsense rivalry between our teams."

"Oh yeah?" Chelsea snaps. "Would you be saying the same if it had been your star player?" And with that, she points straight at Max.

The thought of him getting even the slightest injury makes my stomach churn.

"Yes, it would be the same." Coach Young's eyes shoot daggers at us. "What do you think is gonna happen if we keep swiping at each other? Someone's gonna get hurt again."

Welp, sounds ominous.

She's not wrong. Never in history has fighting ever led to peace. It escalates and escalates until it becomes obvious that everyone sustains losses that way until someone capitulates. Today could be that day.

But it's not like we were entirely wrong either.

"Coach Young," I call out, my voice surprisingly level even though I feel like crap. "I want to speak. Respectfully. And without being interrupted."

She takes a deep breath and lets it out slowly. "Must you?

We're all on thin ice right now. Faculty caught wind of the incident, and there are calls for suspending the whole program. If what you want to say is going to make matters worse, then please refrain."

That makes panicked murmurs ripple across the room. Suspend the program? What about our scholarships?

It's an effective way to sweep other issues under the rug, though.

I steel my spine and say, "Yes, I still want to talk."

"I agree with Coach Young," the Bolts' coach says, sighing. "Can we just table any further discussions? We have to—"

"No." Every eye in the room turns to Max, who crosses his arms. "I want to hear what Luz has to say."

By the way some of my teammates tense, I suppose they take his interjection as a challenge. But I know better. He's trying to back me up. My composure cracks a bit, and I give him a smile.

"Thank you." I hold on to the back of a chair by the table, trying to arrange the words in my head in the best way possible. I'm not a master of oratory, though, so I end up just winging it. "As the captain of the Strikes, I will speak for them when I say that the biggest reason for this rift is a lack of clear communication and direction.

"From day one, no one knew where each team was supposed to go. In fact, most of us didn't even know there was another team."

Whispers of affirmation come from both ends. They make the coaches exchange a confused glance, as if the last thing they expected was for the Strikes and Bolts to come to a consensus against them.

I mirror Max's stance of arms folded and serious demeanor and continue. "We're all supposed to share the facilities and equipment, but the treatment isn't equal." I grind my teeth, remembering the incident with the buses again. "And that's all we've been asking for, all along. That's the fundamental cause of the problem."

"I agree." Max shrugs at the way his teammates stare at him.

"Are you out of it?" Boucher has the cojones to ask. "We can't accept this out of principle."

"And what principle is that?" Max scrunches up half of his face.

Oh, I love the way Max is baiting Boucher. And of course, the latter bites.

"Hockey is a man's sport! See? Girls are easy to injure. They have no place on the ice unless it's to look pretty."

You could hear a pin drop.

Even his teammates cringe. No matter how many of them may agree deep down, they know better than to spew out backward sexist shit with their whole chest.

"Coach Green." I get his attention with a lot more calm than I feel. "Do you understand what I'm trying to say now?"

Brit snorts. "Yeah, y'all are one second away from a discrimination lawsuit."

"The what now?" one of Max's friends splutters. "No one here is discriminating against anyone."

"Oh yeah?" she spits back. "How would you like to travel on the ratty bus all the time? Or hear crap like this every time you walk these hallways?"

The dude throws his hands up. "See, Coach? It's impossible to get along with them."

"Not that we want to be your friends." Chelsea flips them the bird.

The other one of Max's friends pretty much growls as he says, "Maybe if you want to be treated respectfully, you should extend the same courtesy to others."

"Extend your a—"

"Enough!" I yell with all my lungs. Sucks that my voice

squeaks at the end, but it serves the purpose. The commotion that had started dies down, and everyone's attention turns to me again. Through gritted teeth, I say, "It is possible to get along. You just have to care enough to."

"Yeah, right."

"With these pigs? Never."

"Oink, oink."

I think it's Boucher thinking he's burning anyone by imitating a pig that makes me snap. My brain packs up its bags and jumps out the window. On autopilot, I stride alongside the massive table, eyes set solely on Max.

His eyebrows go up as I grab a fistful of his sweatshirt. "Uh, what are you doing?"

"Fighting fire with fire."

No sooner does the word *huh* escapes his lips, than I pull him toward me into a very public kiss.

"Luz?" Max asks against my lips.

I pull away for a second, ignoring the resounding gasps. "Remember I said we needed to find the right time? Well, it's now."

From this close, I can see the specks of black in the blue of his eyes. He blinks them rapidly. "Well, I did say whenever and wherever."

I forget about everyone else as he wraps those strong arms of his around my waist, bringing me closer for a proper kiss. There's some noise around me, but at this point, I couldn't say what it is.

Max is the one who finds the willpower to tear himself away. The worry in the back of my mind that he'd be annoyed is quashed when I see the glint in his eye.

"Bit drastic, but nothing was really getting through to them, huh?" His lips stretch into a little smirk that makes my toes curl.

"Sorry if you were expecting something more romantic for the grand reveal." I chuckle.

He shakes his head. "Nah, I know by now you're unpredictable."

I lift one shoulder.

"What the hell is this?" a Bolts' alternate captain asks, jaw hanging open.

Max clears his throat, and to the larger group, he says, "Yeah. While you were busy fighting like kindergarteners, we started dating."

"Wow, that's the hottest thing that's come out of your mouth," I say low enough so only he hears.

Max looks down at me, perplexed. "This? Really? Not when I said—"

I cover his mouth with my hand and clear my throat. The amusement in his eyes means I'm not quite off the hook yet, but I need to bring this back full circle.

Even the coaches look shocked.

"Anyway." I step outside the circle of Max's arms but hold on to his hand. "I'm sick and tired of this toxic environment. So if you're not gonna change it, I will. *We* will."

"Damn right." Max tugs at my hand. "Hey, let's leave the kids to fight among themselves. How about we go visit your friend instead?"

"Great idea."

And since both coaches seem to need another moment to make some sense of these events in their heads—or that's what I glean when they don't call out and order us to stay—Max and I walk out of that mess. Together. Hand in hand.

# CHAPTER 35
## MAX

Luz has been playing with my hand for a while. In silence. We sit side by side in the small conference room located in the office area. Usually, this room is used for one-on-ones or for staff meetings only, which makes this feel weird. Like maybe Coach Green and Coach Young are banding together to boot Luz and me as captains.

Maybe that's why Luz's lips have remained zipped. And even though it's warm in here, her hands feel like icicles against mine. She runs a finger down the lines of my palm, the other hand cradling mine.

Trying to break the ice, I ask, "Are you trying to see if our love lines are compatible or something like that?"

She blinks up at me. "Actually, no. I was just seeing how much bigger your hand is. But you have a good point. Maybe I should check."

A small smile creeps over her face as I lace our fingers together. Shit, she feels freezing. I shift to cover both her hands in mine instead.

"What's going on, Tinker Bell?" I tilt my head to observe her expression. I can see she's trying hard not to show whatever it is. "I'm nervous too, but… I don't think I've ever seen you this quiet."

Her shoulders shrink just a bit, but the moment she opens her mouth to speak is when both coaches enter the meeting room. I pull our hands under the table but don't let go of her. Something's up, and I want her to know I'm here for her every second.

"Sorry we're late." Coach Green pulls up the chair across from me and plops down with a sigh. "Those guys from the board would not stop talking."

Coach Young follows suit, taking a seat across from her captain. "The good news first. The program is not getting suspended."

"Oh, thank goodness," I say, and I think Luz may have just said the same beside me, but in Spanish.

"Boucher is getting a two-month suspension," Coach Green adds. "So I guess both teams are down a man."

"A player." Coach Young corrects him with a sidelong glance. "We're both down a player."

"Right." He clears his throat, but it doesn't mask the steady rise of red up his neck and face. "So, uh. That's another thing we have agreed upon. Some education. We'll have a professor from the Women's Study department come give Bolts and Strikes a special class on inclusion topics. Staff included."

For the first time this afternoon, Luz perks up. "Oh, that sounds great. And Frankie Boucher will take it too, right?"

"Mandatory for everyone," Coach Young confirms with a nod. "Moreover, we have agreed to use the facilities and equipment according to team needs. So, for example, that means that if the Strikes have an away game that is farther than the Bolts' game, we'll get the bigger bus. And the other way around."

"Yes." Luz lets go of me to pump her fist under the table. I have to bite back my smile.

"These are all great things. But, uh, Rodriguez and I had a talk earlier, and there's something we want to know."

"What's that?" Coach Young glances from Luz to me. Her eyebrows arch, as if she still can't quite believe that the leaders of two formerly warring factions are dating.

I glance at the Strikes captain, wondering if she wants to say the next part. But she nods at me. Below the table, she squeezes my hand.

I focus back on the coaches. "We'll be honest. We both feel pretty guilty about how everything went down. I wasn't as clear with my team as I should've been about what was out of line. Luz maybe wasn't as… cool-headed as she could've been."

"Not maybe." Her brow scrunches up. "I definitely wasn't."

She shouldn't pout like that in public. Makes me want to kiss her.

"Anyway." I fix my stare forward. "So we would like to know, point blank, what the consequences are for us."

There. Now they can rip off the Band-Aid. I take a deep breath and brace myself.

"Well. I personally like this united front and the account-ability behind it," Coach Young starts, pronouncing the words slowly, as if she needs more time to think about the topic. "But since this was purely an accident with no premeditated ill will, there are no sanctions other than Boucher's suspension."

Coach Green drums his fingers on the table, as if needing an outlet. "Things will be changing around here, though. That much is obvious. And as the leaders of both teams, you two will have to set the example."

"We'll do better," I say, feeling the weight of those words settle on my shoulders.

"Absolutely." The second Luz confirms this, I feel lighter already.

We smile at each other. Maybe she feels it too, the relief at having each other. Like lightning striking twice in the same spot. Because it's one thing to go to the same college, but it's another one to meet each other and fall in love. We might be on different teams, but the two of us are forming our own team now.

"Great." The Bolts' Coach nods. "Elaine and I are going to work together more closely too."

"That's right. We'll come up with a plan going forward, but for now, those are all the updates," Coach Young says, making it very clear that we're dismissed.

"Get some rest before this weekend's games." Coach Green waves us toward the door.

"Thanks." I stand up.

It takes Luz a good moment to follow suit. She offers a tight-lipped smile. "We appreciate your time."

I keep mum as I open the door for us, and even as we walk together across the office area and out. My eyes keep shifting to her every few seconds.

The coast is clear once we're in the hallway, so I pull her into the equipment room where we occasionally hide in for a quick make-out session. And I lock the door just in case. The last thing we need is to stir up more drama when the dust is finally settling.

"Okay. You're freaking me out. What's happening, Tinker Bell?"

Her whole face scrunches up and she hunches over. "Ugh, my back's killing me today."

I freeze. "Are you okay? Is there anything I can do? How about a massage? Should I call the PT? Is it severe? Can I—"

"Sheesh. Calm your tits, okay?" She lifts a hand, but a bit more life is coming to her expression now. I take it as a sign that it's not bad enough that she needs to go to the hospital. Which I may yet suggest.

"My tits are calm." I clench my pecs like that's enough confirmation.

"Stop. I don't want to laugh. It'll hurt more."

I rush over to her, placing my hands on her shoulders delicately. "Seriously, I'm worried. Is this my fault?"

"How, exactly?" She's looking at me like I've lost the plot.

Funny, because that's exactly how I feel as I say, "Remember what happened a few minutes before the meeting, right here in this room?"

"Ah, yes." Luz nods, her expression serious. "When you pushed me up against that shelf over there and basically devoured my mouth. I have a vague recollection."

I cringe so hard, I probably shrink to half my size. "Uh, I should be more careful with you. I'm sorry. I just hadn't seen you all day and—"

"Hush, you adorable doofus." Luz puts a cold finger on my lips to shut me up. "And no, it's not your fault. The pain has been flaring up since this morning. I had a nightmare and woke up in a funny position, but more than that, I think it's just all the stress between exams and this whole mess. Plus, Aran told me that Mom and Dad will come watch tomorrow's game and… frankly, I'm nervous. Especially because, um…"

She bites her lip and not in the sexy kind of way, but in the I'm-barely-holding-it-together kind of way.

"Luz?"

Taking a deep breath, she says, "The team we'll face off tomorrow is where the girl who gave me the bad hit plays." She folds her arms, almost trying to make herself smaller. "I should be over it, but I had nightmares about the accident last night, and lo and behold, it's made my back act up."

Air hisses through my teeth. Slowly, and with a loose grip, I circle my arms around her. Looking down at her with a cocked eyebrow, I ask, "Is there something I can do to reduce the stress?"

I've noticed she likes to rest her chin on my chest, and she does that now.

"If my back didn't hurt like a toothache, I would answer that question honestly."

"There must be something *else* I can do." I run my hand up and down her back, keeping the touch light. Maybe it soothes her a bit, because she fully leans against me for a moment and just lets me continue. And then a light goes off in my head. "Luz?"

"Hmm?"

"What about an ice bath?"

Her voice is muffled against my chest. "Nooo."

"Huh, so you did think about it?"

"I hate ice baths." She straight-up whines now. "I've had to take so many of them and—ugh."

I pat her head. "Let's get you one."

*

After that, Luz tries to ghost me, but I know exactly where she lives. It's dark out by the time I pull into the parking lot of the women's dorm. I send Luz a text saying I'm here, but it's her roommate who opens the building door for me.

"She told me not to tell you that she's really in a lot of freaking pain right now." Those words are her greeting to me. "But her whining and whimpering are really distracting me from studying, so I will help you kidnap her."

On the way up, I learn that her name is Lynn, that she's single, and that if I have any clones, I should give them her number. Unfortunately, the only relative around our age who is still single is Leo, and I wouldn't foist that pain in the ass upon my worst enemy.

We make it to their dorm, and I knock on the door. "Tinker Bell, you ready?"

I hear some shuffling before she opens the door. The first thing I notice is her hair up in a bun. The second thing is the big bundle under her arm. And the third is the training clothes under a zip up jacket.

Fourth? She's as pale as a blank sheet of paper.

"C'mon." I tug her by the hand. Luz drags her feet, her sneakers making a racket in the quiet.

"Finally, peace and quiet," Lynn mutters as we leave the room.

I would laugh, except Luz really looks like she's on her way to the slaughterhouse the entire drive around campus to the facility. It's quiet this time of night. Most people are probably cramming for exams. We head past the empty gym to the back, where the shared therapy facilities are. I prepped the ice bath in advance to minimize the odds of Luz running away, and I can tell she's contemplating it as she glares at the filled-up tub.

"Just so you know," she says while unzipping her jacket and taking it off, "I really appreciate your efforts, but I'm also very pissed."

"You're free to be pissed, as long as you get better."

With one last glare, she lowers herself to sit in the freezing water, legs out. Her body locks as she leans back to submerge her back, and a few squeaks make it past her lips. The tub is big enough that she can rest her neck on the edge and keep her torso under water. She wraps her arms around herself and shivers.

I kneel down by her head, looking at her upside down. Pushing a strand of hair off her wrinkled-up forehead, I say, "Maybe you should sit out of tomorrow's game."

"No. Never. It would be like giving in to my parents and to everyone that this is stronger than I am." Her body tightens at the thought. "But even more, it would be like giving in to my own fear."

Leaning down, I kiss her forehead. "Resting doesn't take away from your strength, you know? In fact, I hear it replenishes it."

Luz frowns up at me. "Do you also think I'm being reckless? And that I should quit playing?"

I think about it carefully, and not just because her eyes clearly show that she's close to directing her anger at me. Even then, I can't lie to her.

"I just…" I pause, trying to find the right words. "I can't physically take the pain away. And knowing you're suffering really sucks."

Luz bites her lower lip, which snags my attention for a second before she speaks. "That's probably how my parents feel, huh? Except, funny enough, I don't want to blow your ears off about it."

I beam down at her. "It's probably because of my devastating good looks."

Her eyes narrow. "Annoying, but you're right."

Chuckling, I lean over to give her a quick upside-down kiss. But before I pull away entirely, she clasps my head in her freezing-cold wet hands, forcing me to kiss her for a moment longer. I've been sitting kind of sideways, with a leg tucked under my weight, and the position is so awkward I end up plunging my hands into the icy water to keep myself from collapsing on top of her.

I don't mind freezing my hands off if it means I can kiss her properly. I tilt my head sideways so my chin doesn't push against her nose. Pressing with my lips, I open her mouth. Her hands circle up to the back of my head, fingers threading through my hair. When I swipe my tongue against hers, Luz groans, and it echoes against the tiles all around us.

"Damn," I say against her lips. "If you keep making sounds like that, we're gonna get in trouble."

Luz vibrates with laughter. "We definitely don't want that. Help me up."

After some finagling, we get her standing away from the tub and wrapped in a big towel while I work on draining it.

"Thank you."

Bent over, I swivel to glance at her. "What for, specifically? I've been such a great boyfriend today overall, you know."

Her lips twitch. "For worrying about me so much."

"It's in the job description."

Then her arms wrap around me from behind. I try to turn, but she squeezes tighter. "Will you come watch me play tomorrow?"

I rub my hands up and down her arms, although I don't know how much my own cold hands can warm her skin. "Only if you come to watch my game the day after."

"Deal."

"And every other game you can."

She laughs a bit. "Also deal. But also, if you become my very own cheerleader too."

"Buying the pompons already."

I feel her kiss the middle of my back. "Infuriating, adorable boy."

"How did you know my middle names?" This time she lets me turn around. I wrap the terry cloth around her frame tighter. "Let's go get you changed. You have an important game tomorrow."

Maybe she feels better already, because the smile reaches her eyes like none have all day. I vow to myself to do whatever I can to keep it on her face.

# CHAPTER 36
## LUZ

"Rodriguez."

I stop a second before sliding onto the ice and turn. Coach Young hung back with me at the end of the line, refreshing some of the strategies we'll use for this game, but I thought we were done when the conversation stalled a minute ago while she made some notes. The Northeastern Sirens team is the best in the conference, but our track record so far is good enough that we may stand a chance.

My heart's been beating wildly at that prospect—that, and because I know my family's somewhere in the stands.

"Yes, Coach?"

She's using that stare that is supposed to see right through me. "How's your back?"

Everyone else is already on the ice, skating around the inner circle of the arena. The Sirens skate the outer one, riling up their home audience.

I shift closer to my coach for this conversation. "How did you know it's been flaring up?"

"I know everything."

I'm sure she does. Clearing my throat, I say, "I visited the PT this morning, and she cleared me to play."

"Do you see me asking her?" She shakes her head. "How do *you* feel?"

I bite my lower lip. I'm not at a hundred percent, or what that normally looks like for me. My chronic pain is something I live with every day, but sometimes I almost forget it's even there. On those days, it's easy to pretend like nothing happened six years ago. Like I'm just a regular athlete. But some days, like earlier this week, it very much reminds me that I'm not. And I never will be.

It took me a long time to accept that's just the way it is for me. It took me a very short time to understand that on the bad days, I still deserve to have a life. That I don't want to be treated with kid gloves or looked at with pity. None of that is going to take the pain away, and it pisses me off. That was the biggest source of problem I had with my parents.

And then there's Max. He did what he could to comfort me when the pain flared up. But in the end, he left the choice to me. He trusted that I knew my body better than him.

I focus back on Coach Young. "Today is much better. I feel good enough to play."

I don't even have to brace for the typical patronizing response. All she does is nod.

"Good. You'll let me know if that status changes. Now off you go."

Off I don't go. Instead, blinking back sudden tears, I grab her arm just as she's turning to the bench. "Coach, can I ask you something?"

"What's that?"

"Um." I swallow the lump in my throat and pull my gloved hand away from her. "Even though you've known about my chronic pain from the beginning... why did you recruit me?"

Overhead, a presenter with a mic says something. A wave

of applause explodes in the arena, and the lights turn on all the way. We're probably about to line up and sing the anthem, but I don't want to leave without an answer.

"Pain issues are not uncommon in sports. But—" Coach Young pauses, as if choosing her words carefully. "You're one of the strongest athletes I've met. Mentally. And I wanted that on my team."

"Thanks, Coach."

Before I start bawling my eyes out, I slide onto the ice and join the Strikes' line. We're short a JT, but she tagged along in the big team bus and is in the stands. Sure enough, I spot her easily thanks to the gigantic poster she made. It has a blue background and more yellow glitter than a single craft store had available—she went to two. It reads *STRIKE THE MATCH!* and I love it.

I try to spot the Rodriguez clan, but then the first notes of the anthem hit, and I have to face forward. Across from me is the Sirens' captain. She's looking at me, wide-eyed, as if I'm a truck headed her way at full speed. And as awesome as it feels to inspire awe in an opponent, this is bizarre.

Then it strikes me like lightning. She's taller than me, with a light brown ponytail draped over her shoulder and eyes that match. Her front tooth has a familiar chip. This is the girl who gave me the bad hit that damaged my spinal cord. I knew we'd be playing each other tonight, but I didn't expect a close encounter this early.

My mouth goes as dry as cotton, and I break into a sweat. I feel it trickle down my back under the many layers I'm wearing. I wish I could scratch it. Shit, the pain is coming back with a vengeance.

The anthem ends, and everyone falls into position. I'm supposed to do the faceoff, but I'm stuck staring at this girl. The memories flood back.

It was one of those games in middle school where I played

really, really well, so this girl had it out for me. She would chase me up and down the ice, even abandoning her position if it meant she could block me from scoring. In a tussle, I accidentally elbowed her face and chipped her tooth.

A big discussion between her parents and the refs ensued about what to do with me. Her parents demanded I get kicked out of the game altogether. We were just twelve-year-old girls, not professional hockey players. But in the end, it had been an accident. The refs gave me time in the bin, and I went back out to play. And rather than leaving the game to go fix the tooth issue I gave her, she came after me with a dirty hit.

I still remember her expression when I came to, sprawled on the ice, unable to move. It was the same horror she's looking at me with right now.

"It's you," she says, her voice barely above a whisper.

That snaps me back to this moment. I grind my teeth and squeeze my hand around the handle of my stick. Anything I can do to ground myself. Because the scenes in my head were six years ago, but now is now.

"Yeah, it's me."

She does a double take. "How…"

How can I still play? Everyone keeps asking.

It's stranger that *she* is asking me now. I'm not a budding celebrity like my boyfriend, so it's not like I expected her to have read the news articles about my case. But it's weird to find out she's probably gone all these years believing she took away my ability to play, maybe even move. And like maybe she didn't pay much attention to the Strikes' roster in preparation for this game, and my presence is fully catching her off guard.

Then I see—really see—that there's as much pain in her expression as there is in my back. Almost as if she's grappling with guilt. For how little I've wanted to think about the girl who injured me, I realize in this moment that I've always dismissed her as a two-bit villain in my soap opera. But maybe she's as scared and clueless as I am.

The ref catches my attention, unable to wait a second longer to start the game. I take a deep breath and respond. "I'll show you how."

I get into position for the faceoff. My back feels a bit stiff as I bend forward, but I channel all my emotions into my muscles. Perfectly balanced on my legs and the blade of my stick. A different Siren glares at me as if I stole the last slice of her pizza. Instead, I gift her a feral grin.

The puck drops, and I battle for it like my life depends on it, as if this is the last game of my career. I win the biscuit for my team, and the one who gets it is Chelsea. She plays like the Sirens owe her money. Her attempt at a slapshot not even thirty seconds into the game sets the pace for everyone else.

A few plays later, the puck returns to me, and I come alive. I can see a fairly clear path to the Sirens' goal if I zigzag past two defense players. I send the puck to one of my teammates, but it doesn't take the heat off me. One Siren is determined to be in my way. The poor sucker thinks she stands a chance. She even goes as far as to put her stick in the way of my skates.

I jump it. I can picture Max laughing and calling me Tinker Bell. The queen of the ice sounds cooler, but the fairy on ice doesn't have as bad a ring as I previously thought. I'm up against one more defensive Siren, and it's that girl again, returned from my memories in the flesh, as if life wanted to make me afraid again.

No gracias, mija.

I intercept a pass. The girl is more focused on trying to stop me than on the puck, so I dangle it between her legs. A shout from the stands sounds a lot like my boyfriend. Like maybe he liked that play. My path to the goal isn't clear anymore. There are a lot of bodies between it and me. But my teammates are fighting to clear the way. And then I see it. A hole in the goalie's stance that comes and goes with the motions.

Before I think too hard, I swing my stick and snipe.

There's a fraction of a second where the kerfuffle obstructs my view. But then the buzzer goes off.

I throw my hands up in the air with a scream. It morphs into a wail as Strikes slam against me into a group hug like we just won the world championship and the credits are about to roll. I feel like crying and screaming some more, but the game goes on.

We fight with all our might against the Sirens. Every faceoff is a gladiator fight. Every inch of ice is a conquest. The boards see a lot of action, but even then, no one lands in the sin bin. Which means neither team gets a reprieve. I forget all about my family in the stands, because every second of this game counts toward the goal of winning. This isn't like any game at the start of the season. Winning against the best team in the conference will put the Strikes on the map.

Every cell in my body is focused on that. The pain is still probably there, throbbing like a toothache. But right now, all I care about is keeping the score in our favor.

When the final buzz blows, I can barely believe it. I look up at the scoreboard, and the fight drains out of my body. I don't even know how I'm not falling backward.

Because one to zero, we won. My early goal won us the toughest game of the season.

"Yeah!" One of my teammates slams into me. Fortunately, a second one appears on the opposite side to keep me upright.

There's a lot of booing around the arena, but underneath the noise, I hear my name. Over a teammate's helmet, I glance around and finally spot them thanks to my S'more.

Max waves his arms around, and it's impossible to miss him. He's ginormous. Beside him, Aran is clapping—which is huge coming from him. Then there's Aceituna, her hands around her mouth while she hollers my name. Hers was the incessant voice piercing through the booing. Next to her is her best friend, Brooklyn. He keeps high-fiving my mom, who jumps in turn as if she has too much energy to contain in her small body.

And last, there's Dad. He wipes his eyes with the back of a hand, and then the other, because tears apparently won't stop falling.

The lump in my throat rises with a wail. Right there, in the middle of the ice, I break down in tears.

# CHAPTER 37
## MAX

"How's your condition?" my girlfriend asks. The question itself makes sense, considering I'm about to go play against my nephew again and our entire family is in the stands. What's abnormal about it is the way she asks.

Currently, my face is smooshed between her hands. Which also means I'm forced to be bent over to her level. The position is uncomfortable, and we keep getting wolf whistles from the guys in the locker room who are spying from the open door. I should probably be annoyed.

Instead, I'm trying really hard to not pick her up, slam her against the wall, and have my way with her. She's wrapped in winter clothes like a burrito and all I can see is her face and hair cascading over her shoulders. Even then, my blood is thrumming in my body.

I take a deep breath and wrap my hands around her wrists. Slowly, I pull them down until we're holding hands between us. At a decent distance. Our big off-campus date is tomorrow, and honestly, I'm looking forward to that a lot more than to this game.

Married to hockey, my ass. In a matter of months, Tinker Bell has dethroned what, for years, I believed to be my one true love.

Sighing, I say, "Condition's fine. The issue is more that I keep getting distracted—"

"I know you must be nervous because they're all here, but don't give them that power." There's a big wrinkle between her eyebrows. Her lips pinch with all the seriousness of her feelings. "Listen, Max. You've been appearing in those articles about up-and-coming talent for years. Even your lousiest performance is stellar compared to everyone else's. You don't have to try too hard to impress them, okay? Don't go and get injured on me because of some outrageous play."

A funny pang in my chest leads me to bend down again. This time, I place a quick kiss on her lips. "Thank you."

"Did that help? Because I can still hype you up some more." She pulls one hand away to count with her fingers. "First, you're a S'more, remember? Who doesn't like S'mores? Second, you're *my* S'more, which is even better." By that point, I'm a hairbreadth away from losing my mind, but if Luz notices it, she ignores it. "Third, you're a really, really sexy S'more. I've been trying really hard not to stare at you, but I'm failing—"

"Wait, what?" I start laughing. Like a hyena.

In contrast, she frowns. "Did you not see yourself before stepping out of the locker room?"

I didn't have time to. Before she started shouting for me, I'd been about to put my top pads and jersey on. Right now, I'm in full uniform and skates from the waist down and a performance shirt above the waist. The top is thin and very tight, and I've noticed how her dark eyes keep straying down every so often.

I cock an eyebrow. "Eyes up here, Tinker Bell."

"No." If anything, her expression looks even grumpier. "Let me just get my fill for a second."

I step back and stand up straighter, bending an arm one way and the other in the opposite direction like body builders do. Luz snorts through her nose, but she doesn't stop staring. I know that Coach and the rest of the staff are in the locker room already, and this area isn't accessible to the wider public. So I get a little more daring. Her eyes pop open as I lift my shirt just a little bit, enough to expose the abs she seems to like so much.

"Was that enough or do you need a little more?"

Fast like lightning, Luz jumps at me to stay my hands. Her breath is rushed, as if she ran a mile instead of just one step. "Are you trying to kill me?"

"I thought people called this fan service."

"Big fan, the biggest, but—" She shakes her head. "I'm here to hype *you* up, not the other way around."

"But what if I don't feel sufficiently hyped?" My exaggerated pout makes her frown.

"You mean my grand speech wasn't enough?"

"It was a great effort. But something's missing." I lean back against the wall and pull her up against me. Her hands fall against my chest, which I also know she likes. And sure enough, she can't help splaying her fingers wider and pressing a little harder. I wrap my arms around her waist just enough to leave no room between us, but without hurting her.

"Hmm, what's that?" Luz leans against me until only the wall behind me keeps us upright.

My answer is leaning down for a kiss. Her hand is warm as it holds the side of my face, tilting it so I can kiss her deeper.

That's when Nate chooses to walk out. "Ugh, stop being so damn in love in front of other people! It's offensive."

"Stop being so jealous," Conor calls out from nearby.

I pull away, my forehead against Luz's. "Ignore them."

"Always."

Now, more seriously, I say, "Thank you for being my person."

She offers a dazzling smile. "Always." Reaching on her tiptoes, she pecks my lips. "Now, suit up and go kick ass."

"Yes, ma'am."

I do quick work of suiting up all the way but still end up at the back of the line on our way over to the ice.

"How do you even have time to date, man?" Nate shakes his head beside me. "I can barely keep up with school and training."

I shrug, the movement barely perceptible under pads and a jersey. "It helps that Luz is basically in both of those worlds."

Conor, who has been following the conversation in front of us, glances over his shoulder. "So you're saying we should date Strikes?" He makes it sound as if it's the most horrifying prospect.

"That's it." Nate hits the floor with his stick. "I'm asking Brit Thomas out."

"Good luck, buddy." Conor pats his shoulder with a gloved hand. "You'll need it."

"Yeah, I know. She's way out of my league."

Huh, so maybe Luz and I will have a different problem on our hands. Rather than things returning to how they were before The Incident, maybe we'll end up with a bunch of couples. And if they're anything like Luz and me, they'll have trouble tearing themselves away from each other enough to focus on the game.

I used to only come alive when I stepped onto the ice. When the frigid wind rushed against my face as I skated with all the power in my legs. When the puck connected with the blade of my stick with a cracking sound. When I buried the disk in the net. But now my heart beats as fast when I'm with

Luz. Now I don't feel like hockey is my only reason. I just have more reasons to be better.

The second I slide onto the ice, I feel the answer to Luz's question viscerally. Condition? Never been better.

The home arena is at about half capacity, which is the biggest attendance I've seen so far. By the looks of it, the St. Cloud student body seems to be finally coming around to how cool it is to have a team in the house. One of those is my roommate. He sits with a couple of his econ buddies.

Just a section beyond him, I spot my whole family—sans Alessio, who returned home right after Thanksgiving. Cossimo Jr. holds a big, custom-made sign with Leo's Bulldog jersey printed on it. He takes the thing to every one of Leo's games so his son can easily find him in the stands.

I used to want that, but now it doesn't matter. The fact that Mom and Dad are here is already a miracle in itself. And yeah, I can't lie to myself—I am a bit nervous about it.

Luz is right, though. This isn't amateur hours. It might be their first or second hockey game, but it isn't mine. I'm cool as a cucumber as I get in place for the faceoff against Leo. After tonight, one of us will reign supreme on this ice, and the king will be me.

He gives me a feral grin. "Ready to embarrass yourself?"

I laugh. "Ready to call me Uncle?"

It's pretty sweet how it makes him grind his molars.

The grueling training we've endured since the summer has paid dividends, because even though our first game against the Bulldogs *was* embarrassing, it's clear we're dominating this one from the first period.

For me, the highlight comes at the top of the second period. Sometimes my vision is a bit like a video game. A target visible only to me hangs over the net, and I can find it, I can feel it, no matter where I am on the ice. I skate up to it with a clear intent to kill, because all of a sudden, it feels like there are more Bull-dogs in my way than on the entire ice. I deke one guy so bad he'll have to go home and cry to his momma. And then Leo appears.

The last time he skated over intending to barrel through me, I ended up flipping him over into the air. But maybe my mom will get pissed if I do that, and today, I'm really feeling my stick handling.

Just before he's in my range, I slide the puck wide. It looks like a pass. Confusion slows his roll, but it fuels mine. I pull a Tinker Bell and use some fancy edge work to slide around Leo. Barely grabbing the butt end of the stick, I pull the puck back to me, and it's a breakaway.

Most beautiful goal I've ever scored, and also not the only one in the game.

By the time the final buzz goes off, the St. Cloud Thunder Bolts win, five to two. Three of them were mine.

Coach Green is hoarse again, but this time from cele-brating so much. It feels like a special victory considering we were down Boucher, who is a pretty good D-man, even if he's not really a good person. And with all the drama he caused, it feels great to finally be on track.

"See what happens when you put your minds to it?" Coach asks with what's left of his voice while inside the locker. "You stop sucking, that's what!"

No one said he was great at giving speeches or that he's a perfect person, but he's sure the best coach I've ever had. And maybe one day I'll thank him for recruiting me, because other-wise I wouldn't have left my nephew in the dust like I did tonight. I also wouldn't have met Luz.

I take the world's quickest shower and break the barrier of sound with how fast I get dressed afterward. Earlier, Tinker Bell said she'd wait right outside the training facility. We'll go to O'Malley's with the others to celebrate—and to pregame for tomorrow. I can't wait to hear her play-by-play analysis of my performance.

But instead of just my girlfriend, I find her standing beside the entire Cassiano family. Luz rocks on the balls of her feet, which tells me something's up.

My parents, my brothers, their wives and kids, and even Leo stand outside, blowing puffs into the cold December air. I can't believe I'm irritated that Leo changed faster than me. Maybe one day I'll stop being such a petty baby about him, but not today. Today I'm annoyed.

I glance from Tinker Bell back to the others. "Uh, what are you all doing here?"

Mom steps out of the line to give Leo a pointed look. It's the kind that says his head will get acquainted with the broomstick *unless*.

Leo clears his throat, jams his hands into the pockets of his down coat, and buries his face in his scarf.

From behind my sister-in-law, my baby niece says, "C'mon, Leo. I'm hungry."

"Fine." He clears the rasp from his throat. "Good game... Uncle Max."

Beside him, my eldest brother nods. "Yeah. You played good, piccolo. Maybe I'll make a poster with your jersey too."

Leo glares at him. "Dad."

"I said maybe."

Maria, my other sister-in-law, engulfs me in a quick but hearty hug. "You were unbelievable."

"For real, Max," says Alessandro with a frown. "Why didn't you tell us you were that good?"

I give him a deadpan look. "Would you have listened?"

"We're listening now, son."

The biggest surprise of the night comes right then, when my parents drape themselves around me on each side. And even despite our puffy coats or the massive bag hanging from my shoulder, neither let me go for a good while. I'm taller than either of them, and I can easily see my girlfriend beaming up at me like she had something to do with this.

And she must have. I can't remember the last time my parents hugged me like this.

I'm still blinking like an owl as they pull away. Mom pushes my hair out of my face and says, "Now, let's go home. I'm going to feed you the spaghetti bolognese you like. You're too skinny."

I end up ditching O'Malley's for dinner with my whole family, which now includes my girlfriend.

# CHAPTER 38
## LUZ

**M**y plans of sneaking a quiet, early skate, are thwarted the second I arrive at the arena and find some guy skating alone on the ice.

With a huff, I lean over the edge of the boards to watch him. He's a pretty decent skater, with powerful thighs that his training pants can't hide. They push him to speeds I couldn't compete with even if my technique is better. I could maybe teach him a thing or two, but for now, I'd rather observe.

He handles the stick like an extension of his body, using it to make sharp turns while balanced on the inside foot. His black hair waves against the wind, clear away from his flushed face. I bet his freckles look stark against the paleness of his skin.

Ugh, he's so beautiful it hurts to look at him.

Since the arena is empty except for us, I start catcalling. "Hey, sexy! Why don't you give me a show, huh?"

Max brakes with such force the spray casts a quick rainbow under the light. He puts his gloved hands on that tiny waist of his. "Now that's just disrespectful. Wanna come over and be disrespectful together?"

I don't even wait to open the door. Instead, I slide over it and pump my legs until I slam against his chest. We slide over the ice, but Max is too strong to let us topple over.

"Good morning, Tinker Bell." He places a little kiss on my nose, and I squeeze my arms tighter around him.

"Will you ever stop calling me Tinker Bell?"

"Nope."

"Okay, fine. I'll call you S'more more often."

He shrugs. "Didn't you say that means I'm delicious?"

I choke on my own saliva. And after that, I can't recover fast enough to bite back with a smart-aleck comment. Max throws his head back, laughing at his own joke with all his might. I'd mind it more if the motion didn't give me a prime-time view of the thick chords of muscle up the column of his neck. A hickey just under the collar of his jacket reminds me of the last time I thoroughly appreciated that part of his anatomy too.

"Cat got your tongue, Tinker Bell?"

"No." My voice comes out way raspier than it has any business being. "Just remembering the last time it was on your skin."

Max hisses. His entire expression shifts away from amusement. I recognize the intensity in his eyes. It goes hand in hand with how every muscle of his body grows taut.

"Where did all the teasing go, Cassiano?" I bet my smile looks positively predatory.

He swallows with difficulty.

With a chuckle, I pull away from him to retrieve the stick I dropped on my way to him. If not for special practice starting in forty minutes or so, I would drag him into an empty corner for an extensive make-out session.

When I turn back around, he has one glove tucked between his elbow and his ribs, and he runs his free hand through his hair. The resulting mess only makes him look better.

I can't believe this silly, adorable, far-too-hot guy who irritates me to no end is actually my boyfriend. How did I get so lucky?

Clearing my throat, I say, "Anyway, your skating's pretty good, but it could be so much better. Luckily, I can help with that."

"Only with that?" The corner of his lip goes up, making that little dimple appear. A flash of awareness travels down to the tips of my toes, and I can feel sweat trickling down my back like it's a magic trick.

"Mind out of the gutter, Cassiano."

"Whose fault is it? I was just here, minding my own business, before you came over with the clear intent to seduce innocent little me." Max goes as far as crossing his hands over his chest, as if to protect his modesty.

I snort through my nose. "Innocent my butt."

"Speaking of your butt, I quite like the way it fits in my hands."

"Who's seducing who now?" Unfortunately, Max knows just how wild he can make me with just a single kiss. It's a power I wish I wouldn't have given him, because it's made him even more dangerous than he already was.

We discard our sticks and gloves near the center line. I lace my fingers with his, and we circle around the rink at a leisurely pace, like two lovesick fools on an ice skating date. Max tells me what he has in mind for the special training, and I share my ideas in return. I wasn't bragging earlier when I said my skating skills are better than his. I honed them through desperate blood, sweat, and tears. He's more than happy to leave that section of the training to me.

"And seriously," I add. "You really do need to improve your edge work. It will give you more range of attack when you're able to basically skate in any direction in any situation."

With a side glance, he says, "I know. I also know you'll be my best teacher ever."

My chest puffs up with pride, but I want to throw him a bone too.

"I'll admit your stick-handling skills are superior, though—stop giving me that look, you perv."

With a tug, Max pulls me up against the boards and leans against me. "I can't help it, Luz. You make me electric."

Sighing, I slide my hands up his arms and broad shoulders until I find the short hair at the back of his head. And I bring him closer to me.

Against his lips, I whisper, "Funny, you have the exact same effect on me."

I'll never tire of how his lips feel against mine. Like a promise of the future and a threat to my sanity all at once. They're enough to make me forget where I am, enough to make me lose control in my own skin. I open my mouth wide to let him in, and Max doesn't waste a second. Our breaths mingle, and the warmth travels to every cell in my body. In a matter of seconds, I'm the human version of a melted candle in his arms.

Max tears a guttural sound from my throat when I feel his hands pressing against my butt, pushing me against him until I have no choice but to wrap my legs around his waist. Feeling his smile against my lips sends my pulse skyrocketing to new heights.

"Max." His name comes out like a moan. "This is a dangerous game we're playing."

"I know." His face is buried in my neck. One of his sneaky, sneaky hands lowers the zipper of my jacket. He settles it right on my side. Another promise and threat. "And I'll stop soon."

But I don't let him. I bury my hands in his hair and keep him firmly in place. Max continues kissing my neck like it's my mouth. His own is open, his tongue lashing at my skin, his teeth nibbling.

Mierda, we really need to stop.

I pat his shoulder until he gets the hint. Slowly, he lowers me back down until my skates are firmly on the ice. Our bodies are still glued to each other.

With trembling hands, I fix his hair to make him more presentable. There's no hiding the flush on our faces or the swollen lips, but it won't help to give anyone any further ideas. The fact that his hands are still firmly on my hips as I work doesn't help. I let my hands rest on his chest. His heart thumps at a frantic rhythm.

Biting my lip, I say, "Have I mentioned you make me wild?"

"Once or twice." His voice comes out husky, which absolutely doesn't help calm me down.

"And have I mentioned I love you?"

He startles a bit. "Uh, I think this is the first time."

"Of many." I smile.

As if reading my mind, he leans down for another kiss. Except he stops just as our lips barely touch. His eyes are at half-mast as they bore into mine. His voice envelops me like warm velvet as he says four words.

"I love you too."

Simple words. Life-changing, nonetheless.

Just as he presses his lips against mine again, a sudden bang echoes around the arena.

We jump away from each other, as if what we were doing wasn't obvious. Without Max, I have a hard time keeping upright on legs that have turned to noodles. Only the boards behind me save me from an embarrassing tumble. He isn't as lucky. One of the best center forwards of the league falls on his behind like a child just learning to skate.

His buddy Nate explodes in laughter. "Whoa, I can't believe what my eyes are witnessing."

"Stop sounding so jealous, Garcia," I shout back at him. But from this close, Max can see how I'm about to lose it too. Especially if he keeps scowling like that.

Max gets up and dusts the slush off his delectable bubble butt. "You're early, man."

"So are you all," says a different voice behind Nate Garcia.

He steps aside to let more people through. At the forefront, sitting on a conference chair pushed by Chelsea and Brit, is none other than JT. She looks every bit the queen on her throne, even though her leg in a cast protrudes forward almost comically.

Right behind her is Max's other friend, Conor Mahoney. He shakes his head as if he doesn't approve of the arrangement. But Chelsea and Brit are the queens of chaos, and I have a strong feeling that Nate Garcia gives them a run for their money.

"I'm really excited to witness this special training session brought to us by our two captains, who look like they really want to improve relations between the two teams." JT smirks at us.

The innuendo is not lost on anyone, especially on the still-cackling Nate. "Oh, they're working on those relations, all right. And I got it all on the record." He puts his phone back in his pocket.

I narrow my eyes at him. "I'll smash that phone against your face if I have to."

"She will," JT confirms with a nod.

"And we'll probably help." Chelsea smiles.

"Uh, please don't." Brit clears her throat when all eyes turn to her. She lifts a shoulder delicately. "I have a date with Nate tonight, and I'd like to be able to make out with him without any blood in the way."

"The what?" My jaw drops.

"Damn you." Conor shakes his fist. "How is everyone getting dates but me?"

"Stop being so shy and just ask someone out, man" is Max's advice to his friend.

The other guy turns to JT and Chelsea. Which turns out to be a bad plan when Chelsea tosses her auburn hair over her shoulder and announces, "Sorry, dude. I already have dates lined up all the way till graduation."

From her chair, JT says, "And you're not my type, so don't even try."

Conor throws his hands up in the air. "I give up."

"Want me to introduce you to my roommate? She's newly single," I say, but he still looks sullen at my suggestion.

Max is still chuckling as he says, "Hey, it'll happen when you least expect it."

Don't I know it?

I never imagined that the annoying guy from the first day of bootcamp would turn into my most special person.

More Bolts and Strikes trickle onto the ice for our joint training session, and I look up at Max beside me. I feel like we played the only game where both sides won the faceoff. What a concept.

# EPILOGUE

## MAX

ME

Guys, is everything ready?

NATE

IDK about *everything*

Some stuff is

Some we can't control

ME

This isn't an adventure movie set in Egyptian pyramids. Can you speak NOT in riddles?

CONOR

I think what he means is WE are ready

Pretty sure the employees hate our guts but eh

You? Ready, I mean. I know you already hate our guts

ME

I've never been more ready IN MY LIFE

I'm also terrified lmao

Does that make sense?

CONOR

Well, you're about to take on one of the (if not THE) biggest challenges of your life

I think it's normal to freak out

NATE

Besides your GF is scary

CONOR

Lil bit NGL

Tell her to stop heckling us during games

ME

No one can tell Tinker Bell what to do, trust me

CONOR

THE biggest challenge of your life then, lol

NATE

Anyway, this whole thing wasn't easy to arrange, dork. You better return the favor

ME

Whenever you two are ready to commit, I'll be there rolling down the carpet

CONOR

K, put it on your calendar

See ya tomorrow where I'll crush you in the skills

NATE

No, I'll crush both of you

ME

In your dreams. Buh bye

## LUZ

Sitting crammed between my mom and Max's mom wasn't in my bingo card for today. I lean as far back as the seat allows, but there's no avoiding the flying hands of an animated Venezuelan matriarch on one side or the Italian matriarch on the other. The first time I realized people in both cultures speak with their full bodies was funny—until one of Max's little nieces caught me in the chin. That's what I'm trying to prevent here.

"Whew," I whisper once I evade my own mother's paw.

"And that's why we put butter on it," she finishes with a harrumph and an upward tilt of her nose.

"I'm telling you," Mrs. Cassiano says while throwing her hands in the air, "olive oil is so much better."

From the front seats, Dad and Mr. Cassiano exchange what sound more like grunts than conversation. Mr. Cassiano drives all of us in one of the restaurant's vans toward Madison Square Garden, where this year's All-Star Game is being held. And let me tell you, an elderly Italian man with some eyesight issues driving through the streets of the Big Apple is shaving off years off my life.

As if on cue, we get jostled to the side when he swerves to avoid a taxi. I'm trying to recall how our parents hijacked Max's and my plan of treating today as a date night, but I can't. I only found out this morning when Mrs. Cassiano called and said, "We're on our way to pick you up for the game." And hung up.

Of course, my callbacks went ignored. So there goes my date with Max.

When we finally make it to a parking spot unscathed—except for the allegedly accidental smacks I got, and the weird ringing in my ear after someone blew their horn at us—I almost drop to my knees to kiss the ground.

It's still early enough that we don't have to wrestle throngs of people for the right to take space, so at least there's that. The Cassianos are as familiar with the layout as I am. We kinda compete over who has seen more of Max's games live, so they lead the way.

Side note: I'm winning. And that's even excluding the college games they missed. They just can't compete with a girlfriend who lives in the same city as their son when they live the next state over.

"Anyone want anything from concessions?" I ask once we've cleared the ticket check.

"Oh, we'll help you." My mom nudges the other woman. "Won't we, Alessandra?"

"Yes, of course." She clears her throat. "It'll all be too much for a single person."

"Okay, thanks." I narrow my eyes slightly. Why do they both look so sweaty and jittery? Mom keeps wringing her hands, and Mrs. Cassiano has cleared her throat three times since we walked into the building. Turning to the men, I find them to be the complete opposite. A pair of marble statues straight out of a museum.

What in the what?

"I guess you two should go find our seats, then. Want anything from concessions?"

"A beer," Dad responds in a clipped tone.

"Same." Mr. Cassiano offers a jerky nod.

"Okay…" I drag out the word even as I swivel around and link my arms with the two women. I drag them a few paces away and break the silence with, "Time to spill the beans. What's happening right now? You all are acting super weird today."

"I'm just nervous—" Mom starts.

Mrs. Cassiano cuts her off, saying, "For Max. There are going to be a lot of eyes here."

"Shouldn't I be more nervous than my mother?" I cock an eyebrow.

She laughs awkwardly. "You care about him, so I care about him too."

"Right."

They're clearly up to something.

While they discuss the menu options of the nearest concession stand—and by discuss I mean Mrs. Cassiano taking public offense at what's defined as a pizza here—I pull my cellphone from the pocket of my jeans to text a certain All-Star.

ME

What's up with our parents? They're acting weirder than usual

MY SQUISHY S'MORE

Impossible

ME

Trust me, even New Yorkers are looking at us weird

Max's three dots appear and disappear several times before a response finally shows up.

MY SQUISHY S'MORE

Also impossible

I roll my eyes.

ME<br>
How are the nerves?

MY SQUISHY S'MORE

Non existing

Send me a selfie?

I snort. He's taken to asking me for a selfie every time he's having a lil panic in the locker room before a game. I, ever-supporting girlfriend that I am, always oblige. This time I'm in public, so I can't send him anything too exciting. I angle the phone so our mothers appear in the background, and snap a picture of me grinning from ear to ear. I doodle some hearts on the picture before sending it to him.

He responds back with a selfie too. Max is sitting on his bench, only missing the pads, jersey, and helmet. His hair's already messy, like he's been running his hands through it, and he has one hand over his heart and an over-the-top lovesick expression on his pretty face.

"Este hombre…" I murmur under my breath.

Our line moves, and I have to tuck my phone away. This order will require both hands and my mouth. And sure enough, a few minutes later, the three of us are hugging mountains of overpriced food and drinks as we head over to the seats.

"We're back!" I announce to the patriarchs, and they get on their feet to help us offload.

I have the last seat in our row, and as I wait for all of them to settle, I glance around at the mostly empty place. In about half an hour, it'll be teeming with people, and I bet one whole paycheck that about half of the place will be sporting Max's jersey.

As if to prove my point, a group of what I guess are college girls takes selfies with the ice behind them, and they're all sporting CASSIANO 13 on their backs. I slide quickly to my seat before they spot me in my signed jersey. That's gotten me glared at by grumpy women a few times before, and heckled by a few men who thought I was into hockey purely for the hot guys.

Pfff.

Speaking of, my hot guy didn't text again, so I guess all I can do is hope he's more relaxed after my award-winning selfie. I sit back to start making progress on my enormous vat of popcorn, watching as the crew works on the skills track course. Some crew members set down cones, stoppers, and little flags. Others test cameras around the arena, or check lighting.

This is Max's third All-Star appearance, so I've been here, done that.

I'm halfway through the popcorn bucket when the thing gets going. My eyes spot Max sliding onto the ice right away, and it could be girlfriend-radar, but I think his eyes find me just as easily. He skates a turn around the ice and confirms my suspicions by braking right in front of us.

"Hey." His lips stretch into a wide grin.

I spring to my feet and lean against the glass. "Hey back."

"We're here too, you know," his mother grouches.

"Oh, hi. So glad you could all come. I hope you have a good time." Max's expression shifts to the fakest innocence a son could muster. His parents are categorically not amused.

"You got this," my mom tells him with vehemence. "We're rooting for you."

"Sí." Dad shakes his head. "I mean, yes."

*Weird*, I mouth at Max.

He ignores that. Instead, he kisses his glove and then taps the glass with it, right where my hand is pressed against the glass.

Ugh. He's so sappy. I love it.

Unfortunately, someone calls his name and he pivots away.

My whole body deflates and I plop back on my seat, already missing him. Yeah, I'm just as sappy as him.

Mom says something I don't get over the din, and my attention is still trained on CASSIANO 13 on the ice. He's being interviewed right now, but it must not be for the main production because they're not showing it on the jumbotron.

I brush salty crumbs off my priceless jersey and stand up for the national anthems, all the while ogling my beautiful boyfriend in his full uniformed glory, knowing he's currently the best skating forward in the league because I taught him all my tricks. He's going to crush everyone else tonight, friend or foe. And then I'm going to reward him. If our parents don't stay the night.

Going by how the dads chug beer as the night progresses, I think the answer is unfavorable for romance.

Well, the good thing is that the parental units now know what's what. The first couple of All-Star Games, I had to explain every single nuance, until the one who ended up drunk off her ass was me. I was so thirsty from all the talking that I ended up drinking everyone's beers.

Not tonight. They're all calmly watching. Almost too silent. But that's okay, because it allows me to quietly drool over Max without distraction.

Gosh, does he have to look so gorgeous when he's glistening with sweat? Even the enlarged view of the jumbotron doesn't make him look more down to earth. There's an equal amount of squealing from children as from women every time his face is on the screen. Mine included.

"So, what's the plan after this?" I ask the parents when the whole thing is close to ending. "Are you heading back home right away? I can hitch a ride with Max when he's done."

"Are you trying to get rid of us, child?" Mrs. Cassiano gives me A Look.

"No, no." I shake my hands. "It's just getting late, and it's quite a drive."

"She is *clearly* trying to get rid of us, Alessandra," grunts Max's dad.

"I—uh…" My parents are no help. They keep their attention on the show very intently.

I lean back in my seat, catching the hint that they're staying the night. Even though I was really looking forward to tonight because Max has had an intense away schedule for the past two weeks, and I've had a rough time trying to make my clinic take off. Repeat clients are great, but finding new ones has been more challenging than I expected.

Sighing, I tell myself to suck it up. Of course Max's parents would want to stay for tomorrow's game too. But surely they'll leave on Sunday, and Max and I will at least be able to have an afternoon date or something before we have to get back to work on Monday.

Finally, the last skills challenger positions himself at the start line. I lean on the edge of my seat, almost smushing my face against the glass because of course it's Max. He's the main dish of this whole show.

Sorry to Conor and Nate, who also participated tonight. But this is what half of the attendants came to see.

I clasp my hands against my chest, my ears buzzing with my own excitement. I don't even register the start sound as Max takes off. My head bobs of its own accord, approving every time he skates around an obstacle smoothly. I love how his expression is focused but calm, almost detached from how hard his body's working. His thighs pump fiercely as he eats up the ice, carrying the puck with his stick as if they were an extension of his body. Leaving behind a trail of untouched obstacles, he shoots pucks into comically small nets, bagging them all in one go, before challenging the regular net and the accuracy targets hanging from its corners.

One. Two. My heart pumps harder. Three. Four. Five. And the buzzer goes off.

I wish I could say I'm the first one to jump to my feet, cheering for what *has* to be a new record. My mouth stretches into the most obnoxious shit-eating grin when the jumbotron confirms it.

"Yes! That's my man!" I pump a fist in the air. "Fast as a lightning bolt, am I right?"

"That's my son!" Mr. Cassiano yells and turns to the strangers beside him. "Did you see? *My* son!"

"And *my* son!" Mrs. Cassiano choruses behind him.

They do this every time Max scores or does something cool, and then never tell him as if it embarrassed them.

The show wraps up pretty quickly after Max is interviewed for his thoughts on winning the whole shebang. I stand up, stretching my back, which is aching from sitting in a crammed seat for hours, and turn to the stairs.

Until a strong tug almost topples me backwards.

"Geez!" I recover my balance to glare over my shoulder. My mom retrieves her hand with a sheepish grin.

"Perdón, Luz. But the show's not over."

My face twists into a grimace. "What do you mean? It's pretty over." There'll be some behind-the-scenes interviews after this, then a shower, then some feel-good dinner Max and I were going to attend for half an hour and then skip discreetly.

Mom blinks her eyes super fast, and that's when I notice they're kind of watery. Which makes zero sense, especially because she's still smiling. But then she points up and whispers, "Look."

And I do. Max's face is still on the screen and it's almost as if he were looking through it to me. "Come down here, Luz."

"Huh?" I frown. My eyes sweep the ice and I spot him

standing on a carpet that's been rolled out over the center faceoff circle. He's partially obscured by the cameraman recording him, but otherwise Max's body is angled to face our seats.

Someone taps my shoulder, the one on the side of the stairs. A woman wearing the crew's uniform asks, "Miss Rodriguez, can you please follow me?"

"Huh?" I ask again, super eloquently.

"Go, mija," Dad prompts me. Mom's biting both of her lips but motions with her hands that I should follow the attendant. The Cassianos nod along.

"I—uh. Okay?" I glance back at center ice, but the cameraman is gone and now it's only Max standing in the middle.

Well, sure. I'll go wherever he is.

I pick up speed after that. The attendant takes me around the perimeter of the boards and through a door I hadn't even noticed was a door from the stands. Stragglers from the crowd give us curious looks but I've got nothing for them. I'm not quite sure what's happening. Is this part of the broadcast now? Show the winner's family? But then his parents would've been called up too, so that's not it.

Can it be…

Nah. No way.

And then I remember one night not that long ago, during the summer. We were both at home, taking shots every time the characters of a romcom mentioned the word kiss. Of course, the whole thing ended up with a marriage proposal for the female lead, and with Max and I absolutely plastered on our couch.

He ran his fingers clumsily through my hair while my head rested on his chest, and I was just about to doze off when he suddenly asked, "How should I propose to you?"

"On your knee," I slurred with a giggle. "That's what

knights do to their queen, right?" A hiccup punctuated the question.

"Hmm, any other requests? Should I wear battle armor or something?"

"Just your uniform. You look really good in it."

Now, I follow the woman until she stops at the door to the ice and she's saying something. I shake my head to pay attention and just catch "—slowly and carefully so you don't slip."

Oh, so I'm really going on the ice. I wish it were on skates, but whatever. I know how to walk on the white thing.

"Thanks." I offer what I hope is a polite smile, except I have so much nervous energy coursing through me, I probably look terrifying instead.

Max waits all by his lonesome self in the middle, and I tilt my head, silently asking him what the heck is going on. He pretends like we do this every day instead. I look around, trying to find anyone to clue me in. Our parents are too far now, so they're no help. The crew members are too busy dismantling the props and equipment to give me a second glance.

"Max," I hiss once I'm close enough. "What's all this?"

A corner of his lips tilts into a smirk, and he drops his gloves dramatically as if getting ready for an old school fight. Instead, he offers his hands to help me step from the ice onto the carpet. I crane my head back to meet his eyes.

"Answers, now."

"Calm down, you impatient woman." Max lifts my hands and places a slow, hot kiss on the knuckles of one hand, then the other. All the while, he doesn't drop the smirk or the eye contact.

My breathing turns exponentially more shallow as he guides our hands back down between us, as the curve of his lips stretches into something sweeter, more sheepish, and as the silence between us prolongs. Someone asks for help carrying some equipment. There's a yelp as someone slips on the ice, followed by a crashing sound. And through the chaos, Max strokes the back of my hands with his thumbs. Back and forth. His eyes shining like twin stars.

"Luz."

"Max."

"Do you remember how we first met?" His voice is soft, reserved only for us.

I snort. "How can I possibly forget? I'm still not over how terrible a first impression you made."

He has the decency to blush at that. "Okay, yeah. But my point is that it was on the ice too. Which is why I feel like this setting makes sense."

"For what?" I open my eyes as wide as they can go, shifting my hands to grip his in a vise. "For *what*, Massimo Cassiano?"

Sighing, he says, "For this." And drops to one knee.

"I knew it!" I cry out, pretending like I'm in perfect control even though—hell no, I'm not. This *definitely* wasn't on my bingo card for tonight. This has to be why our parents kidnapped me. Max planned this whole thing.

Oh, crap. That's my huge face on the jumbotron. Are those tears running down my cheeks?

"Luz Maria Rodriguez." I turn my attention back to the man making me weep like a baby. That glorious smile and the blush on his face won't distract me from the fact that his eyes are watery too. Serves him right. "Seeing you that first time felt like a lightning strike. It feels like that every single day I get to spend with you."

I don't even complain about his cheesiness anymore. It's part of him, and I love him with it.

He frees a hand to rummage in the back of his pants.

"The answer is yes," I say seriously. "Even if the ring doesn't fit or is ugly."

Max pauses, pressing his lips to hold back laughter. "Can I at least finish my speech? It was going really well in my mind."

"Oh, yeah. Sorry." I grin, absolutely not sorry.

"As I was saying." Max clears his throat in an exaggerated way. Slowly, he brings forward not a box, but a single ring held between his index and thumb. It's a slim silver band with an oval-shaped diamond that won't break my finger—simple, perfect, with an undeniable meaning. He opens his mouth to speak, and I interrupt again.

"Out of curiosity, where did you hide the ring?"

"*Tinker Bell.*"

"Sorry, sorry. Go on."

"I knew this wouldn't go a hundred percent according to plan because you're unpredictable, but I love that about you. Without you, my life is too boring."

I blow a raspberry. "Sure, Mr-All-Star-Stanley-Cup-Winner."

"Boring without you. But don't tell my team that."

"Deal."

"Instead…" He runs his tongue across his lips, scraping his bottom lip with his teeth until he releases it into a shy smile. "Will you please marry me and make me the least bored man in the world?"

"Really?" The gaggle of butterflies in my belly releases into a fit of giggles. "Is that the best adjective you could think of for such a grand occasion?"

"No, but I literally forgot every damn word I had prepared when I kissed your hands."

I balance on his shoulder pad and also lower down to my knees, my arms circling his neck. "Does it make you feel better if I tell you my heart is beating faster than in the middle of a hockey game?"

"It helps." He leans his forehead gently against mine. "I need your finger to put on the ring."

"You have all of me, Max."

"And you're my light."

His fingers comb through my hair, finding my nape to hold me as his lips descend on mine. There's cheering all around us, or that could just be every fiber of my being. And I don't even care if we're being broadcasted on the jumbotron for everyone to see; I kiss Max right over this faceoff circle like this is the last time, even though this is just the start to the rest of our lives together.

## THE END

*

*Thank you for reading **Faceoff**! I hope you can take a brief moment to leave a review on Amazon.*

*Here are my other works if you're craving more closed door sports romance:*

*Book two in the St. Cloud Hockey Series, **Overtime**, is a grumpy x sunshine romance.*

*Book three and the last in the St. Cloud Hockey Series, **Shutout**, is a childhood friends to enemies to lovers romance.*

***Mistlefoe** is an office rivals to lovers Christmas romance, loosely linked to Faceoff.*

*Preorder **Wild Pitch**, book one in my upcoming Wild Baseball Romance series where the team's hot pitcher becomes our heroine's dating coach.*

*Sign up for my newsletter at MARILOYAL.COM to download **Set Me Up**, a free volleyball romance novella.*

*Happy reading!*

# GLOSSARY OF SPANISH VOCABS

**Chapter 2**

- Mierda: shit.
- "Vamos, que sí se puede.": "Let's go, we can do this."

**Chapter 4**

- Pendejo: dipshit.

**Chapter 6**

- "Mija, *relax*,": mija is a colloquialism of "mi hija" or my daughter but used widely beyond mother/daughter relationships.

**Chapter 8**

- "Qué carajo…": colloquial cuss word used to denote surprise or shock.

## Chapter 10

- "Qué—no. How? *Why*?": "What—no. How? *Why*?"
- No! Qué estoy pensando?: No! What am I thinking?

## Chapter 12

- Correcto, mis amigas: Correct, my friends.
- Cálmate: calm yourself.

## Chapter 13

- "Evening, señoritas.": "Evening, ladies."

## Chapter 14

- "Get home safe, pequeños,": "Get home safe, little ones,"
- Por qué tiene que estar tan bueno?: Why does he have to be so hot?
- *Sí, por favor: yes, please.*

## Chapter 16

- "Yo puedo,": "I can do this."

## Chapter 18

- "Mierda.": (see glossary note from Chapter 2).
- Me gusta. Max Cassiano me gusta: I like him. I like Max Cassiano.

## Chapter 22

- Papirri: Venezuelan slang for a super hot guy, comes from papi.

## Chapter 26

- Cuaimas: originally a type of snake, it became the slang word in Venezuela for an extremely jealous woman.

## Chapter 30

- Pabellón criollo: translated would be "creole pavilion," which means absolutely nothing to us, except that this is the name of the national dish in Venezuela (white rice, black beans, marinated pulled beef, side of arepa and fried sweet plantain).
- Tajadas: deep fried sweet plantain stripes.
- Aceituna: olive.
- Papelón: drink of raw cane sugar and lime in water with ice.
- Mijita: little "mija" (see glossary note from Chapter 6).

## Chapter 31

- Por favor: please.

## Chapter 36

- Mija: (see glossary note from Chapter 6).

## Chapter 38

- Mierda: (see glossary note from Chapter 2).

## Epilogue

- "Este hombre…": "This man…"
- "Sí.": "Yes."
- "Perdón, Luz. (…)": "Sorry, Luz. (…)"
- "Go, mija.": "Go, my daughter."

# ACKNOWLEDGMENTS

This is my first time writing acknowledgments as a self-published author, and I'm working really hard to pretend like it's fine. I'm fine. Everything's fine. It's no biggie.

It's a biggie!

First and foremost, thank you Lord. Contigo todo, sin ti nada.

I truly have to thank Avery Keelan and Tamara Lush. I'll never forget the way you've held my hand through the past year of me preparing to self-publish. More importantly, you both made a huge impact in my life simply by being my friends and encouraging me where others didn't. Y'all are the real MVPs.

To my friend Nati who brought me soup when I was too sick to cook but still had to work on this book's edits: gracias, gracias, gracias!

Thank you to my cuzzy Melissa, who brainwashed me into loving hockey around the Montreal Canadiens Centennial Season. We have to watch another game at Madison Square Garden soon, just saying.

Thank you to Melanie Yu from Made Me Blush Books for the great beta feedback that helped me tighten the manuscript. Eternal gratitude as well to Beth Lawton from VB Edits for helping me polish the book into a legit gem, and for taking the extra time to teach me more in-depth grammar. Thank you also to Enni Amanda at Yummy Book Covers not just for the incredible cover illustration, but also for everything you taught me along the way.

I'll always be thankful to my friend Aimee Crouch for coming in with the save when I added a last-minute chapter and needed someone to edit it ASAP. And also for the pupper pics!

Muchas tenk u to my Wattpad readers, your enthusiasm gave me the confidence to pursue publication for Luz and Max's story. I especially want to highlight readwithkaittt who has been my biggest champion. Thank you also to everyone who discouraged me from pursuing self-publication for fueling my spite to make it happen :)

Last but not least, I want to thank my mom and my sister, and my dad up in heaven, with all my heart for believing in me and giving me the strength I needed throughout this new path. Los amo con todo.

# ABOUT THE AUTHOR

**Mari Loyal** was born and raised in Venezuela, a baseball country that only cared about another sport, football soccer, every four years. As such, she decided to make hockey her whole personality because she had to make a point of being different. These days she no longer suffers from Not Like Other Girls syndrome and is very happy to be in the sports romance fandom. She writes closed door romance with a Latin American flair and an abundance of cinnamon rolls heroes. She also enjoys eating cinnamon rolls (the confections), in her spare time.

**Subscribe to my newsletter at MARILOYAL.COM**